Praise for the delectable Culinary Mysteries
by Nancy Fairbanks . . .

"Clever, fast-paced . . . A literate, deliciously well-written mystery." —Earlene Fowler

"Not your average who-done-it . . . Extremely funny . . . A rollicking good time." —*Romance Reviews Today*

"*Crime Brûlée* is an entertaining amateur sleuth tale that takes the reader on a mouthwatering tour of New Orleans . . . Fun." —*Painted Rock Reviews*

"Fairbanks has a real gift for creating characters based in reality but just the slightest bit wacky in a slyly humorous way . . . It will tickle your funny bone as well as stimulate your appetite for good food." —*El Paso Times*

"Nancy Fairbanks has whipped up the perfect blend of mystery, vivid setting and mouthwatering foods . . . *Crime Brûlée* is a luscious start to a delectable series."
—*The Mystery Reader*

"Nancy Fairbanks scores again . . . a page-turner."
—*Las Cruces Sun-News*

Mozzarella Most Murderous

Nancy Fairbanks

BERKLEY PRIME CRIME, NEW YORK

THE BERKLEY PUBLISHING GROUP
Published by the Penguin Group
Penguin Group (USA) Inc.
375 Hudson Street, New York, New York 10014, USA
Penguin Group (Canada), 10 Alcorn Avenue, Toronto, Ontario M4V 3B2, Canada
(a division of Pearson Penguin Canada Inc.)
Penguin Books Ltd., 80 Strand, London WC2R 0RL, England
Penguin Group Ireland, 25 St. Stephen's Green, Dublin 2, Ireland (a division of Penguin Books Ltd.)
Penguin Group (Australia), 250 Camberwell Road, Camberwell, Victoria 3124, Australia
(a division of Pearson Australia Group Pty. Ltd.)
Penguin Books India Pvt. Ltd., 11 Community Centre, Panchsheel Park, New Delhi—110 017, India
Penguin Group (NZ), Cnr. Airborne and Rosedale Roads, Albany, Auckland 1310 New Zealand
(a division of Pearson New Zealand Ltd.)
Penguin Books (South Africa) (Pty.) Ltd., 24 Sturdee Avenue, Rosebank, Johannesburg 2196,
South Africa

Penguin Books Ltd., Registered Offices: 80 Strand, London WC2R 0RL, England

This is a work of fiction. Names, characters, places, and incidents either are the product of the author's imagination or are used fictitiously, and any resemblance to actual persons, living or dead, business establishments, events, or locales is entirely coincidental.

MOZZARELLA MOST MURDEROUS

A Berkley Prime Crime Book / published by arrangement with the author

PRINTING HISTORY
Berkley Prime Crime mass-market edition / July 2005

Copyright © 2005 by Nancy Herndon.
Cover design by Elaine Groh.
Cover illustration by Lisa Desimini.

ISBN: 0-425-20399-9

BERKLEY® PRIME CRIME
Berkley Prime Crime Books are published by The Berkley Publishing Group,
a division of Penguin Group (USA) Inc.,
375 Hudson Street, New York, New York 10014.
BERKLEY PRIME CRIME is a registered trademark of Penguin Group (USA) Inc.
The Berkley Prime Crime design is a trademark belonging to Penguin Group (USA) Inc.

PRINTED IN THE UNITED STATES OF AMERICA

10 9 8 7 6 5 4 3 2 1

For Jeff, Laura, and Gwen Fairbanks

Acknowledgments

To my husband Bill, with whom I went on the Sorrento trip (we had a wonderful time); to my son and daughter-in-law Bill and Anne, who helped plan the trip and then weren't able to join us because of urgent work commitments (they missed a great time, and we missed them); also to son Bill, who does my Web page (I'd never manage it on my own); to all those readers who e-mail me from the Web page (I love your e-mails, enjoy corresponding with you, and appreciate your comments); to my friend Becky Craver, a wonderful Italian cook herself and the owner of the standard poodle who inspired the creation of Charles de Gaulle (Becky's dog is no longer as rambunctious and has never, that I know of, been guilty of falling in love with or harassing strange ladies); to my friend, fellow Sister-in-Crime, and reviewer Mary Sarber, with whom I discuss my books and other mysteries and attend mystery conferences; to my agent Richard Curtis, who has supported my writing now for sixteen years; to my editor Cindy Hwang, amiable dinner companion, provider of contracts, support, and good advice, and her assistant Susan McCarty, who sends me things in the mail, e-mails me, and keeps me on schedule—to all of these people my thanks.

In writing this book, I am indebted for information to the following authors and their books: Time Out Group, Ltd., *Time Out Naples, Capri, Sorrento and the Amalfi Coast*; Alberto Capatti and Massimo Montanari, *Italian*

Cuisine: A Cultural History; Giorgio Giubelli, *The Sorrento Peninsula*; Insight Guides, edited by Vincenzo delle Donne, *Naples, Capri and the Coast*; Arthur Schwartz, *Naples at Table*; Jacqueline Clark and Joanna Farrow, *Mediterranean Kitchen*; Claudia Piras and Eugenio Medagliani, *Culinaria Italy*; Alfonso de Franciscis, *Pompeii Civilization and Art*; and John Julius Norwich, *The Normans in Sicily*.

N.F.H.

Prologue

Although luxuriously housed on the ninth floor of the Grand Palazzo Sorrento, Paolina Marchetti had been unable to sleep, perhaps because of the failure of her carefully arranged assignation. That failure was certainly not the end of her assignment, but it was irritating. As irritating as the poor excuse for a meal she had shared with a chance American acquaintance after an afternoon spent exploring Sorrento, which Paolina had undertaken so as to be unavailable should Ruggiero call to make excuses for his absence.

He hadn't called. Probably he was chasing after some new woman, which would inconvenience Paolina in that she would have to seduce him all over again. She didn't doubt her ability to do so—even if Ruggiero had caught wind of her inconsequential tryst the night before she left Catania. Could Gracia Sindacco—that nosy, old witch—have found out and told their mutual employer?

"*Basta*," she muttered and sprang from the comfortable bed. She would go for a swim, an activity strictly forbidden by the hotel at this hour. Why have such a series of lovely pools tumbling down the mountainside if they could not be used for midnight swims? Slipping out of the transparent silken nightgown that she had chosen to overwhelm the easily overwhelmed Ruggiero, Paolina donned a skimpy, sea green bikini. She pulled on the soft robe provided by the hotel and dropped a notebook that had lain beneath her pillow into the pocket. Then she grabbed a large pink towel from the bathroom, although it was forbidden to take both the room towels and the hotel robes to the pool area. Towels were rented to swimmers at the bar, which was, of course, now closed.

Most of the hotel patrons she had seen at dinner were middle-aged and stodgy, except for those who were limping and elderly, she mused, as she walked down the empty hall to the pool. That explained their being in bed before midnight and their willingness to eat what the Grand Palazzo Sorrento served for dinner. Hospital fare. It tasted like the food served to her father, the General, after Mafiosi in Palermo had attacked him. Having left her convent school and flown south to be with him, she had told Papa the food was undoubtedly a second attempt to kill him through deprivation rather than violence. Papa had been amused by her indignant opinion, but he had doubted it. Having been hospitalized before, he explained that hospital food was seldom meant to do anything but feed the body, certainly not the soul, as a good Italian meal should.

The night sky was a stunning blue, deep and dark above her, when Paolina nudged open the glass doors at the end of the hall and padded barefoot into the pool area. A light breeze brushed her cheeks, and the stars seemed close and bright. All her irritation disappeared under the gentle blandishment of night in Sorrento. Like a sinuous creature from the sea, she eased herself into the pool and swam. Ten minutes or so was enough to complete the rehabilitation of her mood. Lifting herself from the water, she trailed droplets to a cushioned lounge chair beside a small glass table, draped the forbidden pink towel around her shoulders, and stretched out. In such delicious and beautiful solitude, Ruggiero's absence became something to enjoy. Too bad he would be here tomorrow. Of that she was sure. He wouldn't miss his own meeting.

She removed the small leather journal from the pocket

of the robe, extracted the pen from its holder on the cover, and flipped to a clean page.

A toast to the absent lover
Who disappears, unmourned,
While dark indigo skies . . .

No, she didn't like the lines. They were trite. Uninspired. Ruggiero was not a man to stir her muse. And what of last night's lover? Danger always spurred passion, and he had had that aura about him. Since she had no lover tonight, however, the evening would end nicely if she could at least sample a tasty snack and write a few perfect lines before returning to her room to sleep.

As if her thought had been another's command, a visitor came through the door that Paolina had left ajar, a visitor carrying a tray with two glasses of bubbling wine and two plates. Without rising or offering a greeting, she studied the newcomer and the offering from beneath her eyelashes. Not a particularly welcome person, but as the plates and goblets were set down on the table and a chair pulled up across from her, Paolina could see, in the misty lights that shone on the pool, the rich red of tomato slices, the contrasting white of the fresh buffalo mozzarella, small green basil leaves, a pool of olive oil, and a sprinkle of pepper. She would have welcomed the devil bearing *Caprese*, so she tucked the journal into the pocket of her robe and waved her hand for the visitor to be seated.

The conversation was slow and of no consequence, but the mozzarella was moist and fresh, the tomatoes ripe and sweet, the basil adding a hint of anise flavor to the salad. Perfect. Except that a drizzle of balsamic vinegar had been added. No native of Capri would have approved of that. Still, she would not complain because she was enjoying both the salad and the contrast of the sweet-yet-tart fizz of Spumante from her goblet. Only when she began to feel surprisingly drowsy, too drowsy to follow the

visitor's words, did it dawn on Paolina that she had been
drugged. *Fool*, she thought, as the possibility of poison
drifted through her fading consciousness. She whispered a
curse·in the dialect of her native Umbria, but the words
never rolled completely off the numbness of her tongue.

With silent patience her visitor waited for uncon-
sciousness to overcome the beautiful young woman. Then
the pink towel was pulled from her shoulders and dropped
onto the pavement poolside, the robe left draped on a third
chair, and Paolina's chair rolled toward the water, where a
wrought-iron rail warned swimmers away from the waterfall. The visitor studied the barrier, then hoisted the body
onto the rail and maneuvered it over, head down. Once the
fingers grasping Paolina's ankles released, she plunged in
a clumsy dive over the side, her head glancing off the
edge of the pool below at the shallow end before she sank
into the water. A dark stain trailed her to the bottom,
where she floated, unconscious, in a limp sprawl, the
white of her buttocks glimmering through the water.

With a nod, the visitor rolled the chair back to its place,
retrieved the notebook from the pocket of her robe, having already searched her room for it in her absence, placed
the goblets and plates on the tray, and departed. Below,
the unconscious Paolina breathed in water and drowned.

Sunday in Sorrento

To my mind, *Caprese* is one of the delights of visiting Italy, and I thought of it often during the long flight to Rome. It is a simple dish to fix and can be made at home in the United States, but it will never be the same as eating it in Italy, say, at an outdoor café in a piazza with a beautiful cathedral or basilica looming up in front of you.

Then there are the ingredients: the tomatoes, which are so delicious, fresh that morning from a vine in the countryside, and the mozzarella, also fresh and made from buffalo milk. You can buy little plastic-wrapped blobs of "fresh" mozzarella in the States, but they're made from cow's milk and are much less rich and of a somewhat rubbery consistency. Our buffalo are the wrong kind. Imagine trying to milk an American buffalo. You'd be trampled in one of the stampedes so popular in old western films. In Italy the source of mozzarella is the water buffalo, originally from Asia, and its milk has over twice the fat content. Go to Italy! Eat the real thing!

Insalata Caprese

- Slice *4 ripe tomatoes* (large tomatoes such as beefsteaks) and *9 ounces of fresh buffalo-milk mozzarella*. Overlap the slices alternately on the plate.

- Decorate the slices with *fresh basil leaves* or *chopped basil or oregano.*

- Grate *fresh pepper* over the salad or serve the pepper separately. (*Salt* if desired, but lightly.)

- Drizzle liberally with a good, *extra virgin olive oil.*

- Serve with *balsamic vinegar* for those who like it on *caprese*—I do, but residents of Capri and the Campania would be horrified—and with *chunks of Italian bread.*

- For lunch, as a snack, as a first course—it's wonderful.

Carolyn Blue,
"Have Fork, Will Travel,"
Albuquerque Sun-Times

1

A Lovely Sorrento Morning

Carolyn

On my second morning in Sorrento I awoke feeling much better than I had on the first. And why not? I had a lovely room with a balcony that overlooked the Bay of Naples and even, on the right, the volcano. I knew that breakfast would be delicious, unlike the dinners the hotel had provided last night and the night before. I was truly amazed that such a beautiful—not to mention expensive—hotel could have provided two such mundane entrees.

A young woman I had met in the lobby and with whom I had strolled around Sorrento and dined, said she thought the management must be German, which she deduced from the many signs warning guests of things they were not allowed to do. Perhaps I'd see her at breakfast. She was alone too, her lover having canceled their assignation. She was quite disappointed, although I assumed that he was still paying for her stay here.

I, too, was alone because my husband Jason, who was supposed to meet me in Rome at the airport, had been marooned in Paris by an air-traffic controllers' strike. I suppose I could have stayed in Rome and waited for him, but I decided that I'd rather go on to Sorrento for the sightseeing that Jason was now going to miss—and all because of the French, who are always staging unannounced strikes that inconvenience hapless visitors to their country.

My trip from Rome to Sorrento was an adventure in itself—the train from Fiumacino, the airport just outside of Rome, to the railroad station in the city, the train from Rome to Naples, and then the funny little *Circumvesuviana* with its hard plastic seats, bumpy tracks, and hordes of tourists and school children. Of course, I had to manage my own suitcase on those legs of the trip, and pulling it up and down the stairs that take a traveler from one track to another was dreadful, although on several occasions, while standing at the bottom of a long staircase, looking forlorn, kindly Italian men and boys offered help.

Naturally, I accepted, unless the offer was to lift my suitcase onto the overhead luggage rack of a train car. I reasoned that if the Good Samaritan weren't on hand to take it down at my destination, it would probably land on my head when I tried to do it myself. On trains, I left my bag in the area between cars and sat inside as close to it as I could get, keeping a suspicious eye on my belongings as people climbed on and off at each station. No one, I'm happy to say, exited with my suitcase.

In this manner, miserably jet lagged by my long flight from El Paso to Rome, I did get safely to Sorrento, a place of beauty in the land of romance. Someone said that homosexual lovers go to Capri, the adulterers to Naples, and the divorced to Sorrento. I belonged to none of those categories, being a married, faithful, heterosexual who was in Italy to write about the food of the Campania while her husband attended a scientific conference. Not very romantic, but I was happy to be there on the Bay of Naples.

Once in Sorrento, I had the rather silly idea that I could wheel the suitcase to the hotel, but a friendly taxi driver was quick to tell me that the hotel was well up the mountain. He said no lady but one from northern Europe would think of making that hike, so I took the cab. He was right. I could never have dragged my luggage through the crowded streets of the town and then up the hill, into the driveway, and onto an elevator that took me to the lobby. On the other hand, he charged me eighteen euros for the ride.

The hotel itself was built up and down a cliff and was very beautiful. It should also have been romantic, but it wasn't. I barely arrived in time for the first of the two boring dinners—the evening meal began and ended rather early for a Mediterranean resort. Not that it mattered. Whatever the plans of the meeting Jason would be attending were, I did not intend to eat dinner here again. Our host was a chemical company in Catania. Surely no good Sicilian would be satisfied with such food. The readers of my newspaper column certainly wouldn't be.

I hopped out of bed, thinking of the delicious bread the hotel provided at breakfast, flavored with fennel, if I wasn't mistaken. Jason would, barring any other flight difficulties, be here by midday, as would other members of the conference. I set the coffee machine to prepare me a first cup while I showered and dressed, thinking I'd sip it by the pool on my floor before going down to breakfast; the hotel had a series of pools, one on each floor with waterfalls in between. What luxury. After my many years of being a stay-at-home wife and mother, it was rather nice to be by myself in a foreign resort that offered so many inducements to delight. Not that I planned to swim. A seriously frightening experience in France had made me wary of swimming, even though it was unlikely that I would be caught by a ferocious incoming tide in a hotel swimming pool.

I supposed that I would be happy to see Jason. We hadn't been getting along all that well, if the truth be told, but I had loved him for over twenty years and was no doubt wrong in suspecting that he had taken too warm an interest in a female graduate student. She wouldn't be here, so I'd have no cause for irritation. And it was unlikely that I would come upon yet another pesky corpse whose death demanded investigation, so Jason would have no reason to complain.

My husband had progressed from worry about my safety to anger at my propensity for getting myself into dangerous situations. He had a point. Why was I suddenly giving in to a desire for adventure? Because it was exciting, I suppose. Because, until the last few years, I had led such a placid life—wife, mother, hostess. The new, forty-something Carolyn was definitely beginning to enjoy these recent escapades that had required me to overcome fear and exhibit courage. But Jason was not happy with me! He wanted back his gourmet cook and tidy housekeeper, his docile wife.

Once I was dressed for the day, I took my cup of coffee out to the pool, duly noted the signs that forbade me to take hotel towels out with me, jump or dive over the waterfall to the next level, or bring food or drink into the pool area, although apparently I could purchase it from the refreshment counter, to which I could also report emergencies. I ignored the last one because the refreshment station was unmanned, probably because I was visiting the pool before it was open for the day.

Wondering if the hotel provided a book with an index to its numerous rules, I set my coffee down on a little table, pulled a padded deck chair into place, and prepared to laze about in the fresh morning air for fifteen minutes or so. In El Paso, where I now live, one has to get up almost before the sun to enjoy fifteen minutes of cool air. Most months of the year the temperatures shoot up into ranges that I consider unsuitable for human existence. Of course, as we in El Paso say, "At least the humidity is low, so it's always comfortable." Comfortable if you don't mind stepping from your air-conditioned house into a hot oven supplied with skin-cancer-inducing sunshine.

I took a sip of my coffee, turned toward the pool to sit down, and noticed that there was someone in it. Moreover, the person was resting on the bottom at the shallow end. Some lung-strengthening exercise? I used to see how long I could hold my breath when I was a child. So had a girl child in Donna Tartt's novel *The Little Friend*. Her underwater practice had saved her life. Mine had made my mother very nervous. In fact, the lady in the pool was beginning to make me nervous, and it wasn't just the skimpy bikini with that uncomfortable-looking thong bottom. I reflected on how lucky I was to have missed that style when I was young and foolish enough to have adopted it—not that my father would have approved.

She still hadn't come up. She wasn't moving either. Just resting there. My heart rate accelerated. Surely, she wasn't . . . I kicked off my shoes, jumped in—getting my mint green slacks outfit all wet—and waded toward the woman. The water was about three and a half feet deep where she lay, and I had to duck under to pull her up. *Oh, my goodness*, I thought as I lifted her to the surface and turned her face into the air. It was Paolina, my tourist friend from yesterday, who had been jilted by her boyfriend, who shared my love for the poetry of Edna St. Vincent Millay, who wrote poetry herself, something I have never been moved to try.

2
Pandemonium by the Pool

Carolyn

As a teenager I had been a lifeguard at a lake where my family had a summer cottage. Among the techniques we learned was artificial respiration, so I tried it on Paolina, although I could find no pulse and her face was a bit blue, her skin cold and spongy. My attempts to resuscitate the poor girl had no effect whatever; she had drowned.

I then utilized the phone behind the bar to call the front desk, getting instead room service and then housekeeping. Some poor maid, having heard a hysterical voice saying, "*Morte. Dama morte*," which I hoped meant *dead woman*, connected me with the front desk and an English speaker. While I sat down, weak-kneed, to contemplate poor Paolina's limp, dripping body, the forces of hotel management and then those of law enforcement gathered and stampeded in our direction—Paolina's and mine.

Paolina was an interesting name, I mused sadly. Yesterday I had simply accepted it. Today it occurred to me that it was the name of a Perugian palace, taken over by a pope and turned into a fortress to keep the quarrelsome Perugians in line—Rocca Paolina. Had my late friend been named for the fortress? My thoughts were interrupted by the arrival of Signor Pietro Villani, the hotel manager, accompanied by a phalanx of hysterical employees, all chattering in Italian. He introduced himself with great formality and a disapproving eye for my sodden clothing.

Signor Villani then bent over Paolina and took her pulse. "*Morte*," he announced in sepulchral tones, and made a demand of a well-dressed lady in a chic, black suit. She removed a mirror from her handbag and gave it to him. He held the mirror to Paolina's lips. "*Morte*." His voice deepened with disapproval, and he turned to me. "*Signora*," he asked, "are you a guest of this hotel?"

"Carolyn Blue. Room eight-oh-eight," I replied, wondering whether he thought that I had sneaked in.

He turned to the table at which I had been sitting. "Is that your coffee, Signora?"

I nodded. Why was he asking about coffee? Another of his guests was dead on the cement. Surely he was not about to offer me a refill.

"Food and drink that have not been purchased from the bar are not allowed in the pool area." He stared at me. I stared back, until he gave up waiting for my apology and asked, "Do you know this woman?"

"She is a guest of your hotel," I replied. "Paolina Marchetti. I met her yesterday."

His minion in the black suit whipped out a handheld electronic device over which her fingers flew. "Paolina Marchetti, room nine-oh-five," she announced.

"You were swimming with her, Signora?" Signor Villani asked. "These are not hours during which the pools are open to guests."

"I came out to enjoy the lovely air of this beautiful Sorrento morning," I began. The hotel staffers nodded appreciatively, murmuring "*Bene*," and the like, and breathing deeply to savor the air themselves. "Then I saw the body at the bottom of the pool, so I waded in, dragged her out, and administered artificial respiration, which was of no use, as you can see. I assume she died sometime last night. As for me, I do not swim in my clothing, only in swimwear."

"Night swimming is not allowed," said the manager grimly. "See what happens when guests endanger themselves by breaking the rules." His employees all nodded. Some frowned. One wiped a tear from her eye at the fate of the rule-breaking Paolina.

Can this man be Italian? I wondered. *All these rules, not that the Italians don't have rules—and laws—and layers of governmental bureaucracy. But my impression has always been that Italians pay no attention. The low birthrate is a case in point. Although the Pope resides in Italy, and the Church forbids birth control, the Italians obviously practice it. And the traffic. Italian drivers pay no attention to red lights or stop signs or no-parking signs. They even park on the sidewalks. And race their cars through narrow, medieval streets.*

"Lieutenant Buglione at your service," said a policeman in a delightful uniform. "*Polizia di Stato negli Sorrento.*" He shook the manager's hand. Then he took mine and kissed it. "You must be American lady who drowned. I am so happy to see you have recovered. Sergeant Gambardella," he continued, pointing out the accompanying officer, who shook the hand of Signor Villani and then bowed over mine.

"I am—am not the victim," I stammered. "She's over there." Because the crowd of hotel employees had encircled us, Paolina's body was hidden from view on the apron of the pool. "Behind the lady in the black suit."

The employees stumbled in their haste to clear a path to the corpse, all but the lady in the black suit, who turned and pointed dramatically with her electronic device. "Signorina Paolina Marchetti. Room nine-oh-five."

"And she has drowned, poor lady?" asked the lieutenant. "So young. So beautiful. Such a tragedy," he sighed.

"Actually, since her room was one floor up, perhaps she died in a diving accident," I suggested. When the crowd moved aside, I had noticed that her head was injured.

"Diving is not allowed," said Signor Villani. "Is not allowed even to climb on the railings at the waterfalls. This is most unfortunate. The owners will be horrified."

"Yet, I think this pretty American lady is saying what is true. See the head." The lieutenant bent down and gently lifted aside wet strands of hair, revealing an even larger wound than I had first noticed. "This head has crashed against something, or something has crashed against this head. Is perhaps murder here? Someone throw her over from up there?" He pointed up toward the wrought iron barrier at the edge of the waterfall on the ninth floor. "What do you think, Gambardella?"

"*No Ingles, mi luogotenente,*" said the sergeant sadly.

More uniformed men appeared. A doctor in a white coat and little, round eyeglasses arrived and knelt beside Paolina. The lieutenant, speaking in Italian, evidently demanded that everyone go to the lobby and await questioning. Another policeman rushed to the elevator to roust out all guests on the ninth floor. Soon there was greater pandemonium in the lobby than there had been at the pool. Signor Villani was wringing his hands in dismay because so many of his employees were being kept from their jobs and so many grumpy guests were circling his lobby complaining at the inconvenience and demanding that they be allowed to eat breakfast. I was very hungry myself, having eaten so little of my detestable dinner. I hate mushy peas. It always amazes me that the English actually have a dish called "mushy peas." And why would an Italian hotel want to reproduce it?

Before the lieutenant could begin his interviews, I suggested to him that the guest interviewees be seated at their own tables in the breakfast room, under guard by some of his men. After that the manager looked upon me more favorably. In no time at all I was seated among a covey of guests, attended by two policemen, all of us happily eating things we had chosen from the lavish breakfast buffet of the Grand Palazzo Sorrento. They even provided cake. And champagne. Although the champagne bottles weren't open. Just for show, I suppose. You haven't lived until you've had poached eggs on fennel toast, fresh fruit, and cake with deep, lush frosting. It's hard to believe that one establishment could produce such a wonderful breakfast and such horrible dinners.

3
Meeting the "Executive Garbage Man"

Carolyn

We all lingered over breakfast while Lieutenant Buglione interviewed the hotel staff so that they could return to their posts. Guests who spoke English were avidly interested in my discovery of the body, which was not, in my opinion, the most felicitous subject to discuss over breakfast. And at the back of my mind hovered the thought that Jason, if he actually arrived today, would be unhappy that another dead body had intruded on a trip of ours. Since I hadn't read a newspaper this morning, I didn't know whether the air-traffic controllers' strike had been settled, as he expected.

With any luck, Paolina's death would prove to be accidental. Jason might not even hear about it, or that I had discovered the body, or that I had gone sightseeing yesterday with the dead woman. For all her charm, Paolina had evidently been a reckless young woman. Not only had she complained about the defection of her lover, but also she had confided that she liked variety in her lovers. How many lovers did she have? I had wondered. Had she practiced safe sex, if such a thing were possible when enter-

taining a "variety" of men? And how many was a variety?
If she was reckless in her love life, she might well be reckless in swimming pools, not that I counted using the hotel
pools during forbidden hours as particularly reckless.
Everything here seemed to be forbidden.

"Excuse me." A tall, broad-shouldered man with thick,
black hair, somewhat curly, and an American accent, towered over me. "May I sit down?" Some of the guests had
finished breakfast and filtered back into the social areas
with police escorts. The seat beside me was vacant, although the dishes had not been removed, but I was happy
to meet another American. The closest I had come to
someone from home since arriving in Italy was a pair of
middle-aged Canadian honeymooners on the *Circumvesuviana*. Their main topic of conversation, on learning that I
was from the United States, was a complaint about Asian
immigrants jumping off boats and wading ashore, after
which the Canadian authorities had to research their back-
grounds at great expense in time and money. By then,
many of the Asians had picked up some English and some
money and left Canada to sneak into the United States.

I smiled at the large American and invited him to sit
down, which he did, having brought his own coffee with
him.

"Hank Girol," he said, setting down his cup and shaking my hand vigorously. His hand was so large that I
doubted gloves were made in his size. "I couldn't help
overhearing when you said that you were meeting your
husband here for a chemistry meeting. Are you a chemist
as well?"

"No, an accompanying person," I replied. "Although I
do write a cuisine column, so this is a working trip for me,
too."

Mr. Girol's face broke into a wide smile. "I believe that
I'm an accompanying person at the same meeting. My

wife is Dr. Sibyl Evers from Rutgers. She's attending a conference sponsored by a chemical company in Catania."

I nodded. "That's the one Jason will be attending if he ever gets out of Paris."

"The coincidences multiply," exclaimed my new acquaintance. "My wife is stuck in Paris, too, but she called this morning to say she hoped to get a flight by afternoon or early evening. So are they offering any activities for us significant others?"

"Not that I've heard," I replied.

"Then I suggest that we round up some of the other wives or husbands, if any, to take in Pompeii and drive up the Amalfi Coast. It's spectacular, and I've rented a car. It's a little weird looking, but it's a convertible, which is just the thing for this area."

Of course I agreed. Mr. Girol seemed like a pleasant person, if somewhat oversized, and those were places I wanted to see. I had visited Pompeii years ago with my father, but more archaeological sites had opened there in the interim. "What I'd really like to see," I added, "is Capri. I've never been there, but I've heard how beautiful it is."

"Then we'll go there, too," said the generous Mr. Girol. "There are plenty of boats crossing to the island." He glanced around the room and added, "I think we'd better move into the lobby. The waiters are giving us the evil eye, which is serious business in Southern Italy and Sicily."

Surely he didn't believe in the evil eye. He was an American. Now in Naples, according to what I'd read, people were very superstitious and were afraid of the evil eye. We strolled out together and found seats on a comfy, Italian leather sofa. "How long do you think we'll have to wait to be interviewed?" I asked.

"Actually, the police won't want to talk to me. I just

drove in from Rome and checked into the hotel, so I evidently missed all the excitement. It must have been tough for you, finding a dead body in a swimming pool."

"It wasn't very pleasant," I agreed, remembering how strange Paolina had looked. "Especially since I spent yesterday afternoon exploring Sorrento with her and had dinner with her last night. She was a very lively young woman."

"Really? She didn't seem depressed or suicidal?" he asked.

"Not at all. I thought it might be a diving accident, but the police lieutenant suggested that someone may have thrown her over—murder, in other words."

"Unlikely way to murder someone," Mr. Girol remarked. "The Italian police tend to overdramatize things—the grand-opera mentality, as my dad used to say. Did she tell you anything to indicate that someone might be after her?"

"Actually, she'd been stood up by her lover."

"Poor girl. Perhaps it *was* a suicide."

"Surely not. She seemed more angry than sad."

He shrugged. "Well, the police will work it out. And I hope you won't be too upset by her death to enjoy the week. This is a terrific place to vacation, and I know a number of good restaurants."

I was delighted to hear that since the hotel dinners had been so terrible. We talked about food, especially Italian food, which Mr. Girol, who insisted that I call him Hank, claimed to know all about, being from New Jersey. He called himself, chuckling, "the executive garbage man," because he was the vice president of a company that disposed of waste, much of it highly toxic, that no landfill would accept. Naturally that led to a discussion of our spouses, who were both chemists interested in toxicity.

Hank had met his wife in a Rutgers lab while looking for information on some unusual toxin that had come his way.

"We fell in love beside one of those hoods that carries off poisonous chemical fumes," he said. "I always thought of myself as a more romantic guy than that, but we were obviously made for each other, and I did manage to propose over a great aged Barola in a restaurant where violins were playing and Neapolitan love songs were being sung. The engagement ring arrived stuck into a perfect New Jersey strawberry on top of a dish of great tiramisu."

"Good for you," I said, remembering my own engagement. "Jason proposed to me at a graduation party where all the chemists were pouring or injecting vodka into watermelons and comparing the results. I didn't know that New Jersey grew strawberries."

"It's the Garden State! Our produce is the best in the country. Like the Campania's is the best in Italy. You probably thought New Jersey was all chemical dumps, oil refineries, and toxic waste, right? My wife and I live in a colonial house with a good stand of trees, a stream, and wild violets in the backyard. There's a pre-Revolutionary War cemetery a few blocks down, full of the graves of little kids. Must have been an epidemic or something. Makes you think twice about having kids of your own."

And so the conversation went until I was finally called in to talk to Lieutenant Buglione. He wanted to know, first, about my discovery of the body and anything I might have noticed. I mentioned the injury to her head, which he had pointed out himself, and that I thought her ankles had looked bruised, perhaps from the fall.

Then he asked about anything she might have told me during our sightseeing excursion or over dinner. The truth was, when I thought about it, that Paolina hadn't told me much about herself beyond her name, her love for the poetry of Edna St. Vincent Millay, and the fact that she was to have met her lover at the hotel, only to get a call from him saying that he couldn't make it. I didn't know how long they were to have stayed at the Grand Palazzo Sorrento, so the lieutenant summoned the manager, Signor Villani, and learned that she was registered for a week's stay and that she had made the reservation herself.

"But I thought he was paying for her room," I protested. "That's what she said."

"Ha!" said Lieutenant Buglione after the manager revealed that the reservation had not been prepaid. "He not only no meet her, but no pay her bill. Maybe she did commit suicide."

I told him that she hadn't seemed worried about the bill or even depressed by the lover's failure to appear. She had seemed irritated, but a woman didn't throw herself off the ledge of a waterfall into a cement-lined pool in a fit of irritation, even if she expected to survive the fall.

The manager left, and the lieutenant mused over my statement. "Then he come here and kill her, then go away." He threw up his hands dramatically—even operatically, as Hank had suggested. "Will be very hard case to solve. All night employees must be interviewed to find if strange man, not registered, arrive last night late and leave again."

I had to stifle a giggle. "I must tell you, Lieutenant, that I explored the hotel, and it's full of stairways that don't lead more than a few floors down, and random exits into pool areas and cactus gardens. It's so strangely laid out that if there is a fire, I think the safest thing for a guest to do would be jump into a pool. Unless one can use the elevators, it would be impossible to find one's way to the lobby or ground level."

"So you think he is lost in the hotel?" asked Lieutenant Buglione.

"No, I think he'd have had to take the elevators, so you

simply need to ask the hotel staff if they saw a strange man getting on or off the elevators."

"A very good thought, Signora." He gave me a flashing smile, kissed my hand, and allowed me to go.

4
Bambinis in the Hall

Carolyn

After my interview I went back to the lobby but saw no one I knew. I thought of walking into town to look at the shops with an eye to finding gifts for my children, Gwen and Chris. Or I could visit the museum that featured lovely, almost fragile *intarsio* furniture. It had a gift shop on the first floor that sold amazing marquetry pieces in a more contemporary style. Expensive, unfortunately, but I did long to buy something beautiful, something I'd never find at home. Yesterday I'd been more interested in conversation with Paolina than in shopping. Now, no matter that my inclination to shop had kicked in, I felt obliged to stay in the hotel since Jason might be arriving today. At least, he'd call, so I should be here for that.

Feeling depressed, I headed for the elevator and my room. I could read a book I'd brought along, *Greene on Capri*, a memoir by Shirley Hazzard about the time she and her husband had spent with Graham Greene on the island I so much wanted to see for myself. What a strange man he had been. Greene, and evidently other Europeans, think that the clause in our Bill of Rights about the right to the "pursuit of happiness" is ridiculous, even shallow. I can't see anything wrong with happiness. It's certainly better than gloom. If I got to visit Capri, I was sure I'd enjoy it more than Graham Greene ever had, and Hank Girol had agreed readily to such an excursion for whatever accompanying persons might want to go.

Stepping off the elevator into the long, tiled hall that led to my room, I came close to being bowled over by two beautiful, dark-haired children, a boy of eight or nine years and a younger girl. They were evidently playing soccer in the hall. The boy apologized in Italian for careening into me, or so I gathered, while the startlingly blue-eyed girl peeked at me from under her dark curls and giggled. As I bent to pick up my purse, which had fallen in the scuffle, I noticed the soccer ball at my feet, so I retrieved that as well. The boy looked at me hopefully and asked a question.

"I don't speak Italian," I replied. Pointing to myself with the hand not holding their soccer ball, I said, "Americano."

"For shame, my little ones. Apologize to the nice American lady in English. And why are you playing soccer in the hall when Mama told you not to?" A woman, evidently their mother, squatted down on her heels, although heavily pregnant, and gave each child a hug and kiss after their apologies.

"I am very sorry for knocking you, Signora," said the boy, still looking wistfully at his soccer ball. "I am sorry," added his sister and reached out for the ball from the safety of her mother's arms. I bent to hand it to her.

Their mother, who was as beautiful as her children and as dark-haired, although she didn't have her daughter's blue eyes, tried to rise and failed. No surprise there. I doubt that I could have gotten down when I was that far along in a pregnancy, much less managed to rise again.

"We'll have to call Papa to get her up," said the boy to his sister. "You go."

The little girl, obviously reluctant to obey him, responded with a stream of Italian.

"No one will wake Papa," said their mother. "He drove all the way from Rome while we slept."

"But, Mama," the boy protested.

"I shall sit here until he wakes up and comes looking for us," she decided, easing herself off her heels and onto the floor. Then she smiled up at me. "I'm Bianca Massoni, and these are my children Andrea and Giulia. You mustn't mind us. Just circle around, and I do apologize for my babies. It's hard for little ones to be cooped in a hotel and ordered to keep silent so that their father can sleep. Sit down, children. We'll play a game."

I introduced myself and offered to help her up, imagining how uncomfortable she would become if she had to sit long on that hard tile floor. Her legs would certainly go to sleep, and then rising would become twice as impossible. I'd had that problem while carrying Chris, who had been a big baby. Signora Massoni appeared to be very near delivery, and of a very large child. However, hoisting the lady off the floor was not as easy as it might have looked. First, I tried with one hand under her elbow. That didn't work. Then I took both of her wrists while she clutched mine. Finally with her son Andrea pushing from behind, we got her to her feet, after which all four of us fell to giggling helplessly at what a foolish picture we made while an older couple with a large, black standard poodle on a short leash circled us. They stared with eyebrows raised—well, not the dog. He just stared. In fact, he turned his head to keep staring once they had passed by.

"Oh dear," murmured Signora Massoni when they were gone. "I hope they aren't attending the conference.

Poor Lorenzo will be so embarrassed if he hears about this."

We discovered immediately that our husbands would be fellow conferees, which meant we four were accompanying persons. To show that I was not offended by the collision with the children and to pass the remainder of the morning, I invited them to my room and offered refreshments from the small refrigerator provided by the hotel. Jason would not be pleased, given the cost of such items, but one does feel the necessity to be hospitable. The children, delighted with the opportunity, picked bottled fruit drinks and munchies identified in Italian with garish pictures, evidently some sort of chip colored a bright orange red. To my astonishment, Bianca chose one of the tiny bottles of wine. I had to read the brands off to her because her huge stomach didn't allow her to bend forward and she now knew better than to get too close to the floor. Could she be carrying twins, or had her pregnancy gone beyond term? And if the latter, why was she traveling around the country? Perhaps the Massonis were natives of the area. That, as it developed, was not so. They lived in Rome, where her husband taught.

To amuse the children, I provided Andrea with an Italian Carabinieri doll and Giulia with a prettily dressed Italian peasant doll, gifts that I had bought for Jason's half niece and nephew. The dolls could be easily replaced when I ventured out to find gifts for my own children, who were harder to please, being college students. Andrea's doll immediately arrested Giulia's doll, as Bianca, laughing, explained to me, and a great drama ensued in Italian that kept the children happy for over an hour while we ladies chatted.

First, I complimented my new friend on her excellent English and deplored my own lack of languages.

"But why should you learn languages?" she replied

diplomatically. "You live in a huge country where everyone speaks English."

Of course, everyone doesn't speak English at home, especially in El Paso, but I didn't mention that. It was so pleasant to meet a European who didn't feel disdain for the many monolingual American tourists visiting the continent.

"So much easier, is it not, to be an American? I live in a comparable area of size, but it contains many nations speaking many languages, so naturally I must speak some, especially since I was a tour guide in Rome. You must come to Rome and let me show you my city. Have you seen the Mithraic altar in St. Clement's? The initiates stood under a grate and were baptized by the blood pouring from a sacrificial bull. Gruesome, is it not? The church is a treasure, some of whose delights you can easily pass by without a knowledgeable guide."

I assured Bianca that I would certainly call her for the promised tour when I was next in Rome. In fact, I would have been glad to climb back on the train to Rome with her that very morning, had she not been so hampered by her pregnancy.

"Ah, it is so good to drink wine again," she said, sipping ecstatically. "For six months my doctor insists on no wine. I swear my tongue rusted in the meantime, but in the last three months he says there is no danger."

I hadn't heard any such thing, but there was no use to warn her that in the United States women were expected to avoid alcohol throughout pregnancy. She was already drinking and might have been for several months. "When is the baby due?" I asked.

"You probably think I might give birth this very minute. Yes? We are not quite sure, you see. Even the doctor is puzzled. I am so big, and yet the baby has not

dropped down, and I have no idea when the little one—"
she patted her stomach fondly, "—was conceived."

"You must be a devout Catholic," I observed.

"Oh, not so devout," she replied, laughing. "You think
I don't practice birth control. Yes? I was on the pill, and
was being very good with taking it each night, but then I
found Giulia popping them out of the packet and eating
them one morning. What a scene. My mother-in-law and
I shrieking, Giulia crying, Andrea dragging Lorenzo from
the bathroom to put things to right. Poor baby. We had to
have her stomach pumped at the hospital, and my mother-
in-law threw the uneaten pills away after lecturing me on
my careless behavior, although I keep all the medicines
quite high in a cabinet in my bathroom. That was the day
we discovered that Giulia is a little monkey, aren't you,
mia bambina?"

Giulia, whose doll had just given the Carabinieri doll
of her brother a whack on the head, looked up and giggled. "*Si*, Mama."

"So then I forget about the pills because I did not want
to remember the terror of my baby having her little stomach sucked up, but, of course, being Italian—we Italians
are a passionate people, you know—even my Lorenzo,
who is from Lucca to the north—we made love without a
thought, so—there is another baby soon." She smiled down
at the huge protrusion under her pretty maternity outfit.
With that smooth, oval face and dark hair, Bianca looked
like a beautiful Madonna in a Renaissance painting.

"So you must excuse me. I have been talking and talking. Tell me how you like Sorrento and who, of the meeting, you have met. Have you had adventures here on our
beautiful Bay of Naples?"

"Mama, tell Giulia it is not good for a girl doll to hit a
Carabinieri," Andrea interrupted. "She must go to jail if
she does so."

"And what if the Carabinieri is a girl doll? Could she then hit it? Or if Giulia's doll is a boy doll? What then? It is not proper, *mia bambina*," Bianca said to her daughter, "for anyone to hit a Carabinieri. In the United States they probably hang a doll that hits a Carabinieri. Is that not so, Carolyn? Signora Blue is from Texas in America, where they hang many bad people."

I sighed. Even in Europe, Texas has a reputation for its bloodthirsty judiciary system. "In Texas we use lethal injection," I said, "a shot of poison." Both children shrieked. "But only for bad adults," which wasn't quite true, "and not for children and dolls," I hastened to add. "Utah may have hanging. I'm not sure. I know that a firing squad is an option in Utah." I was trying to excuse Texas, but why? All the headlines about executions bothered me, too.

"We had a death here just yesterday," I said, anxious to change the subject. "A murder perhaps."

"A *murder*?" gasped Bianca. "In Sorrento? You must tell me about this amazing event."

5

A Conspiracy of Women

Bianca

Holy Mother, protect us! I thought as I stared at the American woman while my thoughts whirled like a horde of gypsy girls crowding in on a tourist. To meet a foreigner one day and find her dead in a swimming pool the next! What a drama! Yet my new acquaintance didn't seem to find it as unusual as I did. Of course, she was from Texas, I reminded myself, a place that evidently had a history of murder in its streets and a stream of murderers passing through its death chamber in modern times. In the wild frontier days, the murderers were simply hung from the nearest tree, or so all those American Westerns made in Italy, the ones I saw as a child, had led me to believe.

Here in my beloved Italy, we are more civilized after centuries of warfare. There are, of course, still crimes of passion. Passion does not end with civilization. And there are thieves who will steal your purse, but not your life. Except perhaps in Sicily and Naples where violence continues as a way of settling disputes. Only the weapons are more civilized, the knife replaced by a submachine gun. Remembering that our hosts at this meeting were Sicilians, I crossed myself and glanced at my babies, playing on the floor with the dolls provided by Carolyn. Could the dead woman have been Sicilian?

"Tell me about this poor dead girl," I begged. "Was she beautiful? Was she from Sicily?"

"I don't know," said Carolyn. "I only spent an afternoon and a dinner with her. She mentioned Perugia. Perhaps she was from there, and she was very beautiful. She had come to meet a lover, but he cancelled the assignation. She had dark hair and eyes that were—oh—just a bit slanted, very exotic. And she wrote poetry. We both loved the poems of Edna St. Vincent Millay."

"I do not know this poet," I replied. "An American? Or French, perhaps?"

"Millay was American," Carolyn replied. "Her poetry was very—sensuous. About love. I think that Paolina may have been influenced by it in her teens. She also spoke of her desire for a variety of lovers, not to mention her irritation that the man she expected to meet here had not arrived."

"Ah, sensuality, lovers. A true Italian. Perhaps she was killed by love," I suggested. Smiling, I asked if Carolyn too had been influenced by the American poet.

She blushed. "I read her poetry when I was only eleven or so, and I didn't really understand what she was writing about then. I was enchanted by the words, the rhymes and rhythms, and by the fact that the book belonged to my mother."

It seemed to me that Carolyn disapproved of the dead girl, of her lovers. Americans can be so puritanical about sex. "So how do you think she came to die in the swimming pool?" I asked.

"I'm not really sure," Carolyn replied, her face and voice as serious as a Reverend Mother asked to explain the meaning of a passage in the writings of St. Catherine of Siena. "I suppose it could have been a diving accident, although diving is forbidden in the pools."

I had to laugh. "What is not forbidden in this hotel? There are signs everywhere telling us what we cannot do, and booklets full of prohibitions in the desk drawer of the room. She would not have paid attention to such silly rules. But perhaps, heartbroken over her lover's defection, she killed herself," I suggested.

"She didn't seem like the type," Carolyn replied, frowning.

"But if she was in love—why not? Unless, of course, she was very devout. Sexual liaisons one can confess and receive forgiveness for, but suicide leaves one in sin and unshriven."

"Well, Lieutenant Buglione mentioned suicide, but to me she seemed more irritated than heartbroken. He also thought the lover might have murdered Paolina. Perhaps she was unfaithful, and he was jealous."

That hint of disapproval came through again. What, I wondered, if this American woman had murdered Paolina in a fit of Puritan righteousness? America was settled by all those censorious Protestants, from whom Carolyn might be descended, and now she lived in Texas, a violent place. "Was there any evidence that she might have been murdered?" I asked.

"Damage to her head where it hit the side of the pool," Carolyn replied. "If she dove from the pool above, wouldn't she have aimed at the deep end rather than the shallow? And her ankles. There were marks on her ankles. Bruising. How did the bruises get there?"

"That could be nothing more sinister than the marks left by ankle-strap sandals. My mother-in-law loves them, the higher the heels the better, but as she is older, the straps sometimes leave marks. Was Paolina wearing such shoes when you last saw her?" Carolyn thought not.

"Perhaps then someone held her by the ankles and dropped her over," I suggested, wondering if Carolyn was strong enough to do that. I had read that American women went to gyms and lifted weights. Perhaps under that pretty, if not particularly stylish, outfit, my new acquaintance was a muscular Amazon. Had my poor countrywoman so shocked Signora Blue that the signora had tossed her over the pool railing in a passion of outraged virtue?

"We must investigate this ourselves," I suggested. An adventure, I thought with delight, knowing that I'd have few enough for the next few years. And with my mother-in-law coming to Sorrento to look after the children—but where was she? Violetta was so feckless. She'd probably gotten lost on her way here, or met some attractive man who made her forget completely her offer to entertain Andrea and Giulia. Well, Lorenzo would have to find his mother, I decided, feeling that I deserved to have an adventure before I settled down with the new baby.

Carolyn was looking at me dubiously. She probably thought that I was too fat to have any fun, and who could blame her for thinking that when I hadn't even been able to get myself off the floor? Sometimes, I must admit, I felt I might be carrying a baby elephant, which would mean I had, what—another year or so of pregnancy?

"I had thought I might ask around," Carolyn admitted. "See if I can find any clues."

Interesting. Was she trying to divert suspicion from herself? "But how can you ask questions when you don't speak Italian? I will help you. I can talk to the maids. Hotel maids know everything. They may know who her lover was." *Or if you were the person with her last night before she plunged to her death*, I thought.

"But won't your husband disapprove?" Carolyn asked. "It might be dangerous, and you're—ah—"

"Pregnant? All the better. No one in Italy would harm a pregnant woman. You'll need not only my help but also my protection. What adventures we'll have. Something to while away the days while our husbands are talking about little chemicals too small to see and too nasty to taste."

"But you have your children with you," Carolyn protested.

We both looked at my babies. Giulia had curled up on the carpet and fallen asleep, while Andrea had taken her doll and was bossing it around in the stern voice of his Carabinieri. What darlings they were. Fortunately, I wouldn't have to expose them to a possibly dangerous woman. "My mother-in-law is on her way to watch the children," I told Carolyn. And to watch me, I thought. Violetta was so sure that I would be unfaithful to her son and provide her with bastard grandchildren if she didn't keep her eye on me. Such foolishness. I adored my Lorenzo. Why would I want another lover when I had him? Of course, one doesn't say that to one's mother-in-law, even in Italy.

It occurred to me, not for the first time, that Violetta might be suspicious of me because I wasn't from Lucca, but rather from wicked, wicked Rome. I giggled at the thought, and Carolyn smiled at me. Or perhaps the fact that Violetta herself had had a series of discreet affairs since the death of Lorenzo's father made her think I might do the same, even though I wasn't a widow.

My goodness. Carolyn had just agreed to accept my help in searching out the cause of Paolina's death. She too claimed to think it would be stimulating, as long as I thought it was safe for me to join in. *Poof. Of course I thought I'd be safe. I'd never endanger my baby. Signora Carolyn Blue would do well to consider her own safety. If she'd killed Paolina, I'd ferret out her secret and report*

*her to the hapless Sorrento division of the Polizia di
Stato.*

I'd awakened in the car as we reached Sorrento to find
a member of the Polizia Municipale trying to give my
Lorenzo a traffic ticket for some little thing. "Lorenzo,"
I'd said, "I think I'm starting contractions. Ask him
where we can find a hospital."

Lorenzo, of course, knew exactly what I was doing. If
I'd been having contractions, I'd have been screaming
and on the verge of giving birth. I'm not one to put up
with long labor. We barely got to the delivery room last
time.

"Now, now, *cara mia*," he said soothingly. "Don't
upset yourself." Then he turned to the traffic cop. "See
what you've done. You've upset my pregnant wife."

The fellow stared at my stomach and then at the two
sleeping children in the back seat. "A million apologies,
little mother," he cried. "What a fine family you have.
You must be from the south."

Just careless, I thought, not that I begrudged my little
product of forgetfulness his life. And I didn't tell the policeman that we came from Rome. The Neapolitans and
their southern neighbors sometimes envy our hosting the
pope and having all the beauties of the papal city. And
why not? Naples was a disaster since the war, a modern
disaster with a history of foreign kings and stupid peasants, so unlike the glory of Rome. "Many thanks, sergeant," I said to the policeman with a motherly smile.

He protested that he had not yet reached so high a
rank. Then he offered to escort us to the hospital, and I
told him that perhaps the baby was simply restless and
telling his mother she needed to lie down and rest. Naturally we parted amicably without the citation he had
meant to give Lorenzo.

"What are you thinking?" Carolyn asked curiously.

"Oh, just that, from what I've seen, the Sorrento police will need all the help we can give them."

We smiled at one another, a conspiracy of women, as Carolyn said, "The lieutenant in charge did seem more excitable and melodramatic than logical."

6
Scientists Incoming

Carolyn

The first event of the meeting in the accompanying persons' packet I had received at Hotel Reception when I arrived was to be a cocktail party at seven, followed by a dinner. The program did not say where, but I feared it might be this hotel with its thoroughly boring entrees. It distressed me to think that Paolina's last dinner had been duck, tough, greasy, and overcooked, with a skin like hard plastic. She had tapped her knife against the offending skin and been rewarded with a sharp, cracking sound.

Jason had neither called nor arrived, although he was usually more considerate than to leave me uninformed. Was I expected to present myself, unaccompanied, for the evening's events? I could hardly plead exhaustion. I'd been here two days and had, after lunch, finished the Hazzard book about Graham Greene on Capri while sitting on my balcony in a comfortably padded chair with the gorgeous blue green water of the Bay of Naples before me. Capri no doubt lay somewhere in the distance, overhung with the rain-bloated clouds that shrouded the peak of Vesuvius and the bay. Or was Capri in the other

direction? When the wind picked up later in the afternoon
and ruffled the pages of my book, I went inside for a re-
freshing nap.

I had tried to get CNN or some other news program
that might have information on the French airport strike,
but had, instead, happened upon a pornographic movie,
three sweaty people, a woman and two men, in a tangle
of limbs. Naturally I turned the set off immediately and
called the desk to complain. The young woman seemed
more amused than sympathetic, even when I suggested
that people with children, of whom there seemed to be a
fair number, would not want their children to see such
things. The desk clerk told me that children were not allowed to use the television remotes or ride the elevators
or use the pools if unattended by a responsible adult.
Then she gave me the names of the channels she thought
might offend me. There seemed to be quite a few, and if
I was not mistaken, one had been a cooking channel. I had
clicked over just before I hit the offensive ménage a trois.
A hotel clerk with a sense of humor, however twisted.

Perhaps the thing to do was call Hank Girol, whose
wife was stranded in Paris as well. He might have news
about the strike in France or at the least an opinion on
whether we should attend the party without our spouses.
If not, perhaps we could eat a meal that I could write
about in one of those fine restaurants in the area that he
claimed to know. My readers wouldn't want to hear about
Paolina's plastic duck or my giant meatball entree. But
first we had to escape. It had occurred to me that the
Grand Palazzo Sorrento might try to keep me from eating
elsewhere. Their dinner menu had no prices, at least for
those of us staying here. One just ordered, regretted the
culinary result, and the cost, whatever it was, would presumably appear on the bill at the end of the visit.

Braving the possibility of another telephone encounter

with the humorous desk clerk, I dialed Reception and asked to be connected to Mr. Girol's room. He said that his wife expected to be in this evening, perhaps in time for dinner, and suggested that Jason might have obtained tickets on the same Paris-to-Naples flight. He definitely thought we should attend the cocktail party because, as he put it, "You can count on good wine and wonderful appetizers from an Italian meeting. Think crostini with truffles and mouth-watering antipasto verdure, slices of Parma ham on crusty bread and . . ."

I did consider those delights and agreed that we should attend the party, whereupon he offered to pick me up in twenty minutes and asked my room number. Not something I'd ordinarily give out to a man I'd known for only an hour or so. Still, his wife was about to arrive. What harm could there be? If he proved overly friendly, I could always threaten him with a word to Sibyl.

Interesting name. There had been a famous Sibyl who lived in a cave on the coast near the Greek colony of Cuma in the fifth century BC, one of Apollo's prophetesses. Now what was the story about her? I'd have to look in the history book I'd brought along. However, while I was gathering clothes for the evening, I remembered. She had offered nine books of prophesy to the Roman King Tarquinius for a very high price, and he, not being a worshipper of Apollo, had refused, whereupon she burned three of the books and offered the six remaining for the same price. Eventually, with just three books left, while six had disappeared into the fire and her price remained the same, the king was so impressed that he purchased what was left of the set and took it home to Rome for consultation in time of need. What else could he do in the face of a woman so sure of herself? I wondered if Hank's Sibyl had such a determined character.

But twenty minutes? With so little time, I couldn't

stop to speculate as I struggled into pantyhose—horrible invention—yanked a cocktail dress over my head and zipped myself into it, combed my hair and added jewelry, and dumped a few items from my shoulder bag into a silver evening clutch. Evening bags are so impractical. One's lucky to get a room key, a Kleenex, a lipstick, a credit card, and a bit of money into an evening bag. What do women do who wear glasses? Given my age—forty plus—I might have to wear glasses myself someday.

At the knock on my door, I sallied forth to meet Hank, who complimented me on my teal dress with its silver cording. I thought it was rather nice myself. I had a pretty matching hair clip to hold my hair—blonde—and a matching necklace and earrings. I had bought them in Barcelona the last day there. Jason, my frugal husband, had thought the Gaudi silver earrings I purchased before his arrival were quite enough in the jewelry department for one trip—and this was the first chance I'd had to wear them since I'd found the dress to match—in an El Paso boutique, of all places. The earrings were a little heavy, which brought to mind an image of my earlobes sagging like a dachshund's in my golden years. I'd seen women like that. What could they do? Have their ears trimmed? Perhaps there was a plastic surgery specialty for women with elongated earlobes. I'd heard of an eyelid ophthalmology specialty.

"What's so funny?" Hank asked as we got on the elevator. I told him.

When we got to the desk to ask where the cocktail party would be held, the clerk said, in reasonable English, "I know the voice. The pornography signora. No?"

I was horribly embarrassed and said, "I beg your pardon?" in a huffy tone.

"No rule you must watch sexy films," she assured me. "I go find where is party." She tripped off, Hank looked to me for an explanation, and I said, "Don't ask." So we stood silently and eavesdropped on an English couple at the next registration spot, the man and woman both in tweeds, both somewhat frizzy-haired, although his was disappearing and hers was a strange taupe shade. He had spectacles sliding down his nose, and she was carrying a plant, roots dangling with dirt still clinging to them. Horticulturists? He probably had potting soil in his pockets, which bulged and sagged with the weight.

Dottore and Signora Stackpole, as the desk clerk called them—could they be members of the conference?—were asking questions: Was the bathtub at the end of the hall or in their room? Would they need coins for the water heater? Could soft-boiled eggs and toast fingers be had from the breakfast buffet? What kind of tea did the hotel serve? Not made with tea bags, surely? Could the clerk name the flowers growing outside the entrance, and would they grow in England? Where was this cocktail party mentioned in the chemistry conference brochure?

At this point Hank interrupted to introduce himself and me, and the concierge interrupted to tell us all that the cocktail party would be starting momentarily in the Victor Emmanuel room.

"I can't even think of cocktails, Francis," protested the Englishwoman. "I need to pot this—whatever it is. What is it, young lady?" The desk clerk didn't know and wasn't sure patrons could bring uprooted plants into the hotel. "What I need is a good cup of tea and a lie down," Mrs. Stackpole continued over the clerk's remarks.

Ignoring his wife, Francis Stackpole introduced himself and declared that he could use a nip of something stronger than tea. "Lead on, young fellow," he said to Hank. Then the professor from England waved over a bellman and ordered him to take Mrs. Stackpole and the bags to their room. "Come down when you feel fit, old girl," he said to his wife, and looked expectantly at Hank and me, as if we might have a "nip of something stronger than tea" on us.

Before we could take Professor Stackpole to the party, and while Eliza Stackpole was instructing the bellman as to the exact placement of their luggage on the trolley, the Massonis stepped off the elevator, both children in tow. Bianca spotted me and led her family in our direction. More introductions followed, but not before Bianca assumed that Hank was my husband and had to be told that he was the husband of Professor Sibyl Evers of Rutgers, who had been stranded in Paris with my husband, Jason Blue. The Massonis looked very interested to hear this, causing me to think they might have misinterpreted the information.

"Of course we have no idea whether they saw each other," I hastened to add. "I mean whether they happened across each other—in the airport, that is." I could feel my cheeks turn pink. "Or even if they're coming in on the same plane."

Lorenzo Massoni gave me such a sweet, sympathetic smile that I felt like hitting him. He probably thought I was some pitiful, cuckolded wife. *Although it's husbands who are cuckolded, not wives*, I reminded myself. *What are wives when their husbands are running around on them? Besides angry?* I couldn't think of a word. *Not that my husband even knows Professor Evers. What are the chances of that?*

"There's a dead lady in the swimming pool," said Andrea in his excellent English. "Murdered. That's what Mama thinks."

"Aren't you a darling little curly-haired tyke?" said Eliza Stackpole, patting Andrea on the head. "And with such good English." Then she turned to her husband and said, "Francis, I think we should turn straight around and go back to Oxford." She had turned pale at the thought of a dead lady in the hotel swimming pool.

"Nonsense," said the professor from England.

"She's not still *in* the pool," Bianca explained to her son. "Of course she isn't. Don't cry, Giulia. The lady's body has been taken away, dear, and her soul's gone up to God."

"I'll bet her body was all puckered," said Andrea with relish, "and the police will cut her up to see how she died."

Giulia began to cry, which was probably her brother's intent. Bianca said, "Where in the world is your mother, Lorenzo? She's supposed to be taking care of the children."

"I have no idea, my love," he replied. Then to me, "I know your husband's research and look forward to meeting him, Signora Blue. And now, why don't we look for that welcome party we've been invited to?"

"Maybe I *will* come along to the party," murmured Eliza Stackpole. "Bodies in the swimming pool? How dreadful! You, fellow, take those bags up to our room. I'm certainly not staying there by myself in a hotel that has dead bodies scattered about. The poor woman was probably drowned by the Mafia."

The Mafia? That was a scenario I hadn't considered. Our hosts were Sicilians, and Paolina, when we stopped yesterday to watch a wedding party entering a church, said it was undoubtedly a Mafia wedding; she could tell by the tuxedoed men with hard faces who were keeping the crowd from coming too close. On the other hand, it had been a chance remark, and she had nothing to do with the meeting and the hosts from Catania.

"You saw the dead lady in the swimming pool, didn't

you?" Andrea had edged up beside me and was staring at me with great interest. "Mama said you pulled her out."

Now the Stackpoles were staring at me. Jason was sure to hear about and disapprove of my brief association with the deceased. If he ever arrived.

7
A French Encounter

Bianca

"**W**hat's a tyke, Mama?" my sweet Andrea asked.

I couldn't remember—if I'd ever known. "Something nice, I'm sure, sweetheart." But I thought that it was probably something unkind. The English have always considered us either frivolous or dangerous. And Signora Stackpole thought the Mafia must have killed Paolina? What nonsense. The Mafia doesn't throw people into swimming pools. As for the English—they've been sending their pasty-faced sons and horse-faced daughters to Italy to be exposed to culture and to sow their wild—what's the phrase?—Grasses?—for decades, centuries, and looking down their long noses at us. I used to hate having them on tours. They either ignored me and talked among themselves—"Look, Wycomb, that child has a dirty face." As if their children never got smudged. Or they wanted to argue with me and pronounced all the historical and place names wrong. Or they said disapproving things about the church and the pope. No one has the right to do that but us Italians.

I liked the Americans much better. They were friend-

lier, and why wouldn't they be? Half of Italy immigrated
and bred the joy of life into them. Carolyn, for instance,
was a pleasant woman, even if I did suspect her of mur-
dering Paolina.

At that moment, I heard her say, "What a beautiful
dog," and when I looked around, a huge black poodle let
out a loud woof and launched himself at her. Poor Carolyn
landed on her bottom, looking dazed, while the dog licked
her face.

My daughter, who loves dogs, cried, "Look at the dog-
gie, Mama. He's kissing Signora Blue." Giulia headed
their way to claim a "kiss" for herself, but I dragged her
back.

"Charles de Gaulle, stop that," ordered the woman who
had circled us in the hall.

"Thank you," said Carolyn to the French woman as the
dog obediently backed off.

While Carolyn searched her little silver purse for a
Kleenex to wipe the dog drool from her face, the French
woman said in English—her accent wasn't half as good
as mine, "My apologies, Madame. I don't know what pos-
sessed Charles. His manners are usually impeccable."
Then she scolded the dog so sternly in French that he hung
his head while swiveling his eyes toward Carolyn.

"I believe our Charles has fallen in love," said the
French husband. "You must forgive his clumsy zeal. He
was trying to kiss you, Madame, as the little Italian girl
said, but perhaps you do not understand Italian."

The French couple was very well dressed, I'll say that
for them, but I hadn't missed that covert insult about language. The French are as disapproving as the English,
maybe more so. Poor Carolyn, covered with dog drool,
and, God help us, that big lout of a poodle had bruised her
cheek. I handed Giulia to Lorenzo, who was watching the
scene with amusement, and went to help Carolyn up.

"Adrien, I see you and your wife managed to make it away from Lyon despite the strike," said my husband.

I realized then that the Frenchies must be part of the conference. Something worse than the Stackpoles to look forward to. But no one could complain that I'd brought the children along, not when the French had their dog with them. Maybe the dog would attack our hostess, the very noble Constanza Ricci-Tassone, and the French would be asked to leave. Was that too much to hope for?

Such were my thoughts while Lorenzo introduced everyone and explained the missing husband and wife, who had been caught up in the French air-traffic controllers' strike.

Madame Albertine Guillot evidently took amiss my husband's good-natured teasing about the French propensity to call sudden, inconvenient strikes. She recalled for us the year when a new computer system had been installed in the railroad station in Rome, resulting in twenty percent of the trains failing to run at all, while others were listed for departure and arrival at the wrong times and on the wrong tracks.

"Has a new system of air traffic direction been installed in Paris then?" I asked innocently. "Is that why no one can get here from your capital?" She glared at me.

Professor Adrien Guillot, the French husband, said, "Well, strikes. I remember the labor strike in Rome when so many from all over Italy, wearing their red caps and carrying their red banners, prevented us from visiting the Golden Palace of Nero."

"Not to mention the marathon runners bearing down on those of us trying to cross streets," said Madame Guillot.

"Shall I mediate a truce between the French and the Italians?" asked Professor Stackpole, who had been scratching the ears of an ecstatic Charles de Gaulle. Stackpole's wife had just returned from chasing the bellman into the elevator to give him her uprooted plant, which she wanted him to carry upstairs with the bags and put in a glass of water.

Finally we all set out for the cocktail party, Albertine Guillot and I with our high heels clicking on the tile floors, Carolyn limping slightly in unfashionable, flat-heeled shoes, although her dress was very pretty, especially for the clothing of an American, whose country is not known for its sense of fashion. Still, Americans are much more fashionable than the English. Mrs. Stackpole was still wearing her tweeds and walking shoes. She hadn't bothered to change, although she may have come all the way from England in that outfit. I'm told that the English only bathe once a week. How dreadful, and wearing such unseasonably heavy clothes. Lorenzo and I take a bath together every night in our large, claw-footed tub. It was a wonder we didn't have ten children by then instead of just two and eight-ninths.

Giulia managed to reach out and pat the behind of Charles de Gaulle, who growled.

"I must warn you that Charles does not like children," said Madame Guillot, looking disdainfully over her shoulder.

"How French of him," I muttered under my breath.

"Try to remember, my love, that we're all one happy European Union now," my husband whispered, his lovely blue eyes twinkling. Where did they come from? Perhaps an ancestress had been raped by a soldier in an army of a Holy Roman Emperor from Germany. Fortunately, the rape and its genetic consequences had failed to cast Germanic gloom over my husband's happy and ardent disposition. I sincerely hoped that the late Paolina had been lucky enough to have lovers of Lorenzo's temperament before her death.

8

Sicilian Hospitality

Carolyn

As we entered the room where the cocktail party was to be held, I hung back to avoid the dog. My cheek ached miserably where Charles de Gaulle slammed into it with his hard head. Avoiding the dog left me in the receiving line beside Hank and just in front of the Stackpoles. Mrs. Stackpole dithered on and on in a high voice about whether the bellman could be trusted with the uprooted plant she had been forced to leave with him. Professor Stackpole seemed to take no notice of his wife's concerns.

First he asked me about the woman I had discovered in the pool, so I gave him a brief description of Paolina's death. "I wonder whether the pool water killed her," he speculated, as any chemist interested in toxins would. Jason might have said the same thing. I assured the Englishman that I did not think toxic water had been the problem.

He then looked about him with interest and obvious surprise, which I could understand. The Victor Emmanuel room was so much different from the Roman villa feel of the hotel with its tiled floors and its doors, windows, and

balconies opening onto gardens and pools. In this room
the walls were covered in red brocade (perhaps red for the
flags of Garibaldi, who united Italy and put the King of
Savoy on the throne?), and the floors were marble and lit-
tered with gilded furniture. Heavily draped windows
screened out the sunshine and the grandeur of the natural
world outside and lent a claustrophobic feel to the space.

But more than the room, our hosts mesmerized me.
Constanza Ricci-Tassone was a tall woman with generous
breasts, but otherwise starkly thin, her tanned skin
stretched tightly across her bones. She had blonde hair,
natural blonde but rinsed to control any darkening brought
on by maturity or the encroaching white of age. I knew
this because I rinse my own hair periodically for just those
reasons. A blonde Sicilian. I later learned that she claimed
descent from the Norman, Robert Guiscard, who marched
his army north to Rome in the eleventh century to rescue
Pope Gregory, looted the city, and made off with his prize,
the pope himself—Guiscard and his amazonian Lombard
wife, Sichelgaeta, who rode into battle with him, hair un-
bound and streaming from under her helmet. Was the
haughty Constanza wily, like Guiscard, or warlike, as his
wife had been? Or both?

Her husband, Ruggiero Ricci, owner of the chemical
company hosting the meeting, was dark skinned, perhaps
with the blood of the Saracens who had ruled Sicily before the Normans, with dark hair, whitened at the hairline.
He was shorter than his wife, and stocky. My mind
jumped back to a church in Sorrento I had visited with
Paolina. It contained an altar to Saint Giuseppe Moscati,
who wore, in his portrait, a pale green lab coat and round
spectacles. A handsome man from the early twentieth century, he had taught in the medical school in Naples, where
his chastity and his good works among the poor, to whom
he gave money rather than accepting fees, and his mirac-

ulous medical cures both before and after his death earned him sainthood.

A priest in the Sorrento church had told us about him. After I said he looked like a chemist, Paolina inquired and translated the priest's reply. She had almost laughed aloud when she saw the saint's portrait above the candles that lit up with electric lights when one put a coin in the slot. However, she wouldn't explain her amusement beyond saying that the saint looked like a very unsaintly friend of hers. I had taken a prayer card with his picture to show to Jason.

Now I noticed a resemblance between Giuseppe Moscati and our host, although Signor Ricci did not wear a green lab coat, but rather an expensively tailored suit, and he did not have round spectacles, which might not have been fashionable enough to suit his wife. I had only a moment to wonder if he had been Paolina's friend. Then it was my turn to be introduced. The dog, thank goodness, the French couple, Bianca, Lorenzo, and their children, who had been petted and smiled upon by Constanza, had moved on to be served drinks.

"But where are your spouses?" Signor Ricci demanded after the introductions, as if cheated by the absence of Jason and Hank's wife. Once Hank had explained the problem in Paris, Ricci said, shrugging expressively, "Ah, the French. Their workers have no loyalty to the bosses, unlike our good Sicilians. Well, I must wait a bit longer to meet these two scientists for whom I have such great respect. But not too much longer I hope. Signora Blue, your husband is a very lucky man." Then, much to my astonishment, he leaned forward and kissed me on the cheek. "Lovely, is she not, Constanza?"

"Delightful," murmured our hostess, who then introduced us to Dottore Valentino Santoro, a fine-featured man in his thirties with sad eyes and an expertise in toxicity. "Do have drinks and antipasti," said our hostess, and waved us in the direction of an ornate cabinet presided over by a dashing waiter. We moved on, making way for the Stackpoles.

Because I was an American, I was encouraged to drink bourbon, evidently provided specially for my husband, who was not here, and for me, although I don't like it that much. I had to argue for wine. However, I had no argument with the antipasto and held a small plate of shrimp crostini, mushroom pate on toasts, and little fried zucchini sticks. They were lovely. Had our hostess arranged to have them brought in? Surely the plastic-duck chef had not provided them.

While I nibbled and sipped happily, I endured another round of questioning by inquisitive young Andrea Massoni. Then our host, who said he had overheard me mentioning a woman named Paolina, drew me aside. "May I ask her last name?"

"Paolina's?" I blinked. "I was speaking of Paolina Marchetti."

"And you know this woman?" His wife had glided up beside him with Santoro in her wake.

"I did, briefly, yes," I replied.

"Could you tell me where she is?"

"Well, not exactly. The police took her body away this morning."

"Her body!" Ruggiero Ricci all but glared at me. "Could you clarify that phrasing to me, Signora Blue?"

"She's dead," I explained. He was making me nervous. "Drowned in the swimming pool. I pulled her out, but it was too late. I think she'd been dead for some time. Did—did you know her?"

My host had paled, but more astoundingly, the chemist who worked for him exclaimed, "Paolina is dead?" and began to weep.

Constanza, who didn't seem the sympathetic type, tried
to comfort him while saying to me, "This is quite a shock.
Most unfortunate." She patted their weeping employee on
the shoulder. "You must excuse Valentino's emotional
outburst," and she handed him a handkerchief from her
own beaded handbag. "Do control yourself, Valentino,"
and to me, "I fear that our young friend suffered an unrequited love for Paolina, who was my husband's secretary."

I was dumbfounded. If she worked for the company
that invited Jason to this meeting, why hadn't Paolina
mentioned it to me? Her week's reservation here was now
explained, but not her failure to mention that she was the
secretary of the man I had speculated about in her presence, the man who looked just like the saint, who had
been described by her as resembling an unsaintly friend.
Had Signor Ricci been more than a friend, more than an
employer to Paolina? And what about the grief-stricken
Valentino Santoro? Would his unrequited love or jealousy
of the lover she had come here to meet have caused him
to arrive early and kill her?

"You say she was here in Sorrento yesterday?" Constanza asked.

I nodded, wondering if Signor Ricci might be the lover
who told Paolina he couldn't meet her.

"How strange that she came a day early. You didn't
mention that, Ruggiero," said his wife.

"She was making arrangements for the meeting," he
muttered.

"She told me that she expected to meet a—er—friend
here last night," I said, watching them both closely for
their reactions, especially Signor Ricci's. "But he cancelled."

"By friend do you mean lover? How disappointing for
her," said Constanza. "Perhaps she committed suicide."

Perhaps your husband came after all and killed her, I thought. He looked more stunned than guilty, but that could be an act.

"In Paolina's unfortunate absence, I think we must call Gracia to take up her duties."

"We don't need Gracia," said the husband sharply.

"I can't believe she's dead," mourned the devastated Valentino, and blew his nose into the dainty handkerchief provided by Signora Ricci-Tassone.

I slipped away to whisper the news to Bianca, who said she'd be sure to sit next to our host and see what she could find out. I had to agree that she might be a better interrogator than I since she spoke Italian. On the other hand, I'd had more experience in the investigation of murder, if this was a case of murder. I didn't say that to Bianca, as it's rather embarrassing to admit that my path has been strewn with corpses since I started traveling with Jason. So many murders. Obviously I'd led a sheltered life until recently.

Canapés, in the style of the Campania, are often based on vegetables because, since Roman times, the rich volcanic soil has made the area the vegetable garden of Italy. Interestingly, Neapolitan mushroom pate uses butter, rather than olive oil, which was the oil of choice in Roman times. Butter was introduced by invading Germanic tribes prior to the Middle Ages but was prohibited on fasting days for many years by the Roman Catholic Church. The recipe was inspired by the *Monzu* (corruption of Monsieur) cooks favored by the nobility in Naples, and, of course, the Marsala is from Sicily, which was joined politically with southern Italy from the time of Norman rule in the eleventh and twelfth centuries.

Neapolitan Mushroom Pate on Toasts

- Sauté over medium heat *12 ounces cleaned and sliced white mushrooms* in *2 ounces of butter* and *1/2 teaspoon of dried herbs, rosemary, thyme, and sage*, until liquid from mushrooms has mixed with butter.

- Stir in *1/2 cup dry Marsala wine* and cook until all liquid has evaporated.

- Add *1 tablespoon salted capers, rinsed,* and *1 1/2 tablespoons Gaeta olives, pitted and chopped (purple Greek olives can be substituted)*, and cook at low heat, stirring, for 15 minutes until mushrooms are slightly browned.

- Puree mixture in a blender with *1/2 cup heavy cream* until stiff. If too stiff, add cream 1 tablespoon at a time.

- Put mixture in a bowl and stir in *salt* to taste.

- After smoothing surface with a knife, cover with plastic wrap and refrigerate for 2 hours. Serve on toasts.

Carolyn Blue,
"Have Fork, Will Travel,"
Toronto Mail

9

Dinner Palermo Style

Bianca

I managed to station myself right beside Signor Ricci and mention how comfortable the seat looked to a woman as close to childbirth as I. Naturally he pulled out the chair for me, looking down the neckline of my dress as he helped me into my seat. This happened before his wife could tell people where to sit at the round table in the round dining room whose walls were covered with murals depicting the Roman era on the Bay of Naples. Very decadent—Roman ladies in gossamer gowns reclining on couches with soldierly men in short robes and boots, all drinking and sharing grapes. I wouldn't have objected to a nice couch to recline on while the distinguished Signor Ricci fed me whatever was on the menu. Once I was down, everyone else took seats. There are rewards to pregnancy in Italy. Even if our birthrate is startlingly low, we still pay lip service to the virtues of motherhood.

I directed my darlings to seats beside me, and Lorenzo took the other end of our family to keep them in line. Our blonde Sicilian hostess sat beside her husband with the red-eyed Valentino to her left and the Frenchies beyond him. I could have felt sorry for her if she hadn't been so snobbish and so obviously irritated that I had usurped her right to arrange the seating at her own table. If it was so important to her, she should have used place cards, not that it would have stopped me from sitting next to her husband and questioning him about the dead girl.

Beyond Lorenzo and my children sat Carolyn. She was chatting sweetly with Andrea, which, of course, softened my heart toward Carolyn, but not my brain. I'm sure there are many murderesses who love children. Her companion, Signor Girol, was talking across the table to Professor Stackpole about the disposal of toxic materials in England, and Mrs. Stackpole, who was seated by the professor from France, was asking him questions about his dog, particularly whether the dog gave them trouble by eating plants in their garden, to which Adrien Guillot replied that they owned a very delightful apartment in the old section of Lyon but no garden, and that their dog, whose ancestors were hunting dogs, naturally preferred meat to greens. Where was the dangerous Charles de Gaulle? I wondered. Under the table sniffing out Carolyn for another foray? Between the Stackpoles and Girol were two empty seats awaiting the missing chemists.

The primi piatta, *pasta alla Norma*, a delicacy from Catania according to our hostess, was served, and I asked Ruggiero, as he suggested I address him, if he had any idea who might have been the lover of his late secretary.

"If only it had been I," exclaimed Valentino bitterly.

"No more crying," our hostess cautioned. Then she tasted her pasta and summoned the headwaiter. "Too much garlic," she snapped. "We are neither Sicilian peasants, nor Romans."

"My apologies, Signora Ricci-Tassone," he stammered. "I will inform the chef."

"Very tasty," I murmured to the poor man, catching his

sleeve as he passed by. "But then, I'm Roman, not Sicilian."

"What was that?" demanded Constanza.

"I was asking your husband about Paolina Marchetti. Her death caused quite a stir in the hotel."

"I have no idea who she came to meet," he said, scowling.

"Well, do not worry, my love," said his wife cheerfully. "Gracia will be here by morning to take over. She is a fine woman—nurse to me and to my children," she explained to the group at large. "When her husband died, I saw to it that she went to school so that she could become the manager of my husband's office. Even as we grieve, the meeting must go on, and Gracia will see to it. The Sindaccos have been servants to the Tassones for centuries."

"The woman's an old witch," Ruggiero muttered to me.

"Really? I've never met one," I replied. "I think they're extinct from Rome north."

"One what?" demanded Constanza, who had not invited me to call her by her first name. When I shrugged, she said, "It is very sad that Paolina was so distressed over her love life that she would kill herself. I hope she went to confession before doing so. It might ameliorate her fate in the afterlife, for we all know that suicide is a sin, but suicide unshriven—ah, here is the *tonno alla Palermitana*. That is tuna fish in the style of Palermo. Do not look so gloomy, Ruggiero. Our guests will think you do not like the menu I have chosen. Each dish," she said to the table at large, "I have chosen to make you familiar with the delights of Sicilian cuisine, which is different from any in the world. Signora Blue, may I ask why you are writing on a notepad. Is something wrong with the fish?"

Carolyn looked up and smiled beatifically. "It's too wonderful for words, Signora. I write about food for

American newspapers, and this is a meal that I must describe."

"Ah. I am happy to think that Americans will have a chance to read about fine cuisine."

The woman was as pretentious and arrogant as the Frenchies, I thought, and then smiled at Ruggiero when he patted my knee and asked if he could help me to more fish. "You must come to Rome, where we have wonderful *veal Marsala*, a Sicilian dish, which I recommend to you," I responded.

"Perhaps after the birth of your child," he replied in an intimate undertone. I'd have to tell Carolyn that he didn't seem to be so broken up over the death of Paolina that he wasn't on the lookout for a new love, assuming that Paolina had been his love. I did not know that.

"I shall see that you are provided with recipes for these dishes if you desire them," Constanza said to Carolyn, who agreed enthusiastically. Then laughing with delight at the thought, she told us that recipes in historic cookbooks had interesting size and time instructions.

"For instance, there's a recipe for ravioli that advises the chef to make the ravioli the size of a half chestnut and to cook the pasta while saying the Lord's Prayer two times, then take it off the fire. In fact," she continued, "the Italian word for recipe comes from a Latin word *recepta*, which referred to a doctor's prescription for his patient or for a pharmacist."

Constanza stared at her. "You seem to know a lot about food and its history. Let me assure you that any recipe I provide will have no medicinal quality beyond nourishment and will contain modern measurement instructions, although you may have to translate European measures into—is something the matter, Signora Blue?"

A look of horror had passed over Carolyn's face. Then

her body jerked back, she grasped the edge of the table, and a canine howl followed.

"*Mon Dieu*," exclaimed Adrien Guillot. "Albertine, I believe your wretched dog is again hounding Madame Blue."

The Frenchie rose in as dignified a manner as possible, considering that her dog had obviously been guilty of some antisocial behavior, such as nosing the crotch of a fellow diner. Albertine ordered Charles de Gaulle out from under the table, pointed toward a curved wall, and snapped her fingers, sending him into exile with his head hanging, again. "Sit," she commanded in French, her voice dripping with ice. Poor dog. I'd have been miserable too if she were my mistress.

"Are you all right, my dear Signora Blue?" asked our hostess. Poor Carolyn, whose hands were shaking and whose face was pale, nodded. "Good," said the very self-absorbed Sicilian. "I must add a caution to my offer of recipes," she continued. "The quality of the ingredients is most important in the preparation of these dishes. Such fine ingredients may not be available in the United States, which, I'm told, is a land of food that is preprepared in boxes and frozen lumps." Nonetheless, she looked gratified at Carolyn's interest, although when she tasted the tuna herself, she remarked to the headwaiter that the white wine used in its preparation was not dry enough.

"Well, here you are!" exclaimed a familiar voice from the direction of the door. I turned my head and saw my mother-in-law, dressed for the occasion and all smiles. Where had she been? And how like her to arrive after I'd had to bring the children to the dinner. "Shall I take the little ones up to bed, Bianca?" she asked, although I was sure she had no intention of being left out of the fun.

"Don't make us go upstairs, Mama," cried Andrea,

who had been devouring his fish with gusto. "The dinner's so delicious. We want to finish, don't we, Giulia?"

Constanza beamed at them. "Such sweet children. Of
course, they must stay. It pleases me to see little ones ap-
preciating good food."

My daughter nodded vigorously over a pretty dress,
now dotted with sauce from the pasta and a few sprigs of
rosemary from the fish. Since she had a forkful of fish
waving in time to her nods, a bit of rosemary sailed in my
direction. However, used to such problems, I quickly
draped a napkin over my shoulder in case it landed.

"Can't Granny have dinner here, and then we'll go upstairs?" Andrea asked. "Signora Blue is telling me and
Papa what's in everything, so we can tell you, Mama, and
you can make these things. And then Granny can tell us a
story before we go to bed."

Lorenzo stood up to kiss his mother, who was then
duly introduced and took a seat beside Hank Girol. He
rose courteously to pull out her chair and greeted her
warmly. Violetta is an amazing woman, all curls and
flounces and pretty ways. She flirted right back over the
next course, a *caponata* that raised questions about the capers from Constanza. She detected that they had been preserved in vinegar rather than brine, as was preferable. The
dish was delicious. Obviously, she just liked to complain.

I could hear my mother-in-law telling Lorenzo that she
had taken the wrong plane from Rome and ended up in
Milan, rather than Naples, where a charming employee of
Alitalia had been so sympathetic that he had taken her out
for a wonderful meal, a *risotto*, which the Milanese do so
well, until such time as she could get a plane to Naples.
No one but my mother-in-law could manage to get on the
wrong plane—she'd probably been flirting with the
ticket-taker—and cap that off by getting a free meal and
a free ticket to her original destination. However, she

was good with the children and an amiable woman in general—she'd come to live with us after Lorenzo's father died—except for her propensity to accuse me of a desire to be unfaithful to her son.

"Well, my husband's colleagues are scandalized that we have a third child on the way," I said in response to a remark from Ruggiero about the fecundity of beautiful women.

"There is no scandal in children," said Constanza. "Children are a gift from God. What fault could Romans find in—"

"Oh, the good things of life that are taken away from the first children by each additional child—education, cottages on the beach, cultural opportunities," I replied airily.

"Years of sleeplessness for the parents," my husband added.

"One hires a nursemaid to take care of wakeful children," said Constanza. "You should pay no attention to your husband's colleagues, Signora Massoni. God has blessed you." Then she looked at me narrowly, with the eye of a woman who has borne her own children, and added, "And he will bless you again very soon. I am surprised you felt able to leave Rome in your condition."

"My doctor doesn't seem to think the baby will arrive this week," I replied, and switched the subject. "Having heard of how beautiful Paolina was, I'm surprised that she wasn't married with children of her own."

"You seem amazingly interested in a woman you did not know, Signora," said our hostess.

"I did not know her, but Carolyn spent time with her before she died and was quite taken with Paolina, weren't you, Carolyn?"

Carolyn nodded and swallowed a mouthful of her *caponata*. "Yes," she agreed. "We had a mutual interest in poetry. In fact, Paolina wrote poetry, which I found admirable. Signora Ricci, this *caponata* is marvelous. I do love eggplant, and the strange thing is that when the Arabs brought it to Italy, people were suspicious of it. In fact, the Italian word for eggplant, *melanzana*, comes from *mela insana*, which means 'unsound apple.' It was thought to be vulgar and eaten only by the lower classes."

While Carolyn was telling us more than I, for one, needed to know about eggplant, I noticed that Ruggiero looked surprised to hear that his secretary had been a poetess. Perhaps he hadn't been her lover. Surely he would have known about the poetry if they were intimate. In fact, the only person who seemed to know anything personal about Paolina was Carolyn. I pondered whether their acquaintance had been of a longer duration than the one day Carolyn admitted to. Could Carolyn have been the lover who came to Paolina that night and then killed her? Amazing as it seems to me, there are women who make love to women. I'd definitely have to make discreet enquiries about the time the two women had spent together at the hotel.

"I believe our two missing scientists have arrived," said Ruggiero heartily.

We all turned to see a rather short but handsome bearded man and a tall, red-haired woman, who would have been prettier without her glasses.

Hank Girol stopped flirting with my mother-in-law and rose to greet his wife. Carolyn did not rise to greet her husband. Instead she stared at Girol's wife. I pondered what that might mean. The possibilities were: She was uninterested in her husband. She was interested in Girol's wife. She was jealous of the two new arrivals. Or she, too, thought the glasses Girol's wife wore would be better replaced by contact lenses.

Recipes from Sicily are much like those from the Campania because the cultural influences over the centuries—Greek, Roman, Arab, Norman, French, and Spanish—were similar. In the fish recipe that follows, the Arabs brought lemons to the island, and the sea provides tuna. Wine was a popular flavoring with both the Greeks and Romans. In the vegetable recipe, the use of sweet and sour flavoring was popular with both the Romans and the chefs of the Middle Ages, but the use of sugar, instead of honey, for sweet flavoring, came from Sicily, which grew sugar cane while the rest of Europe was still limited to honey. Both Sicily and the Campania have rich soil because of the volcanic eruptions of Etna and Vesuvius.

Tuna in the Style of Palermo

- Combine *8 ounces dry white wine* with the *juice of one lemon, several sprigs of rosemary, a crushed clove of garlic, salt,* and *freshly ground pepper.*

- Slice *1 1/4 pounds tuna fish,* wash well, and marinate in the wine mixture for 2 or more hours.

- Remove and drain the fish. Grill on both sides, basting with the marinade.

- Heat in a skillet *4 tablespoons extra virgin olive oil* and, using a fork, mash in *3 sardine fillets* to form a paste, which is then spread on the tuna.

- Serve garnished with *rosemary* and *cherry tomatoes.*

Caponata

- Wash and slice *1 pound small eggplants, salt*, and drain in a sieve to remove the bitter juices.

- Dice finely *1 pound onions*, blanch *4 stalks celery* and cut in small pieces, halve *1 cup green olives* and remove stones, and blanch and press *1 pound tomatoes* through a sieve. Rinse eggplants in cold running water, drain, and pat dry with paper towels.

- Heat eggplant on both sides to golden brown in *4 tablespoons hot vegetable oil* and drain on paper towels.

- Sauté onions gently in a saucepan in *6 tablespoons extra virgin olive oil*. Add celery, olives, and tomatoes, sprinkle with *salt* and *pepper*, and simmer 5 minutes. Add *2 tablespoons sugar, 7 tablespoons wine vinegar*, and *3 tablespoons capers*, and simmer 10 more minutes until vinegar odor has disappeared.

- Let vegetables cool before serving.

Carolyn Blue,
"Have Fork, Will Travel,"
Summit, NJ, News

10
The Return of an Errant Husband

Carolyn

My husband entered the dining room beside a strange woman with whom he looked completely comfortable. She was quite tall and, although wearing flats, topped Jason by four or five inches. They both looked somewhat rumpled, certainly not dressed for this dinner party. All smiles, she embraced Hank and introduced him to Jason, making me feel like an outsider, someone watching my own husband's arrival without any part in it. More introductions followed, and Bianca's mother-in-law insisted on giving her seat to Sibyl Evers and taking the two children off with her.

Jason, instead of arranging a seat beside me by asking Lorenzo to move down by Bianca, sat down beside Sibyl, who told her husband that she and Jason met in the Paris airport the day the strike cancelled their flight and had been talking chemistry and writing formulas on Paris tablecloths ever since. Looking horrified at the idea of writing on tablecloths, Albertine Guillot asked if the restaurants had not protested such behavior. Her husband asked what compounds they had been discussing, and

Ruggiero Ricci insisted that they discuss their ideas. They were reticent.

Why? I wondered uneasily. What had they been doing for two days if not talking chemistry? Instead of replying to questions about chemistry, Jason remarked that it was lucky Sibyl had known a hotel where they could stay. Hank chuckled and said he hoped they had managed to get two rooms and that if he hadn't trusted his wife implicitly, he might have been jealous. Having recently worried about my husband taking off for Austin with a female graduate student and realizing that his greeting to me had been little more than a nod and a comment that he'd finally made it to Sorrento, I found that I did *not* trust my husband implicitly, a trust I had taken for granted for years. I was jealous.

"Have you been enjoying yourself?" Jason asked across the table.

"Certainly," I said rather stiffly. "You've missed an excellent dinner."

"The airline fed us on the flight to make up for the inconvenience of being held up two days in Paris," he replied. "What happened to your face?" He sounded rather suspicious, as if I'd been injured while doing something he disapproved of.

"I was attacked by a dog," I replied coolly.

"Your wife has had a bad time of it, Signor," said Bianca gaily from her place by our host. "Not only did the Guillots' poodle knock heads with her, but before that she found the corpse of our host's secretary dead in the pool outside her room. I think Carolyn will need much comforting, Signor Blue."

"Jason," he corrected her, to which she replied with her own name. "I doubt that my wife is in need of comforting. She's become quite accustomed to corpses, haven't you, Carolyn?"

I could see the shock on the faces around the table, particularly Bianca's. She was undoubtedly amazed by my ill luck in finding more than one dead body, but Jason needn't have said that. Now everyone was looking at me strangely, except our hostess, who picked up on Bianca's name and said, "What a quaint, old-fashioned name, Signora Massoni," to which Bianca said, "Yes, isn't it? My mother named me after the good daughter in Shakespeare's *The Taming of the Shrew*. She played the part in the days when she was an actress."

"Thank God she didn't play Kate," said Lorenzo. "I'd have hated to spend my life with a shrew."

"An actress?" mused Constanza Ricci-Tassone, raising her eyebrows as if she'd never heard of an actress who was also someone's mother. "How interesting. And were you an actress as well, Signora Massoni? Before your marriage?"

"No," said Bianca, doing a perfect imitation of Constanza's condescending smile. "I was a tour guide. Lorenzo's mother visited Rome from Lucca and took my tour. A year later when Lorenzo moved to Rome, she gave him my name and telephone number. You might say ours was an arranged marriage."

"And how does one become a tour guide?" asked Constanza. "I would be most interested to know."

I had to swallow a sigh. Given the developing rancor between Bianca and our hostess, the chances of Bianca getting any useful information from the Riccis about Paolina seemed small.

"I can't speak for other tour guides, but I became one by majoring at university in history and foreign languages."

"She has an amazing facility for languages," said Lorenzo proudly. "And it seems to be genetic. Our children can do pretty well in three languages besides Italian.

They certainly didn't get that from me. I hated German and French and only forced myself to master English because it's the lingua franca of science."

Constanza smiled thinly; her husband asked Bianca if he could offer her a job; and the Guillots, who had begun to look irritated when I mentioned their dog, looked even angrier when Lorenzo said he'd hated studying French. I wondered what they thought about English being the "lingua franca." I assumed franca referred to French, which had once been the language of diplomacy, if not science.

Also, given how unpleasant our hostess was being to Bianca, possibly because her husband was showing an interest in the expectant mother, I had to wonder whether Constanza was the person who had killed Paolina because Signor Ricci had been interested in his secretary. Now I had two suspects: the husband and the wife. Possibly three if I counted the toxicologist from Catania. Perhaps he had wept over Paolina's death out of guilt.

"As interesting as your history is Signora Massoni," said our hostess, "I must interrupt the telling to explain the *dulce* which is being served. *Mosto di Ficodindia*. It is a dish that you are not likely to find in your respective countries because it is made from the prickly pear cactus that grows at the foot of our volcano."

For a moment I forgot about Paolina and my unease about my husband, distracted by the interesting dessert placed in front of me. "If growing near a volcano isn't absolutely necessary," I said to my hostess, "I have prickly pear cactus in my yard." I tasted the mold, which was topped by candied orange peel and roasted almonds. "Wonderful!" I exclaimed. Constanza and I smiled at one another. At least she didn't dislike me. Perhaps I should have sat with the Riccis, even if I didn't speak Italian. "This should be very popular in El Paso since we have the cactus, and it is commonly eaten in one form or another by the Hispanic population."

The dinner wound down with espresso and Limoncello, the most popular liqueur of the Campania. Then we diners rose and drifted toward the lobby and our rooms. Jason said to Sibyl that he'd see her the next day and suggested that they continue their discussion at lunch. Hank then laughed and said to me that I needn't feel left out because we were going to explore the beauties of the Amalfi Coast tomorrow while our spouses talked about dull science.

I said, "Umph," because the Guillots' dog had left his isolation beside the wall and then pulled away from his mistress to take another shot at me. "Stop that," I snapped. Thank goodness, he desisted after licking my hand. My ankles and the hose around them still felt damp from his under-the-table attack.

Meanwhile, Hank was inviting the other ladies to join us in the morning, saying his rental car might be a convertible, but he thought it would hold five or six. Bianca accepted immediately, as did Mrs. Stackpole, with a flutter of excitement over the new plants she expected to see. Albertine Guillot announced that she had already seen the Amalfi Coast and planned to rest on her balcony with a good book. Signora Ricci-Tassone assured us that she herself would take us to the Roman ruins in Pompeii on the following day, but that tomorrow she had to see to conference arrangements since her husband's secretary had so foolishly killed herself, and at such an inconvenient time.

She was certainly intent on convincing us that Paolina's death was a suicide, while I was surer than ever that it was murder.

That opinion caused harsh words between Jason and me when we got to our room. "For God's sake, Carolyn," he said. "Can't you leave it alone? The police will sort it out."

"You haven't met them," I retorted, but he wasn't paying attention. He had already turned away and punched his pillow several times in preparation for sleep.

It wasn't so long ago that, after a separation, Jason and I would have fallen into bed to make love rather than to sleep. The thought made me very sad and kept me awake.

Monday in Amalfi

Slow Food, Fast Food

If America is the home of fast food, Italy is the home of slow food, a country where ninety-seven percent of the food consumed is *not* delivered from behind a counter less than five minutes after being ordered. Italians like home cooking, which is interesting because until the nineteenth century, women were not considered fit to prepare fine food. Misanthropic writers said women were dirty, lazy, drunken practitioners of witchcraft. Households where women did the cooking were poor households. In the kitchens of the rich, only the lowliest tasks were considered suitable for females.

But now every Italian male loves not only his mama, but his mama's cooking, which features regional and traditional recipes made with the fresh products for which the various regions are famous or food products produced in small factories, for instance the dried pastas and canned San Marzano tomatoes of the Campania.

So what would an Italian choose instead of a fast-food hamburger? How about this very Italian hamburger patty? You could even put it on a round of toast grilled and drizzled with garlic olive oil.

A Hamburger in the Style of the Campania

- Preheat oven to 400 degrees F.

- At a low heat in a small saucepan place *1/2 slice of crustless, white bread* and *3 tablespoons milk*. Cook gently until bread has absorbed milk. Mash to a pulp and allow to cool.

- Place *1 1/2 pounds ground beef* into a bowl with the bread pulp and *1 beaten egg*. Season with *salt* and *pepper*. Mix well and form 6 patties. Sprinkle *2/3 cup dry breadcrumbs* on a plate and dredge patties thoroughly.

- Heat *1/4 inch vegetable oil* in a large frying pan and fry patties 2 minutes on each side until brown. Transfer to a greased, ovenproof dish in a single layer.

- Slice *2 large beefsteak tomatoes*, and lay a slice on each patty. Sprinkle with *1 tablespoon chopped fresh oregano, salt*, and *pepper*. Cut *one mozzarella cheese* into 6 slices and put a slice on top of each tomato.

- Cut *6 drained, canned anchovies* in half. Make a cross on top of each mozzarella slice with anchovy halves. (If you don't like anchovies, use *slices of sun-dried tomatoes* or dot cheese with *pesto*. You could even form the crosses with strips of long green chiles that have been grilled and peeled.)

- Bake 10 to 15 minutes until cheese is melted. (If you want to, place the hamburgers on top of *toast rounds*

drizzled with *garlic olive oil* and grilled.) Serve hot.
Then enjoy your "slow food" Italian hamburger.

Carolyn Blue,
"Have Fork, Will Travel,"
Kansas City Star

11
Apology with Paint

Carolyn

A **second coat** of makeup didn't help any more than the
first. The colorful bruise on my cheek, courtesy of Charles
de Gaulle, canine abuser of American ladies, was only
slightly less obvious. I wondered if the periwinkle blue
blouse and slacks I had chosen to wear were bringing out
the blue of the injury the way a blue dress is said to bring
out the color of one's eyes. I could change my clothes certainly, but there was nothing to be done about my eye.
From the green lacquered armoire, I selected an off-white
jacket and held it up to my shoulders in front of the mirror inside the door. No help at all. Either the bruise had
darkened or the jacket's color made it seem so. At least
my cheekbone had stopped aching.

Just as I was about to try a black jacket, someone
knocked on my door. Assuming it to be the maid, I opened
the door without inquiring, only to be faced by Albertine
Guillot, looking wonderfully chic at such an early hour in
the morning in her perfectly cut black dress and gold earrings. Her dog, thank goodness, was nowhere in sight.

"Just as I feared," she said, accent dripping with

French hauteur. "Your face looks very battered. However, I have come prepared to help you with that problem," and she brushed right by me without even asking my permission to enter the room. How did she plan to help? Put a bag over my head?

She studied the room, and then proceeded to drag a tall stool from the bar toward the window, drawing open both the green and beige striped drapes and the white sheers behind them. "Sit here, Madame Blue," she ordered. "I can see that you applied makeup in front of the mirror in your bath. I myself find that natural light is much more effective, but then you Americans are so naïve in matters of appearance."

Since I had continued to stand still, amazed by her effrontery, she took my arm and escorted me to the wicker-backed stool. However, once she had me perched there, she was not happy with her access to my face. "You are too tall," she complained. "And why do you not wear eye makeup? A blonde such as yourself will lose the effect of the eyes without the proper color on eyebrows, lids, and lashes." She opened a capacious handbag and laid out various pots, brushes, and the like on a table by the window.

"Really, Mrs. Guillot—" I protested.

She waved me to silence and began to remove, with brisk and painful strokes of some stinging liquid on cotton, the two coats of foundation I had applied. "Your skin is quite good," she remarked, "for a woman of your age and coloring."

"How very kind of you to say so," I muttered.

"It has been my observation that you fair-skinned Germanic types tend to develop fine lines a bit early."

"Earlier than you dark-skinned Mediterranean types?" I asked.

"Exactly." She studied the bruised side of my face and

then selected a small pot of thick white stuff, which she patted, again painfully, onto my injuries.

Clown makeup? I'd have to remove it as soon as I managed to get her out of my room.

"Poor Charles de Gaulle," she murmured. "We were served a spicy pasta on the plane from Milan, and he ate it up before I could stop him. I attribute his naughty behavior yesterday afternoon and evening to a serious case of indigestion."

The pasty white stuff dried almost immediately. I could feel it draw against my skin.

"I do hope you understand," she continued.

I didn't, of course. If he was sick, why hadn't she left him in the room or taken him to a vet?

"I had ordered him something I thought might prove agreeable to him, but the Italians are so inefficient. The stewardess gave us all the same meal and then patted my poor dog on the head with some adoring comment when he plunged his nose into the dish and all but inhaled the whole serving, garlic bread and all." She was now smoothing foundation over the white paste and the rest of my face. "I assure you that the stewardess was not so adoring when he had an accident on the seat. In fact, she was quite insulting, although the incident was entirely the fault of her incompetence." Mrs. Guillot selected a pot of rouge, contemplated the color, and nodded.

Oh God, I thought. *I'm going to have a white face with round red circles on my cheeks. And how will I remove the dried paste?*

"Of course, other Italians, such a noisy people, made a fuss as well. Please stop wiggling, Madame Blue."

"I wasn't wiggling. I was about to say something."

"Oh, very well. What is it?"

"I didn't realize that large dogs were allowed in the cabin of a plane. Is that customary in Europe?"

"Where else would he sit? We paid for his seat, of course. Now, do not talk. I must apply lipstick." And she did. "And now the eyes." She stared into mine, as impersonal as if I were a canvas upon which she planned to paint an eye.

"Actually, I'd rather not—"

"I insist," said Albertine Guillot sternly. "My dog is responsible for your injury to the detriment of your appearance, so I am, as the owner of the dog, responsible for what repairs can be made." And she selected an eyebrow pencil from the array of cosmetics she had laid out, clamped a finger to my temple, suggested that my eyebrows could use a professional plucking, and drew lines. "You may talk while I work on your eyes, as long as you do not become so expressive as to move your head, brows, or eyelids."

Well, that was very thoughtful. Now I could talk. As if I wanted to talk to Albertine Guillot. "Your English is very good," I said grudgingly.

"But of course. I studied it from childhood. I cannot imagine why you Americans allow your children to grow up with only one language." She had outlined my eyes with another pencil.

"Are you well acquainted with the Riccis?" I asked, thinking that I might obtain some information for my investigation into Paolina's death.

"My husband has known Ruggiero for some years," she replied. "Signor Ricci is, as you might imagine, a man given to many indiscreet liaisons with young women. The death of his secretary, however it happened, will no doubt prove to be embarrassing to him and to Constanza for a time."

She was now applying eye shadow. I hadn't noticed the color and hoped that it wasn't red, which does not look good on me, or anyone else, in my opinion.

"And have you met Mrs. Ricci before?" I asked.

"Several times. Her taste in designers is excellent, although her Italian ancestry skews her color selections."

I remembered a trip to Paris and the realization that all the women were wearing black. No doubt Albertine Guillot felt that any choice other than black was in poor taste. "I understood that Signora Ricci was of Norman ancestry."

"Quite true," my snobbish, multilingual cosmetician agreed as she brushed mascara onto my eyelashes. "And she is most fortunate that her Norman-French blood guides her to some extent in her wardrobe selection. There." She put away the mascara brush and box, gathered up the cosmetics she hadn't used on me, and informed me that she would leave the others so that I could take care of my appearance myself in the days to follow.

Then she left! She didn't even hand me a mirror and ask what I thought of the remodeling job. She had closed the door before I climbed off the stool and went over to a mirror. And I must admit that one would never know her dreadful dog had attacked me. In fact, I looked quite dramatic, although I doubted that I'd ever be able to reproduce the effect.

So Ruggiero Ricci was given to many indiscreet liaisons, was he? Did that mean that Paolina had been the first woman to cheat on him, and that he had been so indignant that he killed her? Or did it mean that his wife finally got fed up with his infidelity and killed Paolina to give him a scare?

12
A Chat with Nunzia

Bianca

I blamed Lorenzo for stirring the children into such wild moods, for he wrestled with them in bed and made jokes about the food at breakfast until they were overcome with giggles. What a wonderful father he is to my darlings! And then, once he had gone off to more serious pursuits, there was his mother, who welcomed them to her room, although they were bouncing off the walls, and suggested all sorts of delights to fill their day—a boat ride, for instance. Of course, they wanted to know why Mama wasn't going along, but Violetta told them that I was too fat, that I'd sink the boat, which, of course, caused more laughter, although it was all too true. I hadn't seen my feet in several months, and Lorenzo had to help me on with my shoes because I could no longer do it myself.

But with the children taken care of, I had well over an hour before I was to meet the others in the lobby for our tour of the Amalfi Coast, one of our country's most beautiful sights. As I was coming out of my room, I saw the French woman knocking at Carolyn's door. Even if Carolyn proved to be the murderer of my countrywoman, I wouldn't have wished a visit from Albertine Guillot on her so early in the morning. What could that be about? Was she going to scold Carolyn for getting knocked over by the Frenchies' ill-mannered dog? And Madame Guillot had had the nerve to frown at me and my children while I was sitting on the floor in the hall! I ducked back into my room, peeked out to be sure she was gone, and then headed for the elevator. I'd see if I could find a maid to question on the ninth floor until the coast was clear on Eight. After all, Paolina's room had been on Nine, even if her body was found in the pool below.

I was quite lucky, for there had been no housekeeping carts that I could see on Eight, whereas a cart sat outside nine-oh-four near an open door, which usually meant there was a maid to be found inside, in this case, a friendly woman named Nunzia, whose graying hair was tucked back in a bun and whose nose featured an unfortunate wart.

"Good morning," I said gaily, and entered the room to introduce myself and mention my own room number, asking if she knew when the rooms on Eight would be made up. She replied that she covered both the eighth and ninth floors but could go downstairs if I needed to have my room done sooner. I assured her that whenever she got to it was convenient for me, that I just wanted to apologize for the state of the bedclothes, which were mostly on the floor when my husband and children got through with them.

Nunzia, happily, liked children, as most Italian women do, and asked about mine. We had quite a chat before I managed to work the conversation around to the young woman who had died in the pool. "Such a pity," said Nunzia. "A very pretty girl. She must have gone swimming in the early morning, which is forbidden, of course, since the hotel is owned by the Swiss. They forbid everything, including maids under the age of forty. They don't want the customers flirting with the staff, those Swiss."

Of course I asked why Nunzia thought Paolina had died in the morning rather than at night, and Nunzia said because her bed had been slept in the night before she was found in the pool, a very quiet sleeper she was, only the dent in the pillow to show she had been there.

"What? So young and pretty and no lover?" I asked.

We both chuckled, and Nunzia assured me that Signorina Marchetti had spent both nights alone, although she had an American friend, a woman, who had returned to the hotel with her that afternoon talking of a Mafia wedding. "The Americans, they think all Italians are Mafia. So silly," said Nunzia. "Here it is the Camorra."

With some difficulty I managed to get across to the rather innocent Nunzia that I wondered just what sort of friendship the dead girl and the American had had. Poor Nunzia was shocked when she caught on and wondered if she shouldn't have stayed on the farm with her parents, respectable folk who would be distressed to think their daughter worked in a place where unnatural sexual activities might be occurring. Then she recalled that Paolina and the American had hugged and agreed to meet for dinner when they parted at the elevator, and that the American's bed had been mussed with both pillows slept on.

Ah ha! I thought, very pleased with the information I was gathering. Perhaps Carolyn and Paolina had slept together in Carolyn's bed, then quarreled by the pool, where Paolina had struck her head when pushed. After that she fell or was pushed into the pool, and Carolyn left her there, dead or drowning. It could have happened that way. Instead of Paolina being thrown or jumping from the ninth floor, as the police thought. After all, who would trust *them* to get it right? I considered it very unlikely that Carolyn would be strong enough to dump another woman over the railing.

"Yes," Nunzia was saying, "it was a strange day, the day they found the girl in the pool. I discovered in my cart—" she gestured toward the wheeled cart in the hall— "a tray, two pretty plates, and two wine glasses. The cart was in the housekeeping room on the eighth floor, and the dishes, surely a gift from the Holy Virgin, were hardly chipped at all, and they weren't the hotel's! It is not allowed to bring such things into the hotel with food and drink. Very strange indeed.

"Since the police didn't ask me about them, I took them home. I imagine they belonged to the American. Americans are so rich, you know. They probably carry around their own dishes and throw them away when they're soiled. Or maybe she threw them away after her argument with the dead girl. Such sinful conduct, to seduce an Italian girl!"

"Yes," I agreed. "In some places in America, women are allowed to marry women and men, men."

Nunzia gasped and crossed herself. "I wonder if the Holy Father knows of these things. It must be very hard to be a good Catholic in America. I've heard terrible things about the American priests." She whispered the last. "I don't know whether to believe such things or not.

"And then this morning when I was getting the cart to take upstairs, I thought I saw Saint Giuseppe Moscati. What a fright he gave me. Came right around the corner and bumped into my cart, looking very upset."

Ah, I thought. *Ruggiero Ricci. He does look like the Naples doctor who was sainted not so long ago, although Ricci's no saint. A saint would never squeeze the knee of a pregnant woman and propose to meet her in Rome once she's had her baby.*

"It gave me a shock, but of course he wasn't the saint.

He sounded Sicilian to me, and Saint Moscati was from Napoli, bless his kindly soul. He ministered to the poor without charging a *lira*. My own grandfather, who was burned in a big eruption of Vesuvius, was healed by the saint's very hands. But this one, I heard him shouting, 'What did you do?' and some foreigner—he spoke Italian, but he was a foreigner—he said, 'I wasn't here. Where were you?' and the one who looked like the saint said, 'In Catania, of course.' Then the foreigner said, 'Maybe it was your wife,' and the one from Sicily, where Catania is, said, 'Don't be a fool,' and he came storming around the corner right into my cart. What a day!"

"What did the foreigner look like?" I asked, knowing that when I told Carolyn this tale, she'd want to know, or at least pretend to be interested.

"I didn't see him. He must have gone the other way," said Nunzia. "Shall I bring some candy for the pillows of your children? A little surprise? I make it the way my mother did."

"Why, Nunzia, they'd love it. You must stop by our room tomorrow morning and meet them."

By then Nunzia, having finished making the bed and emptying the waste baskets, was about to do the bath, so we parted good friends, and I stopped by my room on Eight before going downstairs to meet the others. I'd had an excellent and rather amusing idea. I'd dial 112, the Carabinieri, and report the murder. Although they are our military police, their functions overlap those of the Polizia di Stato outside the big cities. Wouldn't Lieutenant Buglione be surprised when they showed up? And maybe something would be done to solve the murder. If not, at least they could entertain us by arguing over jurisdiction.

13
Pre-Trip Detecting

Carolyn

I put away the black jacket I had been considering before Albertine Guillot arrived to make me look normal again—better than normal, actually. I still had over an hour before I was to meet Hank in the lobby, more than enough time for breakfast. Of course, Jason had already been out for a run, eaten breakfast, and was now in a conference room talking about toxins. I'd have to eat by myself.

When I stopped by the desk in the lobby to ask for more hotel stationery so that I could write to the children when I got back from Amalfi, I promptly made a fool of myself by telling the clerk what excellent English she spoke. In reply to my compliment, she grinned and said that was probably because she was a native of Michigan, doing a hotel internship with the Swiss company that owned the Grand Palazzo Sorrento.

"Well, that explains the rules posted everywhere," I remarked, not very tactfully, but she laughed and introduced herself, Jill McLain of Ann Arbor. We fell into conversation about how she liked living in Italy—a lot; how long she'd been here—almost a year; and last, but most important, what, if anything, she knew about Paolina Marchetti.

"Actually, she's been here before," said Jill, "several times. Because I was meeting American friends to celebrate that night, I particularly remember that she was a guest of the hotel on the Fourth of July."

"Alone?" I asked, trying to seem casual about it.

"No, she met an older man, very distinguished looking."

Ruggiero Ricci, I thought.

"They registered under the same name but had separate rooms, and it doesn't seem to me that the name was Marchetti. Odd, now that I think of it." Jill tugged thoughtfully at the brown strands of hair that curved in toward her chin. "What was that name? I can't remember."

"Do you think they were lovers?" I asked.

"I suppose they could have been. They were certainly very affectionate, and she was so upset when he was called away on business. She cancelled her own reservation and left. Maybe it was one of those May-December romances, and they were trying to act like uncle and niece or something." Jill laughed. "You'd be surprised at how many of those uncle-niece couples we get."

Of course I wanted Jill to remember the man's name, but she couldn't. Then she asked me the name of the handsome police lieutenant who was in and out of the hotel investigating Paolina's death. I promised to introduce her to Lieutenant Buglione if she'd glance through the hotel register to see if she could spot the name of the couple that spent the Fourth of July at this hotel.

Then I spotted Bianca coming off the elevator and talked her into having a cup of coffee with me while I ate breakfast. She'd already eaten with her family but agreed to join me because she had information to pass on, things she'd learned from a hotel maid named Nunzia, who thought she'd seen Saint Giuseppe Moscati in the hallway, although it had evidently been Ruggiero Ricci, fresh from a quarrel with a foreigner who spoke Italian.

The reported conversation Ricci had had with the foreigner was really quite interesting: "I wasn't here; where were you?" And Ricci replied that he was in Catania. Then the man said, "Maybe it was your wife." Could they have been talking about Paolina's death, her employer claiming to have been elsewhere when it occurred, the stranger suggesting that Ricci's wife was responsible? If so, who was the foreigner who spoke Italian? And could *he* have killed Paolina? He might be either of the Europeans at the meeting—Professors Guillot and Stackpole. I'd have to pay more attention to them. I suggested that Bianca listen in on anything Guillot might say in French while I monitored Stackpole's conversations, which was not a very exciting prospect.

While we were having this conversation, I was eating a new item from the buffet table. Bianca called it *Sfogliatelle*. She wrote down the name for me. How delicious it was. Crispy dough, not the least greasy, although it evidently had lots of grease in it—including that contemporary no-no, lard—shaped into shells and filled with a soft cream that smelled and tasted of orange and vanilla. Bianca advised me to forgo looking for a recipe. "If no Italian wants to make it, why do you think Americans would?" she asked.

"Because they can't get it at home," I suggested. However, once I'd seen the recipe, I decided not to impose it on my readers.

Bianca made a quick trip up to her room after her second cup of coffee, and I returned to the lobby, where I found Lieutenant Buglione on the job, but unable to give me any news of his investigation because, as he explained, it was too early to know anything about the death or even the deceased. I had to tell him that Paolina had been Ruggiero Ricci's secretary, something the lieutenant had yet to discover for himself, and about Ricci's conversation in the hall on the eighth floor with the mysterious Italian-speaking stranger.

Lieutenant Buglione was appalled at the idea that he might have to investigate a big-shot Sicilian industrialist, so I suggested that he talk to Jill, who had seen Paolina in the hotel with an older man last summer. "It could have been Ricci," I suggested. "And what about the autopsy?"

"Autopsy? There is no autopsy," said the lieutenant. "We don't know the signorina was murdered. She is safely at rest in ice chest until we know—"

Constanza Ricci-Tassone sailed up to us at just that moment, causing me to worry that she'd heard me suggesting her husband might be a murderer. "Of course, Paolina was not murdered," said the lady in her most haughty voice. "In her distress over the desertion of her lover, she must have become careless and fallen over the edge of the pool. Such a sad but romantic occurrence. So Italian, do you not think, Lieutenant?

"As for an autopsy, you certainly cannot send the girl's body home to her parents in such a state. It's bad enough, the rumors of suicide. They will want her buried in sacred ground, as any parent would. Because Paolina worked for my husband, we will stand as her parents in the absence of her own, and demand that her remains be respected. You understand, Lieutenant. There is to be no autopsy and no talk of suicide, and certainly not of murder."

"*Si, Signora*," said Lieutenant Buglione, all but bowing as she swept regally away to breakfast.

I tried to argue with his decision, but he pointed out that Signora Ricci-Tassone, a woman of noble stock, who looked on the deceased as her own daughter, was not to be denied her wish that the body be interred intact. "I can not offend such a woman," he protested.

"Very few wives look on their husband's pretty secretaries as daughters," I retorted. "She's trying to protect her husband or herself."

The lieutenant ignored my comment and fixed his gaze on the front door. "What are *they* doing here?" he grumbled.

They were a man and a woman in fancy uniforms with red stripes down the sides of their trousers and skirt, respectively, a white leather sash stretched diagonally across their chests, and hats with visors and a big gold thing on the peaked tops, sort of Nazi-looking. They whipped their hats off, stuck them under their arms, and strode across the lobby toward us.

"Who are they?" I whispered.

"Carabinieri," said Buglione through tight lips. "Captain. Lieutenant." He saluted. "We've had no terrorist events in the area, no civilian riots, no—"

"Why are we speaking English?" demanded the male, who had the most gold on his uniform, not to mention a number of medals.

"A courtesy," Buglione replied. "This lady is an American."

The two Carabinieri—were they soldiers?—studied me, nodded, and the captain said, "Captain Giorgio Pagano and Lieutenant Flavia Vacci. We received a call about a murder."

"That was yesterday," snapped Lieutenant Buglione. "And it's a suicide. Or an accident."

"It is not," I broke in, so pleased that they were all politely speaking English. "I discovered the body. I'm Carolyn Blue. And this is Lieutenant Buglione of the Polizia di Stato." It wasn't very nice of him not to introduce himself when they had.

"Signora. Lieutenant." The captain made a little bow, looking ever so formal and solemn. His subordinate actually smiled at me.

Maybe they'll take this seriously, I thought, *and not do whatever Constanza Ricci-Tassone wants.*

"I think we should adjourn to the breakfast room, which I'm told has an excellent buffet," said Captain Pagano.

"It does," I assured him. "And this morning they have—" I couldn't remember the name of the pastry— "those shells with orange and vanilla cream inside."

Lieutenant Flavia Vacci, as plump and cheerful as her captain was grim and formal, absolutely beamed.

"Shall I show you the way?" I asked, deciding that I wouldn't mind having another of those delicious pastries. Besides which, I needed to pass on to the newcomers all my information and theories. I really didn't trust Lieutenant Buglione to remember everything. "I have information for you," I added.

"Signora, you are too kind," said the captain, "but this initial discussion must be one between colleagues. We shall be happy to interview you later once we have assessed the seriousness of the case."

Buglione shot me a rather smug look. I suppose if I'd been a pretty young thing, like Jill, to whom he'd missed an introduction, he might have insisted that they listen to me. Well, I'd tell the Carabinieri what they needed to know later, and I certainly wasn't going to wait around for them and miss the trip to Amalfi. Late afternoon would be time enough. Were there two police forces that investigated murders? How odd.

. . . Many of the pastries that are most popular in Naples and the towns of the Campania are complicated and never made at home, but good bakeries abound in the region. One such delight is *Sfogliatelle*—hard to pronounce and spell, wonderful to eat. It turned up at the breakfast buffet one morning while I was in Sorrento, a spiraled shell pastry that is painted before it is baked with a butter and lard mixture (which is so delicious that one can almost forget the cholesterol dangers) and filled with seminolina, ricotta, and egg yolks flavored with vanilla, cinnamon, and candied orange peel. *Sfogliatelle*. I ate two and thought I'd gone to pastry heaven. All over the Campania the inhabitants were devouring them with their morning coffee, probably thinking the same thing.

Carolyn Blue,
"Have Fork, Will Travel,"
Albany Morning Post

14
Four for Amalfi

Bianca

What a drive we had! Hank chose to take the scenic Nastro Azzurro route from the west side of Sorrento across the peninsula on twisting roads through farmlands, terraced orchards, and vineyards. Both women in the back seat asked to stop every few miles. Eliza Stackpole saw people selling bags of wild oregano on the roadside and wanted to ask them questions about native herbs, but neither Hank nor I offered to translate. Carolyn wanted to buy a bag, but I assured her that the U.S. government would not let her bring it back into her country. "Or maybe you plan to eat it before you leave," I suggested. Of course, she couldn't. She didn't even have cooking facilities.

Then we passed through Saint Agata Dei Due Golfi, where, Carolyn remarked, there was a Michelin-starred restaurant. Hank said it was too early for lunch, and we'd never get to Amalfi if we stopped and waited for the restaurant to open. She then talked him into a quick stop to see an amazing marble altar, multicolored and immense, at Santa Maria delle Grazie. Carolyn had found it in a guidebook as soon as she saw the name of the town on a road sign. Eliza thought the altar gaudy and declared that she much preferred the more austere churches of England. Then we maneuvered out of the parking lot, which, for some reason, was crowded with farm vehicles and equipment, and continued across the peninsula to Positano and the Amalfi Coast.

The coast road was intimidating, and Hank grumbled that it would have been easier to come by boat. He was probably right. Cliffs towered above us and sheared away hundreds of meters down to the water where the tide dashed itself into spray against the rocks. The road twisted, clinging to its ledge, in turns so sharp that large vehicles had to edge back and forth to get around, taking up both lanes in their efforts to keep from tumbling in a long, long fall to the wild waters below.

Hank Girol's rented car, sleek and sporty with its top folded down, had only two doors. Of course, that meant I sat in front with him because I could never have scrambled over the folded down front seat into the back—not carrying my immense stomach before me. I felt bad for Carolyn. Eliza Stackpole, who had replaced her heavy tweeds with loose trousers and blouse, boots fit for rock climbing, and a floppy cotton hat that blended nicely with her khaki hair, insisted on sitting where she couldn't see how far we had to fall if we went off the road. After they had squeezed in back and Hank moved my seat back far enough to accommodate my tummy, Carolyn had to pull her knees up under her chin. No wonder she wanted to get out for everything that interested her.

Eliza, of course, prattled about the trees and bushes. At one point she remarked that the protective black nets on the lemon groves looked like hairnets on green hair in a punk beauty saloon. I was astounded to think that she'd ever been in such a place. I asked her what her favorite hair-dye color was, but she thought dying one's hair was a waste of time. Did that mean that her strange hair color was natural? I asked whether the English girls with green hair favored mohawks or long frizzes. Eliza said she never talked to girls like that; she'd just peeked into the window of such a shop and then hurried away.

Poor Carolyn couldn't have been at all comfortable, stuffed in back there, but she didn't complain. In fact, the possibility of tumbling down the cliff once we got on that road didn't seem to enter her mind. She folded herself into awkward positions, hung over the side of the car, stretched out her arms and hands holding her tiny camera, and took photos of everything on both sides of the road. Then, when she got a picture that looked particularly good to her, she passed the camera around so the rest of us could look at the little window where the picture appeared.

I couldn't fault her enthusiasm because the water foamed against jagged rocks, shimmered blue-green away from the cliffs, and sparkled like diamonds in sunshine beyond the swathes of color. Still, I'm afraid that we were never sufficiently excited about her pictures. Hank had to keep his eyes on the road, which was crowded with cars, tour buses, and even people walking to stairs that dropped down the rock face to hotels and houses beyond our range of vision.

I was clinging to the arm rest to keep my baby from being hurled against the dashboard when Hank had to brake sharply for foolish drivers or the warning honk of a bus that was about to attempt a dangerous curve on the other side of the road. So I had only one hand to take the camera and often no desire to look away from the road. And Eliza was still going on and on about flowers, trees, and cacti. What was the name of the blue flowers that hung in lovely sheets on the cliff? We didn't know. What

tree was that, clinging like an upright greenish black umbrella to a jut of stone ahead to the left? Plane tree? I
wasn't sure. I was a city girl. Did those cacti bloom and,
if so, when? None of us could say, although Carolyn, a
desert dweller, thought cacti bloomed whenever it rained.
She had to promise Eliza copies of any vegetation she
photographed.

What all of us could identify were the orchards, growing on the terraced cliffs, walnuts and peaches (for which
Sorrento was famous; Carolyn said some food writer,
goodness knows how many centuries ago, had called Sorrento peaches "delicious enough to raise the dead"), and
particularly the lemon groves. They were so pretty, and
they reminded me, not of hairnets on green hair, but of the
region's favorite liqueur, Limoncello. I wouldn't have
minded a little glass right then to take off the edge of fear
engendered by the road. Probably I should have been a
sensible mother-to-be and stayed safely at the hotel. The
baby certainly seemed to think so. It kicked so hard from
time to time that its little foot poked my dress against the
dashboard.

Nonetheless, I was happy to be on this gorgeous coast
again with the wind in my hair and the sun warming my
face. How lucky we were. When we left Sorrento to cross
the peninsula to the coast on the other side from the Bay
of Naples, we left heavy clouds and the dark thrust of the
volcano behind us and drove into the sunshine. The
stacked hotels of Positano, marching down the cliffs to the
sea, glittered white under blue sky as we crawled through
the narrow, crowded streets, and Hank flirted shamelessly
with me and I with him.

I could almost forget that I had passed the dreaded age
of thirty, that I had a baby the size of an elephant waiting
to be born, and that my companions were in early-to
middle-middle age. But we were so happy and light-

hearted. Every time Carolyn spotted a shadow on the horizon, she thought it was Capri, which she evidently had a great desire to visit. She told us about the Emperor Tiberius, who had built castles and villas for himself there, and ruled the empire from the island for the last twenty-three years of his life while he seduced beautiful young boys and had those who became boring tossed into the sea. Eliza was horrified. I noted with interest Carolyn's knowledge of homosexual history. Perhaps it was important to my theory of the murder, although Tiberius and his reputation were well known, except perhaps to a shrubbery-besotted Englishwoman.

Hank promised Carolyn that she would see Capri, and I, laughing, insisted that I be taken along. Eliza asked only about the vegetation on Capri, and when we were all disappointingly vague on the subject, she lost interest because she had so much to look at right there at the side of the road.

15
In a Shady Amalfi Piazza

Bianca

When we pulled into Amalfi at last, I was in need of a comfortable chair on the shady side of a piazza. Carolyn, having used up all the memory on the smart card in her digital camera, had to replace it with another card. Eliza bent vigorously to tighten the laces of her hiking boots (Hank had refused to stop along the road when she wanted to take off up a cliff to pull up some plant that had caught her eye) and insisted that we hike straight up the hill away from the cathedral. Hank agreed, so I sat in the piazza and ordered a cool drink while the others, Carolyn not looking particularly pleased at the steep hill she faced, went off to explore because Hank said it was too early for lunch and Eliza pointed out that the cathedral would not open until two.

What a pleasure to sit in the shade with a cool lemon drink and no one to hand me a camera or ask me about a plant, as if I were a botanist instead of a retired tour guide and mother of two and eight-ninths children. My feet and ankles were swollen, but the baby had fallen asleep. I bought flowers from a wizened, shawled woman making the rounds of the tables and stared lazily up at the dark and light patterns of the cathedral stones, the colonnade of rounded arches, and the many, many steps leading up to the door of the church. Perhaps I wouldn't visit the cathedral either, although I remembered a lovely cloister and a dark crypt that had beguiled me years ago. Could Carolyn be both a murderer and a lover of cathedrals? A bisexual and a prude? It was too much for me, and I gave up wondering.

They were back in fifteen minutes—or thirty; I may have dozed off—Hank still cheerful, Eliza disappointed in the plant life but invigorated by the climb, and Carolyn eager to tell me about a cultural contrast she had witnessed and taken pictures of: a slender young man working at a laptop computer at a table in an outdoor café, while another young man, sun-browned and muscular, drove a donkey loaded with bags of rough stones to the top of the street. There he tumbled the stones into a pile, leapt onto the bare back of the donkey, and road it downhill. "The past and the present," she exclaimed triumphantly, and showed me the pictures. Dear God, but the man on the donkey was handsome. I admired her pictures and forbore to tell her that the past and the present rubbed up against each other everywhere in Italy—nowhere more so than here where Greeks and Romans had fought for and colonized the land, where maritime kingdoms (Amalfi had been a powerful one in the Middle Ages) had flourished and waned, and where despotic foreign kings had held the people in thrall and delayed the birth of the modern world.

When Eliza looked at the photo of the donkey man, she exclaimed, "My goodness, he's as brown as oil."

Now that was a disgusting simile. What kind of oil was brown? "Do you cook with brown oil in England?" I asked, wondering if I'd been so unfortunate as to eat something cooked with it while on a visit to London. The idea made me a bit queasy.

"I know where that saying comes from," said Carolyn. "Actually, it's quite interesting. From about the fourth century the Catholic Church wouldn't let Christians eat meat on what they called "lean" days—Lent, feasts, and whatnot. Even lard and butter were prohibited because they were animal products. So only olive and vegetable oils could be used for cooking until—I don't remember—some time in the Middle Ages. That meant people in northern Europe, where there were no olive trees, had to import oil. The traders in Spain and Italy took advantage of the situation and sent bad oil. That's why the English began saying 'brown as oil,' referring to the nasty imported stuff, which was all they could get."

"Wouldn't you know!" exclaimed Eliza. "I read in the *Times* that the olive oil, vinegar, and wine that are supposed to be from Italy are really fakes. Personally, I think the European Union should put a stop to that sort of thing. How can they expect us to give up the pound for the euro with all that cheating going on? I'm against the euro *and* the European Union. We English should keep to our own ways."

I had to laugh. "Which do you dislike more?" I asked. "The fake Italian olive oil or the euro?" Whoops! The baby woke up and gave me a hearty kick. I gave him a gentle, calming pat. I myself was offended that Italy was being accused of exporting brown oil and goodness knows what else these days.

"My goodness," said Eliza, staring at my stomach. "You've got a football player there. Definitely a boy."

"She already has two soccer players," said Carolyn, "and one is a lovely little girl named Giulia."

With that, we went into a café that had been recommended by the flower lady and dined on *fritto misto*,

French fries, wine, and *dulce*. Fish and chips, Eliza called the entree, but she was wrong. In England the batter is never so light and crisp, and there are no calamari to be found in the English version of mixed, fried fish. In fact, Eliza wouldn't eat hers; she thought squid were "nasty." I noted that Carolyn was happy to take a share of the spurned delicacy. I tried to talk my companions into Amalfi's famous chocolate eggplant dessert (a medieval import from Turkey during the Amalfi empire days), but no one wanted to try it, not even Carolyn. She opted for lemon torte, and the others had mixed gelato. How boring! They didn't even want to taste my *melanzane in salsa cioccolato*.

During lunch most of the talk revolved around Paolina Marchetti. Hank seemed very interested in her, or perhaps he was very interested in Carolyn. She certainly looked pretty that day, more vivid somehow, and where was the Charles-de-Gaulle bruise? Gone. At any rate, Hank quizzed Carolyn about every word the dead girl had said. Maybe he planned to launch his own investigation into her death. And the tale Carolyn told us was interesting. It made me wish that I had known Paolina.

The story revolved around the small, red leather book in which Paolina wrote poetry that was inspired by an American poet, Edna somebody, not a very poetic name, and I had never heard of her, although she must have been a very sexy lady. *Promiscuous* was the word Carolyn used to describe her. Paolina had found a book of the woman's poetry in a musty bookstore while the girls of her convent school were visiting the town on a day out. When the nun teaching her English class had required a translation of a piece of English poetry, Paolina had chosen a long poem from that book, evidently something about death and re-birth. The teaching sister found the poem confusing and probably not in accordance with the Faith, as did the Reverend Mother when the translation was passed on for her opinion.

Thereafter, Paolina was praised for her skill in translating the work—the title had something to do with the Renaissance, although the bit that Carolyn quoted seemed to be about mountains, woods, and water—but our late, adventurous secretary was reprimanded for her choice of subject matter and told to read no more of the American's poetry. Naturally all the girls then became interested, searched out books, translated them, and giggled in the dark at the poems about love and infidelity.

Carolyn ended this tale by saying that she herself had read an excellent biography of the poet and had offered to send one to Paolina. But then the young woman died, and the offer was moot. Remembering my own days in convent school, I found the story and its heroine delightful. I wished that I had known her.

Over *dulce*, Carolyn told of a wedding party she and Paolina had seen outside a church in Sorrento with burly men in black tuxedoes prowling the perimeters and keeping the tourists away. "She evidently had great contempt for the Mafia," Carolyn remarked, "and she said that it was definitely a Mafia wedding. But really, does Sorrento seem like a Mafia-type place?"

"The Mafia are everywhere," said Eliza. "Not just Sicily and America. Anyone at these tables might be one." She glanced around the café suspiciously.

"Bull!" said Hank. "All that talk of the Mafia—it's just rumors."

"How very naïve of you, Mr. Girol," Eliza retorted. "Your New Jersey is probably full of them."

"You're absolutely right, Mrs. Stackpole," he agreed. "They own all the pizzerias. You take your life in your hands when you want to pick up a pepperoni and mushroom to go."

Carolyn started to laugh, and Girol grinned at her. "Very dangerous, New Jersey," he added, glancing at his watch. "If we want to see the cathedral, we'd better get over there. I'd like to beat the heavy, late afternoon traffic."

I didn't go. Why climb all those steps when I could count on Carolyn to bring back pictures? And she did take a lovely photo of the cloister with its surround of white columns and pointed arches, and its garden of palm trees ringed by flowers, edged walkways, and a fountain in the middle. If there hadn't been so many steps up to the church, I'd have enjoyed sitting in that garden. Instead the baby and I dozed in the piazza, waited on by a solicitous waiter who plied me with cool, fruity drinks and gelato.

When they returned, we walked to the car, and Carolyn told me that two Carabinieri officers, a man and a woman, had arrived that morning. "They have very fancy uniforms, and I had high hopes that they'd do a better job of investigating Paolina's death than Lieutenant Buglione is doing. Anything Signora Ricci-Tassone wants, he agrees to. But then, the Carabinieri didn't even want to talk to me. They were more interested in having breakfast at the hotel buffet. And why are there two police forces that investigate murders?"

"They're the military police." I grinned. "They fight wars, crime, and any attempts to redesign their pretty uniforms or to interfere with their right to carry submachine guns. I called them myself, but since I never saw them, I thought they'd ignored the whole thing—found a terrorist to chase or a riot to quell."

"I should have guessed that anyone in a uniform that elaborate would be worthless in a murder investigation," said Carolyn. "They probably won't even bother to interview me."

On a visit to Amalfi, a friend, who chose to rest in a shady piazza instead of going sightseeing, confessed that while we more ambitious tourists were climbing hills and cathedral steps, she had consumed, in our absence, three helpings of gelato (*stracciatella*, which is plain ice cream with crunchy chocolate bits; *zabaglione*, extra-creamy ice cream made with eggs and Marsala wine; and *fragola e limone*, strawberry and lemon), four cold fruit drinks, a goblet of cold white wine, and a coffee *granita*. Tired and somewhat damp with perspiration, I must admit that I envied her.

Italy is ice cream heaven and has a long history of liking cold treats. The Romans, for instance, liked cold drinks and got them by storing snow in the mountains in pits and trenches. During the summer the snow was carried down to the cities on mule back at night. A sixteenth-century Italian physician named Pisanello wrote that cold drinks would lower a fever. He recommended a drink made of water, wine, and chilled fruits, the chilling agent being, of course, snow from the mountains, and claimed that not only did everyone want to drink these cold fruit drinks, but also that doing so was necessary to good health in the Italian climate. Italy was following his advice by the end of the century. In the second half of the seventeenth century, *De Sorbetti*, the first book on making frozen desserts, had been published, and Naples had a shop that sold very sophisticated sorbets. There was even a word for a sorbet maker—*sorbettiera*. Of course, Catherine de Medici introduced ice cream to France.

Italians usually buy their gelatos, sorbets, and ice creams in stores and restaurants, but here is a *granita* you can easily make at home.

Coffee Granita

- Fix *coffee* as you like it, with or without cream, sugar, and caffeine (I also suggest the addition of Frangelico, a Northern Italian hazelnut liqueur, or even Irish Mist, which, although not Italian, is really tasty in coffee). Pour the coffee over crushed ice. You may wish to garnish your hot-weather drink with *whipped cream* and *chocolate covered coffee beans.*

Carolyn Blue,
"Have Fork, Will Travel,"
Boloxi Bay Messenger

16
Lobby Inquiries

Carolyn

When we arrived back at the Grand Palazzo Sorrento, my clothes were rumpled, my hair tangled, and my face sunburned, even under all that makeup, although maybe Albertine's applications had worn away in the wind and sun. We didn't lose the sunshine until we crossed the peninsula, and then the wind had picked up and dark clouds, lit red by the setting sun, made an ominous picture. It would probably storm that night, I thought as we all climbed, as stiff as arthritics, from Hank's convertible. The day had been lovely, but I could have done without the hill climbing, the steep cathedral steps, and being uncomfortably scrunched up into that back seat where there was no room for my legs. Every muscle ached as we rode the elevator up to the lobby.

I had planned to go straight to my room for a nap. Maybe I'd sleep right through dinner. However, we walked in to a squabble in front of the desk, where Valentino Santoro was protesting to Lieutenant Buglione that he would never have killed Paolina, that he had loved her. If Bianca hadn't been there to translate, I wouldn't have known what was going on. The lieutenant demanded to know where Santoro had been the night of Signorina Marchetti's death. The chemist said that he was in his lab until after midnight working on a problem that had to do with toxic volcano gases. An incredulous Lieutenant Buglione stared and threw up his hands, announcing that he doubted Santoro, given his professional interests, was a romantic enough man to have killed for love or to have inspired such love in a pretty young woman that she would commit suicide over him.

What an astonishing piece of reasoning, if it could be called that. A man could be neither romantic nor violent just because he harbored a scientific interest in toxic substances? Perhaps I should write a letter to the *Journal of the American Chemical Society* to let chemists know that the Italian police considered them wimpy and boring. They could commit crimes at will in Italy and expect to be overlooked as suspects. I had to clamp my hand over my mouth to keep from giggling, a sign that I really did need a nap. And where were Captain Pagano and Lieutenant Vacci of the Carabinieri?

Again the nap was forestalled, this time by the arrival of Constanza Ricci-Tassone, who told the lieutenant in no uncertain terms that Paolina's death had been either a suicide or an unfortunate accident, that he was to stop harassing Dottore Santoro, a valued employee of her husband's company, and that Paolina's body was to be sent home immediately to—"Perugia, is it not, Ruggiero?" Her husband had followed her into the room, so evidently the conference had broken up for the day. "Perugia has marvelous truffles, Lieutenant. If you have not been to Umbria to try them, perhaps you should accompany the body." Lieutenant Buglione looked understandably confused and hastened away to confer with Sergeant Gambardella.

I, meanwhile, was staring at Signor Ricci. He did look *exactly* like Saint Giuseppe Moscati, just as—What was her name?—Nunzia, the maid, had said. The handsome, square face, the hairline that ran straight across his forehead, the neat, dark mustache.

"Is my necktie crooked, Signora Blue?" Ricci asked, smiling.

"You look so much like Saint Giuseppe Moscati," I replied. "I saw his picture in a church here in Sorrento. It's an amazing resemblance. And he was a scientist and a medical doctor, a professor in Naples."

"I am most complimented, Signora, to be compared to a scientific saint." He smiled at me. His wife smiled at me. Then he leaned over and kissed my cheek. "*Molte grazie*, sweet lady," he murmured in my ear.

His wife stopped smiling and said, "The Holy Father has made hundreds of saints, more than all the other popes together, and you, Ruggiero, are not one of them." Then she turned to those of us who had made the trip to Amalfi and told us that we would be escorted by limousine to Pompeii the next day. "Please be here in the lobby at ten," she ordered, and walked away.

"After driving for a day in Italy, a limousine sounds good," said Hank. "Italian drivers and roads make you appreciate a nice interstate highway. Even the Pulaski Skyway looks good after the Amalfi Coast road."

I had to agree. "In Texas we don't have that many cars on our interstates. I wonder how the lieutenant found out about Valentino's connection to Paolina."

"Maids," said Hank. "They know everything and tell everything. Try not to smoke any pot in your room. You'd be caught for sure."

I must say that I found that remark rather offensive. "I have never smoked pot," I said.

"Never?" He laughed. "Even if you didn't inhale?"

I noticed that Lieutenant Buglione was about to leave, so I scurried over to intercept him, leaving Hank to make tasteless jokes with someone else if he was so inclined. "Lieutenant, a moment of your time," I called.

He turned and bowed over my hand.

"Are the Carabinieri going to help with the investigation?"

He threw up his hands. "I do not know. We talked much. Then they left. And I remain."

Then my question would have to be asked of him, which was just as well since he had been involved from the beginning. "Tell me, was a red leather notebook found in Paolina's room?"

He assured me that no such thing had been found there or in the pool area.

"Then I don't think you need to consider accident or suicide as the cause of her death. If either of those had been the case, the notebook would have been in her room. The murderer must have taken it. Find the book, and you'll know who killed her."

"An interesting theory, Signora," said the lieutenant, nodding and stroking his chin as he gave it his attention. "However, is possible a maid steals the book when she cleans the room."

"Why would a maid steal a book of handwritten poetry?" I asked. "And didn't your men search Paolina's room before the maids were allowed in to clean it?"

"*Si*. We look in her room first, but maybe the maid go in before we get there, take the book, and leave."

"That sounds unlikely to me," I retorted.

"Maybe we search the swimming pools for the book. She could drop when she fall in."

"I doubt that people carry notebooks into a pool with them." If it were left up to Lieutenant Buglione, this case would never be solved. He was more interested in pleasing the Riccis. "And now I want to introduce you to Jill McLain, an employee of the hotel who has seen Paolina here in the past with an older man, perhaps the murderer."

"Perhaps tomorrow," suggested the lieutenant.

I pointed to Jill behind the desk. "Such a pretty girl," I murmured.

"But maybe I can spare the moment to hear her," said the lieutenant, who evidently thought her very pretty, too, if his dawning smile was any indication.

I left them smiling and talking. There were certainly more questions that I needed to ask, but they would have to wait until after I'd had a little nap. Then it occurred to me that I needed to write a column. After all, I did want my expenses to be tax deductible. I'd write about lemons.

Sorrento and the surrounding area is a magical place, and not the least of its beauties are the lemon groves that rise in terraces on the cliffs. The Arabs introduced lemons and oranges to Sicily and Southern Italy in the eighth, ninth and tenth centuries, and from the fruit come some of the Campania's most delightful recipes: the liqueur, Limoncello, which you can easily make yourself if you can't find it at home or don't want to pay the price for an imported fruit liqueur, and lemon torte, a cake that will bring the sunshine and lush green life of the Campania and the beautiful islands off the coast of Southern Italy right onto your plate in, say, rain-shrouded Oregon or snowy Maine.

Homemade Limoncello
If you sell it, the Feds will get you

- Peel *2 pounds of washed, very fresh lemons* (or, in the U.S., *green and yellow lemons*), taking only the peel, not the pith, which is bitter.

- Put the lemon zest in a 1/2 gallon jar with a tight-fitting lid. Add *1 quart grain alcohol* and allow to stand from 2 to 4 days, away from sunlight. Shake the jar several times a day.

- When the zests become pale and crisp, strain them out and keep the lemon-flavored alcohol.

- In a saucepan, mix *6 cups water* and *2 1/2 cups sugar* and stir over medium heat, never boiling, until the sugar dissolves and the liquid is clear. Take off heat and allow to cool to room temperature.

- Stir syrup into the alcohol and pour the resulting cloudy liquid through a funnel into 2 clean, dry bottles. Close with clean corks.

- Limoncello can be enjoyed immediately but tastes better when it sits for a week or so. Serve in small glasses, Campania-style, at room temperature or cold and syrupy from the freezer.

- For a sweeter liqueur use more sugar and less water.

Lemon Torte

- Preheat oven to 350 degrees F. Butter and flour a 9-inch bundt pan.

- Cream together *6 ounces butter* and *1 cup sugar* in a

large mixing bowl for about 5 minutes or until light
and fluffy.

- Add *4 eggs*, 1 at a time, beating well between addi-
tions. Beat in the *grated rind of four large lemons,
juiced (reserving at least 1/2 cup of juice)*.

- Sift *3 cups all-purpose flour* and stir in a *pinch of salt*
and *2 teaspoons baking powder*.

- Fold in half the flour and *1/4 cup milk*. Fold in remaining flour and another *1/4 cup milk*.

- Pour into 9-inch bundt cake pan and bake 40 to 45
minutes.

- In a small saucepan over high heat, boil and stir *1/4
cup water and 1/2 cup sugar* until sugar is dissolved
and syrup is clear. Let cool a few minutes and add
reserved *1/2 cup lemon juice*.

- When cake is done, take from oven and cool on rack
for 15 minutes.

- While cake is in the pan and still warm, make holes
with skewer or toothpick; then slowly spoon lemon
syrup over cake, letting each application become
absorbed before adding more. Reserve a few tablespoons of syrup.

- Turn cooled cake onto serving plate. Boil reserved
syrup until thick. Brush outside of cake with thick
syrup to form a light glaze and press *slivered almonds* onto surface of cake.

Carolyn Blue,
"Have Fork, Will Travel,"
Cape Elizabeth Journal

17
Gracia Sindacco's Revelations

Bianca

I fell onto the bed without even checking to see where Violetta and the children were. The one yet to be born occupied my thoughts, and that birth couldn't be soon enough for me. He was kicking again, all the way up the elevator. People noticed and stared. Picking Lorenzo's nice, fat pillow from its place beside mine, I tossed it to the end of the bed and hauled my swollen feet and ankles up, me who had been known for my pretty legs, for the most slender and shapely ankles in Rome. I groaned at the luxury of resting my back, which ached from the weight of the baby, and at the pleasure of raising my feet and ankles so that the throbbing eased. If Signor Girol had been able to see my ankles, he wouldn't have been such a flirt.

I had left Carolyn in the lobby lecturing poor Lieutenant Buglione on his sloppy investigation and knocking down his ill-conceived reasoning. Sighing, I thought of something that I myself should do for the late Paolina, poor girl. She must have had a lot of fun while she lived. Gracia Sindacco, the office manager to Ruggiero, should be here and on the job by now. If anyone knew the gossip about his secretary, it would be she. I'd heard that she had six sons, all of them grown now, but still there would be the bond of motherhood between us, as well as the bond of being Italians, although Sicilians—were they true Italians? Well, I would see. And so I lazed on the bed for a few more minutes and then rolled to my feet to search out Gracia Sindacco. She proved to be the very stereotype of a witch, just as Ruggiero had said, although he may have been referring to her personality as well as her looks.

Her skin was dark and lined, her nose long, her hair gray and pulled into a tight knob at her neck. Add to these characteristics a stringy body draped in black, baggy clothes—ah well. I prided myself on being able to charm anyone. "Signora," I called as I limped into the office beside the conference room at the end of the hall. "You must be Gracia Sindacco. I am Bianca Massoni, wife of Lorenzo. I have heard that you have six sons. What a fine thing! Your husband must have been delighted with his good fortune to have such a wife in his house."

She had been looking me over. "Have you come, Signora Massoni, to ask me to deliver your child? Big as you are, I do not think the time is now. Your baby has not dropped."

Not an easy woman to charm. I laughed and asked permission to sit, which was granted. "I do know that, Signora Sindacco, although you are the only one to say my time is not yet. The foreigners are sure I am about to give birth before their eyes. So I do not need a midwife today, but advice from a mother of six—that would be welcome. Both my husband and I are only children, and the baby—" I patted my stomach, "will be only my third." And so I did manage to charm Gracia, who sat down and insisted on pouring me a glass of some strange, cool drink—from a fruit of unknown origin.

I wouldn't have minded the juice of the blood orange,

for which Sicily is famous, but this was not it. Still, what she provided went down well, and we mothers of Italy were soon chatting away about husbands and children. It didn't take me long to work the conversation around to the unfortunate death of Paolina Marchetti, whose mother, I surmised, would be grief-stricken at the loss.

Gracia shrugged. "If that one was my daughter, I would not grieve too long," she said grimly.

"Really?" I must have looked as interested as I felt. "I did hear that she came here to meet a lover who called off the assignation. It's thought she committed suicide from grief."

Gracia snorted and leaned forward to pour herself more of the mystery drink. It had certainly perked me up. "Have another glass," she urged. "It will help with that swelling in your ankles."

I slid my glass forward for a refill. How nice it would be to attend the dinner tonight with normal ankles and feet that did not lap over my shoes.

"She would not commit suicide over a man. She'd just find another. She was sleeping with Signor Ricci, but I know that she took home someone else the night before she left for Sorrento, and the one who failed to meet her here must have been a third. They were alike, those two— Ruggiero and his young secretary—sleeping with anyone who was willing and some who weren't, but I doubt he, Ruggiero, knew she was as unfaithful to him as he was to Constanza."

"Mother of God!" I exclaimed, crossing myself. "Men are such fools. Here he has a fine wife, yet his eyes seek out other women."

Gracia scowled ferociously. "I told Constanza not to marry him. I was her nurse, you know, and nurse to her children. Then when my husband died, Constanza had me trained to run Ruggiero's office and keep an eye on him for her. By then she knew she should have taken my advice. A handsome husband with no sense of decency or discretion is not a good choice."

I nodded sagely. "But perhaps it was arranged between the families. I have heard that hers is of the Sicilian nobility."

"Hers, yes," Gracia agreed. "But the Riccis—a bad family, very rich, but very bad. Mafia. The old man is evil. Satan in the household. Constanza thinks that's all in the past, the Mafia connection, but she's wrong. And that Paolina. I was glad to hear she'd been killed. There was something wrong about that one. A slut, surely, but a secretary? That didn't make sense."

"My goodness!" I exclaimed. "And here I thought it was a tragic accident or a suicide, although no one wants to believe that because of the sin. I wonder who could have killed her?"

"The old man," said Gracia. "Probably found out she was cheating on his son and hired an assassin to avenge the family honor." Again she snorted. "As if the Riccis were men of honor. The old one, he's too weak and crippled now to do his own killing, but he has the money to buy what he wants, even murder."

Now there was an innovative idea. I'd have to pass it on to Carolyn. "I heard a whisper, just gossip, that Paolina liked women, too."

"Women didn't like her," said Gracia stoutly. "No good woman is friends with a slut."

"I meant women who like women." I think I managed a credible blush. It wasn't too hard because I felt as if the blood was migrating from my swollen feet to my flushed cheeks.

"Ah, I see what you mean." Gracia nodded thoughtfully. "It could be. There are some who will try anything, but it was the men she always went for as far as I could see. She'd no more than signed her employment papers than she was rubbing up against her boss, who never turned down a pretty girl. Aren't you going to the dinner?"

"Oh, my goodness. I've enjoyed our conversation so much I forgot the time. I'd better get dressed." I twisted to the side to get a peek at my ankles, which felt better and, in fact, looked better. "You are a miracle worker, Signora Sindacco," I said sincerely. "I wish you were my doctor."

She almost smiled at me—not quite—and advised me to empty my bladder twice before I went downstairs to dinner. Mother of God, would her miracle drink have me peeing at the dinner table?

13
Another Fine Dinner

Carolyn

At the predinner cocktail party, I fended off a suggestion from Francis Stackpole that I have a Scotch neat, his choice, by laughing and telling him that wine had the longer history, having been favored by the Greeks and Romans. "For centuries people drank it with their meals and without—for instance, when they got up in the morning, or to rejuvenate themselves while traveling, or even to cure whatever ailed them. Pope Paul III's wine steward had to choose wine for his master with all kinds of activities in mind, not just to go with the Pontiff's meals, but for dipping biscotti and gargling," I explained earnestly.

"That's all very well, my girl," said Professor Stackpole, "but in Scotland, where I grew up, there was not a grape growing, and a good nip of Scotch did just as well for everything you mentioned. Never gargled with it myself, but Eliza always fixes me a toddy for a cough or sore throat. Maybe that's why the pope was gargling with wine. Poor fellow. Probably couldn't get his hands on Scotch."

Even having heard such a fine tribute to Scotch, I decided on the *Greco di Tufo*, a Campanian white wine made, I assumed, from grapes that had been brought to the area by Greeks in ancient times. With it, I ate fresh anchovies and fried artichoke pieces that had been dipped in batter.

While I was savoring the delicious tidbits on my plate and sipping my wine, Bianca whispered to me the news that Ruggiero's father was an evil Mafia person, according to Gracia Sindacco, and might have hired a hit on Paolina to avenge her infidelity to his son. It sounded a bit far-fetched to me, but I suppose it was something that needed to be considered. I did think this Sindacco woman's opinion, that Paolina was a slut, very unkind. Of course, the woman would take Constanza's side rather than the side of Ruggiero's mistress or girlfriend or whatever Paolina had been to him.

Had she really expected to sleep with three different men in as many nights? Poor Paolina. Perhaps she was one of those girls in search of love that she hadn't found in her family life. Surely just reading Edna St. Vincent Millay's poetry hadn't brought on that sort of behavior. I had read it younger than Paolina, and it hadn't had that effect on me. But then at eleven I probably missed a lot of the sensuality. I liked the words and rhythms and needed an escape from the fact that my mother was dying.

After she died, my father took a look at the collection and said it was too old for me. I, of course, said that it was Mama's book, so there couldn't be anything wrong with it. Daddy said she was an adult when she read it. Maybe so, but my mother certainly hadn't been promiscuous. I think I'd have noticed if she'd been entertaining men other than my father.

And speaking of mothers, Lorenzo's mother was flirting with Francis Stackpole, whose wife didn't even seem to notice. Eliza had cornered poor Valentino Santoro and was quizzing him about plants that grow on Mount Etna and how they were affected by lava. How else would they be affected? They'd burn up.

"Look at my mother-in-law," said Bianca. "How can she flirt with that Englishman? I'm sure he's a sweet man, but his clothes look like he slept in them. And I had to pay a local girl to look after the children so that Violetta can practice her wiles on an Englishman."

"I'm sure she doesn't mean anything by it," I said absently.

"Well, she's not looking to marry him, if that's what you mean," said Bianca, "but she probably wouldn't mind a fling with him. Maybe he looks better without that dreadful tweed suit."

"A—a fling?" I stammered.

"An affair. She has several a year. Maybe she's settled on him as her next man."

"Your mother-in-law has affairs?" I was amazed. What would I think if my mother-in-law had affairs?

"Violetta's a widow, and she doesn't usually sleep with married men," said Bianca, looking at me as if I had called her mother-in-law a slut when I was thinking no such thing.

"Of course not," I mumbled, but then I couldn't help thinking of Violetta, the beautiful courtesan who died of tuberculosis in Verdi's *La Traviata*. Although Bianca's mother-in-law was probably twice the age of Verdi's heroine. Then my mind jumped to my own mother-in-law, and I was hard put not to burst into laughter as I imagined Gwenivere Blue, radical feminist, professor of women's studies, luring some unsuspecting older man into an affair.

"Carolyn, are you laughing?" Bianca demanded. "It's not funny, you know. Sometimes it's embarrassing, all that flirting. As for the affairs, she's very discreet about those, but the really irritating thing is that all I have to do is talk to another man for a few minutes, and she thinks *I'm* having an affair.

"She's decided Hank Girol is after me because I sat in the front seat with him today. I ask you? How likely is it that a woman in my condition is going to inspire lust, or feel it, for that matter? When I go to bed these days, I'm only interested in getting a full night's sleep. Too bad the baby doesn't feel the same way. Ah, it's time to go in to dinner. More Sicilian cuisine probably. Did Constanza bring her own chef or just send menus and recipes to the hotel's chef?"

"She hired someone local," I replied, having heard from Jill at the desk that Constanza refused to let the hotel's Swiss chef prepare anything for the conferees.

And in we went, for a Neapolitan meal this time: a spicy tomato-based bean and pasta soup (so deliciously warm and tasty when the thunder was rolling over the cliffs and heavy rain lashing the hotel), then individual roasted pepper casseroles and monkfish in wine and tomato sauce, with which we drank the most famous white wine of the area, *Lacrima Christi*, and finally a really wonderful dessert. It was made from layers of la-dyfingers dipped in brandy, topped with cream, marmalade and, last, grated dark chocolate. The conversation, none of it about Paolina, flowed around me as I savored each dish. Of course, I made notes. I had columns to write, columns about the joys of dining in Italy, any part of Italy.

During the soup course, Albertine Guillot remarked that French soups, and cuisine in general, were much more refined because the French were more oriented to the savoring of fine food. Bianca took offense and pointed out that haute cuisine had come to France when Catherine de Medici became the French queen and brought her chefs with her. *Good for you, Bianca*, I thought, and stopped making notes so that I could put a word in for Italian cuisine.

"Actually, the Italians were so serious about food and its preparation that Petrarch complained Italians spoke only of food and that cooks were required to take examinations while copyists were not."

Albertine shrugged. "A poet's jealousy and an examination for cooks does not mean that the cuisine is—"

I interrupted her to point out that the French in the time of Montaigne had thought the Italian interest in food peculiar and condemned it as an immoral attempt to make people eat more than was good for them.

Albertine settled into a sulk, and the monkfish entrée was served. I do like monkfish, and this was served without the intimidating teeth. Smiling at me, evidently pleased with my defense of her country's cuisine, Constanza asked, "And what can you tell us of historical interest about monkfish, my dear Carolyn?"

Again I put off note taking and thought about her question. "Well, nothing particular to monkfish, but I've read that the Romans preferred saltwater fish, which the monkfish is. It's also called a devilfish because of its huge mouthful of dangerous-looking teeth and scorpion configuration, or an anglerfish because it unrolls a shiny filament to lure other fish in and then gobbles them up. But people in medieval Italy preferred freshwater fish. They thought the saltwater variety unhealthy because it made the diner thirsty. Eels were a particular favorite all over Europe as well as in Italy because they could be eaten on fast days and could be transported for periods of several days, fresh but out of water. As I remember, they were carried in grass baskets."

"Did they eat the grass?" Eliza asked, taking a sudden interest.

"I have no idea," I replied, wondering what eels ate.

"Eels? That sounds disgusting!" exclaimed Sibyl Evers. "Sort of like eating a snake."

"I've never eaten a snake," I replied, "although people do. There was an excellent restaurant in Washington, D.C., that served rattlesnake, but my father and I didn't order it. Eel is actually tasty. Sort of meaty, with a high fat content, I would imagine."

"You eat eels in Texas?" Sibyl asked. "I thought it was all desert. Don't they need *some* water to live in?"

"Carolyn had eel here in Europe," said my husband, smiling in a friendly way at Sibyl. "I've never seen it on a menu in Texas, even in areas that have lakes and rivers in plentiful supply."

Since there were only three courses and espresso, we broke up early, the better for the chemists to meet in the morning, and went to our rooms, all on the eighth floor. Ruggiero's company had taken the whole floor, conference rooms and all. After booting up my laptop and writing a column, I got ready for bed and turned on the television. Jason was already under the covers reading. A little channel surfing got me past the Italian stations to something in English, Sky News. First there was a news report about a "lorry" accident out in the English countryside and a sheepdog contest in Scotland, then sports, a boxing match. Normally I wouldn't watch boxing, but Jason seemed untalkative and grumpy, while the announcer was hilarious. He had a Cockney accent that wasn't to be believed. "I *fink* this" and "I *fink* that"—all referring to a pale, skinny pair of fighters who looked as if one hard punch would shatter them both and end the match.

"Jason, you've got to listen to this man's accent. It's incredible."

Jason looked up from the reprint of an article on chemistry, listened, and shrugged. "English," he said.

Duh, as my daughter would have replied. I turned off the television and asked cheerfully, "How's the meeting going?"

"Oh, wonderful," my husband replied. "It's turning out to be an attempt by Ricci to pick our brains without paying a consulting fee. A little free R & D for them—"

"And a free vacation for us in a beautiful place."

"Maybe for you," said my disgruntled husband. "I take it that the trip to Amalfi was a success."

"Delightful, except that I was squished into the backseat and have bruises under my chin where my knees knocked into it at every bump in the road." That really wasn't doing the trip justice, so I added, "Aside from coming back partially crippled and definitely sunburned, I did really enjoy our outing. The coast is spectacular. I have hundreds of pictures. Shall I get out the camera?"

"Some other night," said my husband.

"Well, did you notice my new face?"

Jason gave me a quizzical look. "You looked fine to me when you came back. I couldn't even see the bruise on your cheek."

"That's because Albertine Guillot forced her way in the room this morning and attacked me with expensive cosmetics, her way of apologizing for her dog's unprovoked attack. I wonder what Alitalia thinks of Charles de Gaulle. He had his own reservation on their flight from Milan, scarfed down some spicy pasta, and threw up on the seat. Or pooped. I'm not sure which. Albertine blames the airline."

"So Adrien told me. He's actually a good man, and an excellent scientist, not to mention quite embarrassed about the dog's behavior. I hear you think Ruggiero Ricci is a saint."

"I do not. I said he looked like a saint whose picture I saw in Sorrento. And he does. You'd be amazed. As for his character, I think he may have murdered Paolina, his sec-retary. He was certainly having an affair with her."

Jason snapped his book closed. "Carolyn, I hope that you're not getting mixed up in this murder investigation."

I scooted down under the covers and said, "I'm listen-ing to gossip, Jason. I'm not investigating. The police are doing that, but not very effectively. The lieutenant in charge is so overwhelmed by the importance of the Riccis that he's let them convince him Paolina's death was prob-ably an accident or a suicide."

"Probably was," said my husband and turned out the light.

"And the Carabinieri evidently aren't even interested in the case," I muttered as I turned on my side and settled down to sleep.

"Good for them. I wish you weren't," said my husband.

Tuesday in Pompeii

Vesuvius — Disasters and Blessings

In the eighth century BC, Greeks sailed to the Island of Ischia in the Bay of Naples, but many were discouraged by the volcanic activity that drove them to settle on the mainland at Cuma. Ironically, that move brought them into the shadow of Vesuvius. The largest eruptions in Europe occurred here in 5960 and 3580 BC, and the area suffered devastating earthquakes, but we have no written records of these. Now a grim reminder of disasters ancient and modern, Mount Vesuvius rises from a plain in the Campania with Naples to the north and the Sorrento Peninsula to the south. Over two million people live near it today.

Preceded by a violent earthquake in 62 AD, Vesuvius erupted in 79 AD and destroyed Pompeii, Herculaneum, and other Roman towns. Between 3,400 and 16,000 citizens were killed—no one is really sure how many. This was the first earthquake to be described by a historian, Pliny the Younger. Fifty more eruptions followed into modern times. Between 79 and 1037 AD the volcano brought fear and disaster every hundred years or so, and then it went dormant for 600 years. In 1631 it reactivated and destroyed a dozen towns or more, killed another 4,000 people, and continued to erupt off and on into the twentieth century, devastating Naples in 1906, with lava flows invading towns up to 1944.

During eruptions Vesuvius has expelled columns of smoke, ash and fire, mud, boiling water, lava, and poisonous gases. The descriptions in historical times are terrifying. Yet between the earthquakes and eruptions, the lava breaks down into rich soil, trees and plants grow, people forget that Vesuvius is a volcano, and they move back to reap its blessings. They plant fields, orchards, and vineyards and produce delicious food, wonderful wine, and a superb cuisine. They build houses and public structures on the land, while Vesuvius, the only active volcano on mainland Europe, lies in wait for a greater disaster than ever with two million people at risk, and more every year.

Carolyn Blue,
"Have Fork, Will Travel,"
Raleigh Star-Telegram

19
Carabinieri — Absent but Revered

Bianca

We had a little family argument because Lorenzo didn't think I should go to Pompeii in my delicate condition, while Violetta and the children wanted to go in my place. I insisted that I'd be fine, that I could always go back and rest in the limousine if I got tired, and that there wouldn't be room for three people to take one place, even mine.

Downstairs I found Carolyn breaking up an intimate conversation between Jill at the desk and Lieutenant Buglione so that she could tell him about Gracia Sindacco's Mafia hit-man theory. The lieutenant insisted that he had interviewed all guests on Paolina's floor and found them to be ordinary tourists, not Mafia hit men, and on our floor, he added, smiling triumphantly, everyone was a guest of the Ricci convention, either a scientist or the spouse of a scientist. When Jill suggested that the criminal might have been a Mafia hit lady, Buglione chuckled appreciatively while Carolyn's lips pressed together in irritation. I noticed that the bruise was back on her cheek. How strange.

"Haven't the Carabinieri returned?" I asked Lieutenant

Buglione. "I called them myself because I thought you could use some help."

He frowned at me. "Do you know why they have that red stripe up their trousers?" he asked slyly.

"So they can find their pockets," I replied. "And I also know what a tumor does on the brain of a Carabinieri. Nothing." Carolyn was looking shocked, so I told her to pay no attention. "The Carabinieri are national heroes. Everyone loves them. That's why they're called *la Bene-merita*, the well deserving."

"Collodi didn't think so," snapped Buglione. "He made fun of them in *Pinocchio*."

"That was a long time ago, Lieutenant," I responded, "when they were poor, uneducated lads. And Collodi was from Florence. The Florentines are known for thinking they're better than anyone else. These days the Carabinieri officers are the top graduates of the military academy."

"That's wonderful," said Carolyn. "But when are they coming back?"

"I see that you ladies are not satisfied with my investigation," said Buglione resentfully, "and I, you will notice, am here every day with my men."

"Doing what?" Carolyn muttered as he stomped off. Then she told me that Pompeii, as she remembered it, was short on shade and long on sun. She had come prepared, with comfortable shoes, a hat, sunscreen, and drinking water, and hoped that I had done the same. As if I'd never been to Pompeii. "Are you sure you'll be up to so much walking?" she asked, looking worried on my behalf.

"If I'm not, I can just sit down on a rock. They're everywhere. Or go back to the limousine and take a nap. Or faint so that handsome medics will come and carry me away." I grinned at her. "When I was pregnant with Giulia, we went hiking in the Dolomites. It was lovely." I didn't mention that my feet hadn't swelled so much during my first two pregnancies.

"Hiking?" Carolyn looked horrified. "How could Lorenzo do that to you?"

"He didn't want me to get too fat," I explained. "He should be very pleased to hear that I'll be walking all over Pompeii. You can spend six hours or more there if you want to. And of course walking is good for bringing on labor."

"It is?" she asked weakly. Then she squinted at me. "You're putting me on, aren't you?"

"Just a little," I admitted. "But I *am* getting a bit tired of hauling this child around. Labor is beginning to look better and better." Then I took pity on her and asked, "So what should we do next in our investigation?"

"Well, we need to find out where Constanza and Ruggiero were the night Paolina died," said Carolyn, readily distracted. She got no further because Constanza and the guide she had hired shooed us into the elevator for the trip down the cliff to the road. I considered suggesting that we ask Constanza herself where she and her husband had been when the murder occurred. She was right there, our hostess for the day. However, I reconsidered that idea. Carolyn might do it.

20
Expectant in Pompeii

Bianca

There were nine of us in all in the limousine taking the SS145 north, the heavily traveled, twisting road to Castellammare di Stabia, where we turned onto the A3, the Naples-to-Salerno highway with the Pompeii turnoff. The chauffeur and the tour guide sat up front, separated from the rest of us by a glass window. In back were Constanza, Hank, Eliza, Albertine, Carolyn, me, and Charles de Gaulle, who was assigned a place where luggage could be stored behind the last seat. Evidently thinking the dog would sit with Albertine, Carolyn leapt in first and scooted to the back, which is how she ended up with Charles de Gaulle's head resting on her shoulder. I suppose it must have been a shock to her when the chauffeur opened up the back and let in the dog. It immediately gave a low, lovesick woof and nuzzled Carolyn's neck.

She shoved him away with a hand on his nose and didn't say another word except to answer when Constanza asked if she was comfortable back there.

"Lovely seats," said Carolyn politely. "Much nicer than the plastic ones on the *Circumvesuviana*." She was trying to edge away from the dog, but there was no room to do so because I was taking up the rest of the seat.

Constanza was, of course, amazed to learn that Carolyn had ridden, with her luggage, from Naples to Sorrento on the little train. I was just glad it hadn't been me; I'd been on the *Circumvesuviana* and knew that it was no place for an expectant mother, whereas this delightful limousine made traveling like floating down the road on a cloud. I even dozed off while Carolyn, Constanza, and Albertine discussed opera in Catania and Palermo. Composers' names drifted into my sleep—Verdi, Mozart, Puccini, Donizetti, Bellini. I dreamt that I was in the opera house in Palermo, with Johnny Stecchino, played by Roberto Benigni, in the balcony threatening the audience with a banana. After waking up with a start, I said, "I saw that movie."

The three women looked at me in surprised confusion. Then Carolyn said, "Oh, for goodness sake!" after glancing down at her blouse. "He's drooled on me. Madame Guillot, would you please tell your dog—"

I spoke quickly to the dog in French because I could see that harsh words were about to be exchanged. Charles de Gaulle actually lifted his head and turned to look at me, so I continued to talk to him in French, but how much can you think of to say to a dog, especially a French dog? Finally I murmured softly, "Look you ill-behaved, froggie mutt, if you don't leave my friend alone, I'm going to climb back there and hang you up by your designer dog collar."

"What did you say to my dog?" demanded Albertine.

"I don't know what she said to him," Carolyn intervened, "but his head is off my shoulder, and I think he's moved away." She glanced into the back compartment, where Charles de Gaulle was now lying down, staring at me in an unfriendly way. *Does he bite?* I wondered. He hadn't so far.

Nobody got into a squabble because the tour guide turned on her microphone and began to tell us the history of Pompeii. Iron Age settlements in the ninth and eighth centuries BC, influence of Etruscans, Samnites, Greeks, Romans, the 62 AD earthquake—nap time again. I knew all that. Carolyn woke me up by exclaiming, "I didn't know they thought Vesuvius was just a green mountain until it erupted!" The guide continued by describing the awful plaster casts made of agonized people who had tried to escape and died and the excavations of the city that had begun in the eighteenth century.

She droned on, and again I dropped into a pleasant snooze. Naps are good for pregnant women, and I needed to store up strength for hiking through dust and clambering over stones on a very large site, carrying my very large baby. At least, I hoped that my mountainous stomach was mostly baby; if it wasn't, I had a lot of dieting to look forward to if I wanted to retrieve the body my husband was so fond of. I was very happy to hear Constanza announce that we would break for lunch around one. I was hungry already, and I'd certainly need a rest by then.

Evidently the plan was to see major civic and religious ruins in the morning, so of course we looked at a lot of pillars without roofs, something I'd seen so many times in Rome: the remains of temples to Fortuna Augusta, Jupiter, Apollo—that was a good one because the statue was of Apollo naked except for a scarf over his arms, and he had a nice butt, but his bow and arrow were gone—and Isis, who had a lot of worshippers in Pompeii before they were gassed or buried under falling buildings when Vesuvius exploded. The temple had little rooms in which to keep water from the Nile and sacrificial ashes and a big room for worshippers. It's a wonder Europe ever became Christian when the Roman soldiers kept bringing new religions home from the East.

There were theaters and amphitheaters holding from a thousand to twenty thousand people, not enough for soccer, but not bad. Near the amphitheater were a gymnasium and a pool for gladiators with graffiti left from their stay. I imagined them, coming in from practice, all sweaty, scratching things into the wall. The guide didn't translate the graffiti. In her place, I would have, if it had been interesting. Needless to say, I did not climb up and down any crumbly, grass-choked amphitheaters. I was watching out for myself and the baby.

Probably the most unsettling sight was the view of Vesuvius, gray and forbidding, through the columns of the Forum. Or maybe it just looked gray because the clouds had rolled in, shadowing everything beneath. Of course we visited the thermal baths at the Forum, which had statues, carvings, pools of different temperatures, heat from boilers under the floors, dressing rooms, and separate sides for men and women. It was very elegant in its day. I remember reading that, after the earthquake when the baths were rebuilt, they dropped the separate sides for different sexes. I wonder how people felt about that? Titillated? Embarrassed?

I was thinking about that when we went out into the streets, which in Pompeii were full of obstacles. Big stepping stones had been set crosswise so the citizens could get from sidewalk to sidewalk without stepping into rushing water that couldn't be contained by an inadequate sewer system. Down the center ran a rise in the stone pavement low enough that the wheels of carts and chariots could roll along with the stones in between. You could see the tracks worn in the road by the heavy traffic.

Those streets are not easily negotiable, not only because of the obstacles but also because the step down from the sidewalks in front of the buildings was often a long one. When I made the attempt, disaster struck: I lost my balance, stumbled toward one of those large stones, and would have fallen stomach-first onto it except that Constanza was right behind me. She grabbed me under the armpits and jerked me onto my feet, right off the ground, in fact. I don't know when I've been more frightened. She'd saved my baby, and yet she just shrugged off my thanks and said in a surprisingly kind voice, "Be more careful, Bianca. How sad it would be to lose a baby from a misstep."

From there to the limousine either Hank or Carolyn walked beside me, holding onto my arm to keep me from falling again. It occurred to me as I plodded along, still a little shaky and keeping an eye out for anything that might trip me up, that Constanza was not only quick for a woman her age, but also very strong. Lifting me up and off my feet was no small accomplishment. I'd gained twenty-five, maybe even thirty pounds with this pregnancy. *Is Constanza one of those women who exercises and lifts weights?* I mused. *No wonder she has such a good figure.*

I mentioned the thought to Carolyn as we waited at the Porta Nocera for the limousine, and she nodded thoughtfully. "That might mean that she's strong enough to have thrown Paolina over the waterfall."

I didn't much like her saying that about the woman who had saved me from a miscarriage or a stillbirth, and I made a point not to sit with Carolyn at lunch. She, however, made a point of sitting beside Constanza, and I got stuck with Albertine Guillot, who gave me a lecture on my responsibilities as a prospective mother. A woman with no children! I told her that dog owners had responsibilities, too, and hers had drooled all over Carolyn's blouse. She turned her back on me and struck up a conversation with

Eliza Stackpole. Just what Albertine deserved, in my opinion. She got an earful about the cacti outside Eliza's balcony, while I flirted with Hank Girol, which was a soothing pastime after my frightening tumble.

21
The Two Faces of Constanza

Carolyn

At first, all the walking was dreadfully hard. The guide raced along much too fast for me, but I had to keep up if I wanted to hear what she had to say. A very knowledge-able woman, if a little dry. Perhaps Constanza had hired an archaeology professor. So I climbed, panting, up and down curbs and stairs, and hurried through the dust and stones when hurrying was necessary. After what seemed like a very long time, it got easier. I couldn't believe it. And after that, I began to feel very cheerful, and my breathing, even under dire conditions, deepened and evened out. Was I experiencing a runner's high? Jason did things like that, but I hadn't been running. Still, my lungs seemed to have expanded, and a lot more oxygen was ob-viously being pumped to my brain. I felt almost euphoric.

When Bianca, after her fall, commented on Con-stanza's strength, I knew immediately what that meant. Accordingly, I made sure that I sat beside Constanza so that I could ask her wily questions. However, it didn't quite work out that way. For one thing, the restaurant had lovely food and pitchers of delightful wine from the Campania, not one of the famous brands, but very good, nonetheless, perhaps from one of the terraced vineyards we'd seen on our way to Amalfi. I should have paid more attention, but I'd been too busy taking pictures of the cliffs and the sea.

I ordered the *pasta puttanesca*, and it was so spicy, so delicious, and so colorful with its olives, capers, tomatoes, red peppers, and parsley. Many possible explanations of the name have been offered, most of them quite scandalous. It may have been named by a brothel madam in Naples because it was something easily fixed for her customers, or by the girls between tricks. It might be named for the colorful undergarments the girls wore to entice their customers, or because it smelled so good that it lured customers in off the streets. Or it could have received its name from a wife, returning from an afternoon adultery, who needed a quick dinner for her husband. At least, it can be agreed that the sauce was so named during the twentieth century, that it looks, smells, and tastes wonderful, and that it can be quickly prepared.

Turning to Constanza to comment on the perfection of the dish, I noticed that she had placed a little meter gadget on her skin. It popped out a bit of paper, which she studied for a minute. Then she pushed away her own pasta and signaled the waiter. "The pasta's wonderful, really," I assured her.

Constanza sighed and said, "I know it is. I've had it here before, but my glucose level is too high. You'll have to excuse me for a minute." She rose and left the table. While she was gone, a salad was delivered and her pasta taken away. *She must be a diabetic*, I decided. I'd always thought of that as an American thing. Half the population of El Paso has diabetes. But Constanza was so slender— well, except in the breast area.

I did feel sorry for her. She wasn't going to be able to

eat this wonderful pasta. I twirled up some more, ate it, and snagged a piece of crispy-edged garlic bread from a straw basket. She couldn't have that either. I'd noticed a list of gelatos on the menu, wonderful flavors, many not available at home. Perhaps I'd order a bowl with several flavors. No, that would be so cruel to my hostess.

She returned, sat down beside me, and calmly began to eat her salad. "It's not the hereditary type of diabetes," she remarked. "I find it a bother, certainly, but at least my children will not inherit it from me, or so my doctor assures me. They will have their blood checked when the time comes and take measures if they must. I was caught completely by surprise when I was diagnosed. No one in my family has had it that I know of. Of course, these are different times. Maybe I have ancestors who ate the local diet and died before their time, completely unaware of what killed them."

Because I had stopped eating, she smiled at me and advised to me enjoy my pasta. "I intend to enjoy my salad," she assured me. "The artichokes are excellent. Would you like to see pictures of my children?"

Of course, I said yes, and they were a very handsome young man and woman: Luca, the son, blonde like his mother; Elizabetta, the daughter, dark and exotic. The son lived in Catania and traveled widely as an executive ambassador for the family business. The daughter was in England taking a science degree. "Strange, isn't it," said Constanza, "that it would be my daughter who is interested in the medical side of the business? Valentino says she will be a brilliant scientist. Perhaps now that he must relinquish his infatuation for Paolina Marchetti, he and Elizabetta will marry. They would have beautiful children, just as Ruggiero and I have done. My son has already married, an American girl he met at school in your country. They have twin boys with the prettiest curly, blonde hair." She showed me pictures of her grandchildren as well.

Then I showed her pictures of my children, Chris, the scientist-to-be, and Gwen, the aspiring actress, and we exchanged stories of their childhoods and their triumphs as young adults, just as any two mothers might. I couldn't believe I was having this pleasant, normal conversation with Constanza Ricci-Tassone, whose descent from old Norman-Sicilian royalty had made her seem so snobbish. I never did get to the matter of her strength or where she had been the night Paolina died—Paolina, who had caught the eye the man Constanza had picked out for her daughter, as well as the eye of Constanza's own husband. Hmmmm.

Then, after dessert, which Constanza skipped except for an unsweetened espresso, we were off in the limousine to Pompeii again. She very kindly arranged the car seating herself. Albertine and Hank sat in back with Charles de Gaulle behind them. I doubt the dog drooled on his mistress, and I hoped that he'd leave me alone. Bianca decided to take a nap in the limousine, so the chauffeur stayed with her to keep the air-conditioning going. The rest of us spent most of the afternoon visiting areas of Pompeii with houses and shops.

Shops were on first floors with signs to advertise their merchandise, marble benches to display it, and gods to afford them protection from ill fortune. There were bakeries where flour was milled, kneaded, and baked, and shops with amphorae of wine, oil, corn, and sarum, which was a popular Roman fish sauce made of mashed fish intestines and used to add a salty flavor to dishes. They even put it on salads. Doesn't that sound disgusting? There were taverns where people could eat and drink and, of course, brothels. The structures were often incomplete, but they gave one a feeling for the city and its life. I was fascinated, as I had been when I visited with my father years ago.

And the houses! Life must have been very pleasant for those who could afford the villas with atriums housing fountains and ponds, and rooms for all the uses of a family, even bathrooms, decorated with frescoes and mosaics, statues and portraits. In the House of the Faun, named for a delightful third century BC statue of a faun in the atrium, there is a floor with a reproduction of an early Greek mosaic depicting a battle between the armies of Alexander and Darius of Persia. And who could forget, even when Eliza was rattling on about the Mafia, the House of the Large Fountain, with its two stone heads that sported curling hair and beards, large eyes, and gaping mouths from which the water must once have flowed? I wished Eliza would stop chattering.

Constanza heard her and said, "One seldom meets Mafiosi these days, even in Catania. My husband's family were affiliated in the old days, but no more. Now the Riccis make medicines and beautiful children." She laughed, and Eliza, shocked, said no more about the Mafia.

Our last visit was to the Villa of Mysteries, where we saw a frieze in the great hall with life-sized figures painted on a blood red background. Our guide said it was thought to show the initiation of a young bride of Dionysus. Whatever it meant, it sent shivers up my spine to see the scourged woman, the scenes of sacrifice, and the naked bacchante in their orgiastic dances.

I didn't remember this house from my visit with my father. I remembered things like the statue of a deer attacked by dogs; "fast food" shops with bowls inset in the counters, where soup was sold; and the statue of drunken Hercules, one hand holding a huge fish, the other the penis beneath his protruding belly. As we walked at a leisurely pace to the waiting limousine, I mentioned these to Constanza—well, not Hercules—and she said they were at Herculaneum.

"If you have a chance to go to Naples, you must be sure to see the painting of Medea at the Archaeological Museum. A very powerful depiction, the mother so grim as she decides to slay her children because Jason is to marry another woman; the children, watched over by their old teacher, playing innocently, unaware of what she plans. I have never understood why she killed the children. She should have killed Jason."

As my husband is named Jason, I felt somewhat discomfited by her opinion, but not as shocked as I was with what Constanza said next.

"And the fate she chose for the bride-to-be—you remember? The fiery bridal dress she sent to Jason's princess?" Constanza laughed. "That was a satisfying episode in the myth."

Again I shivered. Constanza, whom I had so liked in her role as a mother, approved of the agonizing death Medea meted out to Jason's new love. To get my mind off an unpleasant subject, I asked her if she knew what sharp cabbage was, explaining that I'd read Pompeii had been famous for onions and "sharp cabbage." However, my hostess said that, without hearing the name of this cabbage in Italian, she couldn't tell me and thought of cabbage as peasant food anyway.

"I read somewhere that in the Campania garlic and onions are never used in the same dish," I remarked.

"Of course not," she replied. "Why use both? In fact, a little of either is quite enough, and both together entirely too much. One does not want the breath to be offensive, after all. Breath smelling of onion and garlic is so lower class."

I had to chuckle. "That's a very medieval attitude, Constanza. Quite in keeping with your Norman heritage.

Leeks, garlic, and onions were considered the food of the lower classes, who could be identified by their breath. There's a story of the Duke of Ferrara, Ercole d'Este, who was asked by a peasant for knighthood. The duke agreed and ordered the knighting ceremony prepared, but when the peasant's coat of arms was presented, it was a bulb of garlic on a blue background, and everyone laughed at him."

"I'm sure you think that story unkind on the duke's part," said Constanza, "but it does show that garlic, historically, was held in low esteem, as was the peasantry. They ate coarse food which would have given the nobility indigestion."

"So I read. There's one story about the introduction of the potato to Italy. It was called a white truffle and no one would eat it until a time of famine in the eighteenth century, and then the peasants took potatoes up. It was suggested that bread could be made from potatoes, which might cause indigestion, but would make peasants happy because indigestion made them feel full. That's sort of sad, don't you think?"

Constanza gave me a stern look. "In a time of famine, which perhaps you do not have in America, a peasant is glad enough to eat and to feel that his stomach is full when his fields have been destroyed by the volcano or by marauding armies."

I suppose she was right, but it was the attitude that grated on me. Did she really believe, as some nineteenth century writer had said, that indigestion was good for the poor? Maybe she did. This was the woman who approved of Medea's solution to Jason's marriage plans. It made you appreciate divorce laws that imposed civility on the separating couple. And yet Constanza could be so pleasant, and she was obviously a loving mother.

22
A Green-Eyed Evening

Carolyn

I didn't even take my shoes off before falling onto my bed after the Pompeii trip. Jason wasn't there; I had seen him downstairs talking to Sibyl as they headed for the bar. Hank joined them, but I was too tired for anything but a nap. Then, just as I was drifting off, I had a thought that sat me back up on the bed. Gracia Sindacco had told Bianca that Paolina slept with someone other than her boss the night before she left for Sorrento. What if it was Valentino? That would give Constanza two reasons to kill Paolina—because she had slept with both Constanza's husband and with the man Constanza had chosen for her daughter. I immediately called Bianca's room and asked her to see if Gracia knew who that man was, Paolina's last lover. Then I did take off my shoes and went to sleep.

Jason got back to the room so late that I didn't have time to do more than wash my face and change my clothes before dinner. He chatted about some interesting toxic idea he and Sibyl had come up with at the bar while I was worrying about my unwashed state after an afternoon of wind, dust, and sun. My husband didn't say anything to indicate that I needed a bath, but then, he wouldn't. There was no predinner gathering for drinks and appetizers, maybe because Constanza was watching her glucose levels. Alcohol isn't good for diabetics, is it? We were to go straight in to dinner, but Bianca pulled me aside to relay her conversation with Gracia.

"She thinks Paolina slept with a man who came to visit Ruggiero that day. He stopped to talk to her on his way out of the office."

"Who was he?" I asked, glancing at my husband, who was now chatting with Sibyl on the way in to dinner.

"Well, this is the weird part, and I have to say, I think maybe Gracia is a provincial type who hates foreigners."

"What did she say?" I asked impatiently.

"She said it was a foreigner, maybe an American, maybe someone from this meeting. That I should ask my friend Signora Blue if she knew where her *professore* was that night. I wouldn't pay any attention, Carolyn," Bianca added.

I noticed that she was watching me rather curiously as she reassured me, and Gracia's remarks did send a shiver up my spine, which had been doing entirely too much shivering today. Still, it was nonsense. Jason had been in Paris with Sibyl, for all the consolation that gave me. I shrugged. "It couldn't have been an American from the conference. Jason was in Paris, and Hank was in Rome. I wonder if she has something against me. But why would she? I don't even know the woman."

"Ignore it," Bianca advised again, and we went into the dining room together, where I saw that some people were seated, but not Hank and Ruggiero, who were in intense conversation. Hank? Why was he talking to Ruggiero? I managed to sit beside Hank and asked him.

"I'm trying to drum up business," he replied as he took the bottle from the waiter and poured wine for both of us.

"Why do they give us only half a glass?" he muttered. "It's not like they won't be back every five minutes with refills."

"Business with Ricci Chemicals and Pharmaceuticals?"

"Sure. They have toxic waste. We're trying to expand into the European market. It's not like we're just in New Jersey. We do business all over the U.S. Might as well expand. I'd love to get into Eastern Europe and Russia. They have toxic waste coming out their ears. And China—that would be a gold mine if it weren't such a pain to do business there."

He turned to talk to his wife, and I considered what he'd said. It made sense. More sense than Gracia accusing Jason. We ate our way through another wonderful dinner. How was Constanza getting this fantastic food out of a hotel that served such awful dinners to the other guests? Maybe the breakfast chef was doing her dinners? No, wait. She'd hired a local chef. I knew that. Obviously my nap had been too short.

Among other things, we had lovely pork cutlets with Marsala and juniper—I do love the sweet, rich taste of Marsala with meat—and an excellent polenta. A form of polenta goes back to Roman times. People in Pompeii had probably eaten it. But an interesting thing I'd read about polenta concerned the eighteenth century. This was after maize from America had become popular in the area and was a staple food of the poor. Because the method for treating the maize killed the vitamins, there were terrible epidemics of pellagra among the people in the countryside and the poverty-stricken urban dwellers in Naples and other cities. I didn't even know what pellagra was, but I presumed I was in no danger because I'd eaten polenta on one evening.

At dinner the chemists were quite animated—mostly

about chemistry—but those of us from the Pompeii tour were half asleep. Wouldn't you know? Ruggiero announced dancing after dinner and led us into a small ballroom with a musical foursome on a little stage. I wanted to groan. As soon as I got up from the table, I discovered that all my leg and back muscles were aflame. Of course I understood the progression: first climbing around rocks, then oxygen euphoria, then horrible pain. There were chairs in the ballroom, and I longed to commandeer one, but I had questions to ask.

First, I cornered Ruggiero and said I understood Constanza had been in Sorrento the night before the conference to help Paolina with the organization, adding that we had had such a lovely time together today that I now wished I could have had dinner with her that night. Her husband said he didn't think she'd been in Sorrento; she'd never offered to help Paolina before, but he and his wife hadn't come to Sorrento together the next day. Maybe she'd been off shopping. His wife was an ardent shopper.

No alibi for Constanza. Then I limped over to her and said that the conference was so well organized that her husband must have come ahead to see to things himself. She stared at me with raised eyebrows. "The president of the company does not come ahead to organize the conference, my dear Carolyn," she replied at last. "However, being a professor's wife, you might not know that. I suppose if your husband were organizing a conference, he might well have to come ahead to see to the details. He probably doesn't have people to do it for him."

Well, we were back to the old snobbish Constanza, and I still didn't know where her husband had been the night of Paolina's murder, or in fact, where either Ricci had been. And that, I felt, was all the detecting I could handle in my present condition, so I sat down. Eliza plopped herself right down beside me. She was wearing a crepe dress that matched her hair—taupe. "I was so curious about that dish you ordered at noon. Isn't the name rather—er—salacious?"

Goodness she looked interested, as if she expected me to tell her a dirty pasta story. "Well, *puttanesca* does refer to women in the sex trade."

"Hmm." She nodded knowingly. "How very obscene. A perfect lunch choice after a visit to Pompeii. The guide did say it was the site of the famous Roman orgies."

I'd always wondered exactly what sound a titter made; Eliza was tittering, and I couldn't resist teasing her a bit. "Oh, Romans were quite straight-laced compared to earlier inhabitants of the Campania—the Oscans and the Samnites. Romans considered their drama so disgusting that the word obscene grew from the name of the tribe—Oscan."

"Really? Whatever could their plays have been about? Sex, I suppose, which explains why *pasta puttanesca* is so spicy."

"Actually, it's the red pepper flakes," I replied.

"Pepper was used for a long time to disguise the flavor of spoiled food." Eliza nodded knowledgeably. "My mother always said that."

"Oh, I'm not sure of that. It became popular around the first century AD and was used in everything—even wine. And desserts. I suppose the wine wasn't all that good in Roman times, but I doubt that the desserts were spoiled. And people in the Middle Ages believed that spices helped to dissolve food in the stomach. They sprinkled spices on everything as a digestive."

"Really?" Eliza stared at me, puzzled, and then suggested that I might like to try reading books on botany, which were so very interesting.

After mentioning a few fascinating botanical facts to prove her point, she popped off her chair and left to spread her love of plant life elsewhere. I relaxed and watched the action. Ruggiero was dancing and flirting with Sibyl, of all people. She was taller than he. I studied Constanza surreptitiously to see if she cared, but she didn't seem to notice. Maybe she was as tired as I was. Then I watched Jason to see if he was jealous. He wasn't even looking at Sibyl; he was talking to Adrien Guillot, a conversation that had the look of chemistry. I could usually tell.

Constanza, when I looked again, was glaring at Valentino and Violetta, who were laughing together. Was she jealous on her daughter's behalf? Did her daughter know that Constanza had Valentino picked out as a prospective son-in-law? Then, as Ruggiero danced by, I heard him bragging to Sibyl about how fit he was. That meant, if true, that he would have had the strength to throw his unfaithful mistress over the waterfall, he or his wife, who had picked up Bianca.

About then Hank sat down beside me. Too bad. I wanted to watch, not talk.

"Ricci's a good dancer," Hank observed.

"So is Sibyl," I responded politely, although actually she was more enthusiastic than graceful, in my opinion, but maybe I was just jealous since my husband seemed to like her so much. At least he wasn't dancing with her. Had they danced in Paris?

"She's a jewel," he agreed. "I can see why Ricci's putting the moves on her, but he doesn't have a chance. Neither does your husband, in case you're worried about that."

Well, that was tactless, I thought, embarrassed that Hank had noticed my uneasiness about Jason and Sibyl. "That's very reassuring," I said dryly, and started looking for someone else to talk to.

"The fact is that Sibyl knows she's not likely to find a lover better than me." He grinned at me and added without the least appearance of modesty, "Not to blow my own horn, but I do know my way around a woman's body."

The man was drunk, I realized, though it didn't excuse the poor taste of his remarks.

"So how about Capri tomorrow, Carolyn? Are you up for it? Us accompanying persons have to stick together."

Fortunately Jason arrived and suggested that we call it a night. I was only too happy to agree, even if he did grumble all the way to the room about the deficiencies of the meeting and all the undercurrents between the participants. I was surprised that he'd noticed, but he mentioned Constanza's reaction to the flirtation between Lorenzo's mother-in-law and Valentino Santoro. "What's that about?" he muttered. "Violetta must be twice his age. And he's supposed to be mourning his lost but unrequited love, what's-her-name."

"Paolina," I replied, and headed straight for the bathroom. I was going to soak in a hot tub until my muscles stopped aching, and then I might even sleep through breakfast—or not. That fennel bread was so good. And there was the possibility that they'd have the shell pastry with the orange-vanilla filling again. I wouldn't want to miss that, even if I couldn't pronounce it.

Pork and other meats didn't find an important place on the Southern Italian menu until the Roman Empire decayed and the Barbarians from the north invaded, bringing with them their penchant for hunting and for raising livestock, their taste for butter and lard, and all the problems a meat menu caused Christians, who were expected to observe "lean" days, weeks, and months. Although not an acceptable Lenten dish, this pork recipe is tasty and relatively quick to fix.

Pork with Marsala Wine and Juniper

- Pour hot water to cover *1 ounce dried cepes or porcini mushrooms*. Let stand.

- Brush *1 teaspoon of balsamic vinegar* on *4 pork cutlets* and sprinkle with *salt* and *pepper*.

- Cook *10 cloves garlic* in boiling water for 10 minutes until soft. Drain and set aside.

- Melt *1 tablespoon butter* in a large frying pan. Cook pork quickly until browned on one side. Turn and cook another minute.

- Add *3 tablespoons Marsala wine, several rosemary sprigs, mushrooms, 4 tablespoons mushroom juices, garlic cloves, 10 juniper berries*, and *1 teaspoon balsamic vinegar*. Simmer gently for 3 minutes or until pork is cooked through. Season with *salt* and *pepper*.

- Serve with polenta or noodles and a green vegetable. Broccoli, for instance, is so well loved in the Campania, that a young man leaving Naples for foreign parts is reported to have bid a poetic and tragic farewell to broccoli.

Carolyn Blue,
"Have Fork, Will Travel,"
Iowa City Call-News

Wednesday in Sorrento

The Pasta Epidemic

You probably think Marco Polo brought pasta to Italy from China. I thought that from childhood, but evidently it isn't so. The Romans had a flour and water dough called *lagana*, which was flattened out, cut into strips, and then cooked with sauce in an oven. The Etruscans, too, had pasta from the fourth century BC. Some scholars of the subject think pasta came from Persia and was spread by the Arabs to China, the Middle East, and Europe. The Arabs were using pasta dried in the sun (which could be carried around in the desert without spoiling) by the ninth century, and dried pasta was being made in Sicily in the twelfth century in such quantities that it could be shipped to other cities. By the Middle Ages in Italy pasta was being made in different shapes, but instead of being baked, as it had been by the Romans, or cooked in boiling water *al dente* as we do now, it was cooked for several hours and flavored with cheese and spices, a recipe that held pride of place in Italy until the

1700s, when tomato sauce was introduced. However, that didn't become popular until the early 1800s.

For many centuries pasta was considered an expensive dish because it cost so much more than bread. When an Italian peasant family, used to eating bread, soup, and vegetables with an occasional bit of meat, ate pasta, it was considered a feast. Then in the 1600s various production innovations lowered the cost, and the problems of feeding large city populations brought it onto the table of the urban poor. Neapolitans were being called macaroni eaters by the 1700s, and pasta could be seen flapping on drying racks in the city, where it was also manufactured and exported.

And how did pasta become so popular in America and everywhere else? It immigrated with Italian immigrants, particularly immigrants from Southern Italy, where war, earthquakes, volcanic eruptions, plague, famine, and endemic poverty encouraged hundreds of thousands to leave the region for greener shores, taking their love of pasta with them.

Bucatini alla Caruso

And one shouldn't discount Enrico Caruso, famous tenor, pasta lover, chef. In the early twentieth century when all America loved his beautiful tenor voice, he was in the habit of dashing into Brooklyn restaurants with his adoring followers in tow and cooking pasta—*bucatini alla Caruso*. He sautéed *garlic* in *olive oil*, added *chopped fresh tomatoes*, sprinkled on *basil, parsley*, and *red chili flakes to taste*, mixed in the *bucatini*, and garnished the whole with *fried zucchini disks*.

He loved it; his fans loved it; Americans loved it; and it is simple to fix. It's said that Caruso was more interested in his fame as a pasta cook than his renown as a tenor.

Carolyn Blue,
"Have Fork, Will Travel,"
Trenton Sentinel

23
Dog Days

Carolyn

Nine o'clock! If Hank really planned to take us to Capri this morning, I was late. In fact, if I didn't hurry, I wouldn't get any breakfast. Brushing my teeth, applying a bit of makeup, and throwing on some clothes took me only ten minutes. I am a woman who can be ready to leave in record time when necessary. I checked my purse for the room card and other necessities, dashed out the door, and slipped in a puddle. At the end of the hall I could see Albertine Guillot disappearing into the elevator dragging her wretched dog on a short leash. I turned my head to see yellow liquid dripping down my door, and I was sitting in the puddle that had formed on the tile of the hall. This was unbelievably disgusting. That woman had let her dog urinate on my door.

Gingerly I pushed myself up, desperate to keep my hands out of the mess. Then I called housekeeping to report the antisocial actions of my French nemesis and demand an immediate cleanup. Finally, I locked the bathroom door, undressed, put my clothes into the sink to soak, and took a long shower. A very long shower! By the time I had finished and redressed in clean clothes, house-keeping had removed the evidence of Charles de Gaulle's bad behavior and left me a note of apology, which was all very well, but they didn't say anything about punishing the culprits. *Well, we'll just see about that!* I thought, and stalked to the elevator.

And what did I see as I approached the desk to complain in person? Madame Guillot and her dog. If a dog of mine had done such a thing, I'd have gone into hiding. She was at the desk complaining at length to some poor girl about the quality of a cheese she had ordered from room service. "It is not fit to eat with a good wine," she said. "I have a relaxing afternoon planned, reading on my balcony, sipping white burgundy, and what do you send me?" The girl looked completely befuddled. "A bland, rubbery cheese that no sane person would eat," said Albertine.

"Maybe the Signora should be—ah—call to her travel agent," suggested the young woman, who obviously hadn't understood a word and looked on the edge of tears.

Jill intervened at this point to ask if "Madame" planned to drink a fine wine not provided by the hotel.

"Your hotel does not stock fine wines," said Albertine haughtily.

"Our hotel does not allow food and drink to be brought here from outside," said Jill.

"How like the Swiss," retorted Albertine. "They can't make decent wines themselves, and they won't buy decent wines for their hotels. No French hotel would—"

"This hotel is owned by French-speaking Swiss from Geneva, Madame." Jill looked very prim and reproving as she spoke. "And we have received a very serious complaint about your dog," she added.

I stepped up at that point and said, "A complaint from me. Charles de Gaulle urinated on my door, Madame

Guillot, and I slipped in it. It's a wonder I wasn't seriously injured. My clothing had to be changed and will have to be washed, and I am missing breakfast."

"The hotel will see to your clothing, Mrs. Blue," said Jill sweetly. "Just put it out for the maid in a laundry or dry cleaning bag. "I am sure Madame Guillot will wish to pay for any damage her dog has caused. Shall I call a doctor to be sure that—"

"Why are you assuming that my dog is responsible for—"

"Because I saw you dragging the dog into the elevator," I snapped. "And there were no other dogs in sight, unless you think a guest—"

"And because Charles de Gaulle's behavior had been dreadful all week," said Bianca, who had come up to the desk in time to catch the last of the argument. "Look at Carolyn's face. The dog did that."

"If she would just use the proper makeup, which I provided—"

"And then he licked her ankles at dinner the day before yesterday, which was really disgusting, and drooled on her yesterday in the limousine," Bianca continued with enthusiasm. "If I had a dog who behaved so badly, I'd have him put down."

"Charles de Gaulle is a model of propriety compared to your children, Signora Massoni. You let them run wild in the halls and ride the elevators up and down so other guests cannot get to their rooms."

Good heavens, I wondered, *is she suggesting that Bianca's children should be put down?*

"You are a very nasty person," said Bianca. "My children are delightful. Only a horrible Frenchwoman—"

"*Mon Dieu!*" exclaimed Albertine. "I do not have to listen to insults against myself and my country." She yanked on the dog's leash—he had been edging toward me as we argued—and left in a huff.

"I'm going to ask Jason to take this up with your husband," I called after her. Then to Bianca and Jill, I said, "I don't think Professor Guillot likes that dog any better than I do, although he keeps excusing it by saying the dog has fallen in love with me, which is no excuse at all."

Bianca started to laugh. "Then he was marking his territory when he peed on your door—the dog, not Professor Guillot."

"I've missed breakfast," I said dolefully, thinking of the fluffy eggs, the delightful toast, the fruit and, best of all, the cake. I wondered how Jason would feel about cake for breakfast at home. Of course, he got up so early—

"I will see that breakfast is brought to your room," Jill offered. "What would you like?"

I made some suggestions. Bianca said to send something along for her. She was hungry already and had some things to tell me. Of course, I reminded her about the trip to Capri, but Bianca said, "That's all off. We're grounded. Isn't that the English phrase?"

24
The General from Rome

Bianca

Before we could take ourselves off to Carolyn's room and breakfast, a very satisfying thing occurred. I had dialed 112 as soon as I finished talking to Gracia the night before and demanded to know why local representatives of the Carabinieri hadn't returned to continue investigating the murder at the Grand Palazzo Sorrento. I told the sergeant to whom my call was transferred how disappointed I was to find that my heroes had not answered my plea for help, beyond having breakfast with some lieutenant of the Polizia de Stato in the hotel buffet.

"Are these the men who follow in the footsteps of the beloved Carabinieri martyr, Brigadier Salvo D' Acquisto, who gave up his own life in front of a Nazi firing squad so that innocent citizens of Rome would not be killed for the death of a German soldier?" I asked. "Are these the followers of Carabinieri who died with honor and courage on the battlefields of our country?" I demanded, even more theatrically.

The sergeant, almost in tears over the heroic history of his compatriots, assured me that he would find out what had happened and get back to me. Perhaps, he suggested, they had been called out because of terrorists threatening the peace and safety of our beautiful Italia. These were dangerous times. And so forth.

He'd done better than return my call. They were here—a tall, handsome captain and a pretty, plump lieutenant. What a nice uniform she wore. Very well cut. We Italians do love a fine uniform, and now that we have women in our military, even more attention to fashion design is necessary.

The captain marched up to the desk and said to Jill in Italian, "I am Captain Giorgio Pagano of the Carabinieri, Campania unit. It has come to my attention that General Luca Bianconi and his aides are here in the hotel. The lieutenant and I have come to offer our assistance in their investigations."

"General Bianconi is questioning suspects, Captain," said Jill. "I was told not to bother him."

"Then you will send a message to the general that we are here. We will await his answer in the breakfast room."

Ah ha! I thought. *He's not here because I called. He just wants to butter up a general from Rome and have another free breakfast. Wouldn't you know? Even the Carabinieri are losing their reputation for stern attention to business. Soon there'll be nothing to say for them but that they have pretty uniforms.*

I went to drag Carolyn out of the gift shop, where she was choosing postcards. Once she'd paid for them, we went upstairs to her room. Without Gracia's magic fruit drink, my ankles had swollen up again, and my feet were lapping out of my sandals. Sitting on Carolyn's balcony with my puffy feet propped up on her little glass table was heaven, not to mention the cup of coffee and the piece of chocolate cake on a plate that was carefully balanced on my immense stomach. Now if the baby would just stay asleep and not kick the plate off, maybe I could get though the weird story I had to tell Carolyn.

She didn't seem in any hurry to hear it because she was forking up scrambled eggs and munching on toast, which she extolled between bites for its wonderful fennel taste. That didn't sound so wonderful to me, but she was American, so what did I know? I'd been surprised when she wouldn't let me have both pieces of cake. Naturally, I'd assumed that she'd think eating cake in the morning was horrendously decadent. Maybe she wasn't such a Puritan after all, just a lesbian, and I hadn't seen any sign of that lately.

"So why are we grounded?" she asked, having finished the eggs and toast, the fruit and coffee, and reached for the cake.

I hated to see it disappear. I really wanted a second piece. "Some general from Rome showed up this morning. None of us are allowed to leave the hotel."

"Us who?" she asked, licking the chocolate off her fork like a child with a cookie bowl.

"Us people connected with the Ricci conference. There's a guard at every entrance to keep us in, in case we get any ideas about running."

Carolyn pushed back a strand of hair that had been blown loose in the wind, which was picking up. Every day around lunchtime, the wind began to blow, and the clouds formed. Well, this wasn't the high season. If we were going to have another storm, today was a good day since we couldn't go anywhere anyway. "And don't ask me what it's all about," I added. "He may be a general, but they say he's not wearing a uniform. Nunzia said he's probably the head of a government spy group or a Mafia-chasing, undercover federal outfit. She's got some paranoid ideas for a woman from the country. Oh, and the

Carabinieri showed up again while you were buying post-cards. They wanted to see this general."

Carolyn sipped her coffee thoughtfully and pushed back another straying lock of that loosely tied-back hair. I wondered how old she was. No sign of white in the blonde.

Carolyn grinned at me. "Maybe they all heard about Eliza and her insistence that the Mafia is everywhere."

"Then they should talk to her. I wanted to go to Capri," I said. "Don't you think the English are weird?"

"Better than the French," she replied. "Of course, Gracia did say that Ricci's family was Mafia. Even Constanza said they used to be. Maybe these federal agents are investigating the Riccis."

The telephone rang in the room, and Carolyn went in to answer it, taking her cake with her. I followed because I was tired of getting slapped by the wind, which was about to blow my empty plate off my stomach. Of course, it took me a while to get out of the chair, so I missed the conversation, but Carolyn passed it on.

"That was Jill at the desk. She just saw the general, and she said he's the man who met Paolina here last summer, same name he used then, Bianconi, Luca Bianconi. She looked it up. Paolina was registered as Lucia Bianconi. Since we know that isn't her name—" She stopped and thought the latest news through. "I know what's going on," she exclaimed. "They were lovers, and then he found out about her affair with Ruggiero, so he made arrangements to meet her here—he must be the lover she thought stood her up—but he didn't; he came here and killed her."

"So what is he doing here now?" I asked. It didn't make sense to me that he'd return to the scene of the crime. "You know, maybe you should put that laundry bag out in the hall. I can smell it."

Carolyn turned her head to stare at the plastic bag that

held her clothes. "If that dog harasses me one more time, just one more time, I'm going to kick him, and then I'm going to kick Albertine—" She stopped and shook her head. "He—the general—obviously thought the police would take her death for suicide. Now that they're looking into it—"

"You're looking into it. I haven't noticed Lieutenant Buglione doing anything but flirting with Jill and side-stepping the bigwigs. As for the Carabinieri, they only seem to come for breakfast."

"Now that questions are being asked," Carolyn continued, ignoring my opinion of both the military and state police, "he's returned to cut off the investigation." She picked up the bag and, holding it at arm's length, opened her door and dumped it out in the hall. "There's a strange man standing at the elevator," she whispered as she came back in. "Maybe he's there to see that we don't go downstairs. Well, I need to get hold of Lieutenant Buglione and no *Federale* from Rome is going to stop me."

Federale? What was that?

Carolyn called the desk and told Jill that it was "imperative" that Buglione call her room right away. The lieutenant must have been hanging around Jill again because it wasn't more than half a minute before Carolyn was telling him that the general was the person who had killed Paolina and was now using his position to cover up his crime. Evidently Buglione didn't think much of that idea because Carolyn listened and then said, "Of course it's still your case, and you'll be a hero when you prove that he was the murderer." More listening.

"But Lieutenant, I know how to prove it. We just need to get into his room. If the red book is there, he's the murderer." She listened again. In fact, I could hear him myself. He was saying they'd end up in jail if they tried to break into the room of a general from Rome. Finally, dis-

gusted with the Carabinieri and with the state police—
and I could have told her how much help they'd be—she
asked to speak to Jill. She wanted the general's room
number, and from the smug expression on her face, she
got it.

"Now we've got to find Nunzia," she announced.
"Maids usually have a master key."

"Come on, Carolyn," I protested. "You want to get a
nice woman like Nunzia into trouble? And what is this
we? I'm on the verge of giving birth. I can't be searching
the room of some wild-eyed, high-ranking murderer from
Rome."

"I'll search the room," she promised. "You can stand
out in the hall to see that nobody catches me at it."

"Absolutely not," I said firmly.

"I'll give you the rest of my cake," she offered.

I shook my head.

"I saw you eyeing it, Bianca. Wouldn't you like some
more?" She held up the plate. "See, there's more than half
left. All you have to do is cough and walk away if you see
someone coming."

25
An International Confrontation

Carolyn

Bianca didn't ask Nunzia for the master room card, as I'd suggested. Instead she introduced us, and as I was shaking hands with Nunzia, who had been standing in the open door of a room she was about to clean, Bianca picked up the card from the cleaning cart and slipped it into the pocket of her maternity blouse. Then she gave Nunzia a hug and hustled me off. "It takes her fifteen or twenty minutes to do a room," said Bianca. "That's how much time you've got to search the general's room before I have to get the key back to the cart."

The general had a suite on the tenth floor, which I entered while Bianca stood outside eating my chocolate cake. His bed hadn't even been made up yet. What if the maid for Ten and Eleven showed up with her cart? I considered my options and decided that I'd pretend to be dressing, buttoning the last button or something. She'd think I was the general's mistress and pay me no mind. *Thank goodness the Italians are so amorous*, I thought. Given Sorrento's reputation for sensuous liaisons, no maid would doubt that the general had been entertaining a lover. After all, he'd done it before.

This region was the home of the famous sirens of mythology, fish or bird women—the stories don't agree—whose irresistible songs lured sailors to their deaths on the rocks of islands. When the canny Ulysses plugged his sailors' ears with wax and had himself tied to his mast, the siren Parthenope was so crushed by her failure to add him to her list of trophies that she threw herself into the sea and washed ashore at Naples. If the maid caught me, she would think of me as a siren luring the general into sexual disaster with my siren song. The only problem with that scenario was my singing voice, which was unlikely to befuddle anyone. These were my thoughts as I scanned all the surfaces for the red leather notebook. It wasn't in sight.

Then I quickly pulled out drawers, but they had nothing but hotel literature and rules in them. He hadn't unpacked. Over on the luggage stand I spotted a heavy leather suitcase. *Goodness*, I thought. *Nobody carries those anymore. They're too heavy.* But the general did, and his was locked. How was I going to get it open?

Coughing. Good heavens, Bianca was coughing. I darted over to see if the maid was coming, but what I saw was my friend disappearing down the hall with an exaggerated pregnant waddle, cake plate in hand, while two men strode toward this door from the elevator. I ducked back, afraid they had seen me. Quickly closing the door and locking it, I looked around desperately for an escape route. Maybe they weren't coming here. I headed for the balcony and was in the act of trying to climb over the railing into the side cactus garden when they hauled me back. They certainly didn't look very friendly. Why hadn't I thought to put on the security chain? And how did they get past the locked door?

Maybe they were criminals. Burglars. Just like me. A hysterical giggle rose in my throat as they snapped at me in Italian. As if I understood a word they were saying! I gave them as blank a look as I could manufacture, considering that I was terrified. Maybe they'd take me for some mentally retarded person who had just wandered in. I tried a bit of nonsensical babble, while smiling at them. What a really bad idea this had been, and I hadn't found a thing! The red notebook was probably in that locked suitcase. In fact, he'd probably left it in Rome. Or burned it. Why hadn't I thought of that and stayed safely on my balcony, eating my chocolate cake? In the meantime, my arms had been twisted up behind my back by a short man, as the taller one shoved me toward the door.

Who *were* they? "Do you speak English?" I asked, forgetting for the moment that I had just been impersonating an idiot. Evidently they didn't speak English because they muttered to one another in Italian. Were they kidnappers? Or secret agents of the Italian government? We rode the elevator down to the lobby. I'd made up my mind. As soon as we got into a populated area of the hotel, I'd scream as loud as I could and keep screaming.

The doors opened; I was hustled out. The doors closed, and I let out a loud shriek. "Help! Help!" I screamed. The two men just kept shoving me along. What was the Italian word for *help*? I'd read it in the American Express Italian handbook, but I couldn't remember. "*Help!*" People were staring, but no one moved to rescue me. Italians must be as bad as New Yorkers in that respect. These two men could shoot me in the head and carry my body out the door, and nobody—wait, actually, if they wanted to get away from the hotel, they'd have taken the elevator all the way down to the road-level entrance.

By then my chance of rescue had passed because I was pushed through a door into a conference room. One of the men made some remarks in Italian to an older man in a very well-tailored suit. Possibly a designer suit.

"You are an English speaker, Signora?" he asked.

I nodded reluctantly.

"What is your name?"

Let him find out for himself, I thought, and stood there silently.

"And what were you doing in my room?"

"How did you know I was in your room?" I retorted, now rather indignant with the treatment I was receiving. After all, I hadn't stolen anything. Either these people were hotel security, or the older man was the general from Rome.

"My room is wired, Signora," said the older man. "As soon as you entered, an alarm I carry went off. Who was the pregnant woman who ran away?"

As if I'd rat on Bianca! "I don't know whom you're talking about."

"Why were you in my room?" he demanded again.

"I just got the wrong door." I'd settled on this story while he was questioning me. "It's rather upsetting to think that the room cards may open all the doors, isn't it?" I said earnestly. "You should complain to the management." I thought I was doing very well, handling myself with aplomb. If Jason hadn't been so disapproving of my occasional involvement in detection, he'd have been proud of me.

"See if she has a card on her," ordered the leader. The short, broad man with the mustache let go of my arms, took my purse, opened it, and extracted my room card. Of course, it didn't have the number on it, so they couldn't identify me that way. Then the one who had been shoving me hither and yon stuck his hand in the pocket of my blouse.

"Stop that!" I snapped. "How dare you be so—so familiar."

He pulled out the card Bianca had taken from Nunzia's cart. Oh dear. Nunzia would be discovering its loss just about now.

"My aide is not trying to be familiar with you, Signora. You are being searched by lawful agents of the Italian government." Then he ordered the short man to take the cards to the manager and find out what they were and how I might have come by them.

Worse and worse, I thought. *It must be the general. If he'd killed Paolina, he probably won't hesitate to kill me, even though I made a big scene in the lobby.*

"Have the local authorities lock this woman up, Marsocca." He waved a hand. His aide nodded, handed the general a credit card slip from my handbag and a credit card, both of which had my name on them, and then pulled me toward the door.

The mention of local authorities was probably a code for, "Take her out and shoot her."

"I demand to see a representative of the American government," I said bravely. "Everyone in the lobby saw me dragged in here. You'll never get away with this."

"There are no representatives of the American government closer than Naples," said the general.

I was now sure that's who he must be.

"However, I'm sure Lieutenant Buglione of the local Polizia di Stato can call Naples for you." Then he nodded again to his aide. "Take her away."

"The local authorities know all about you, General," I said, trying to slow my unwilling progress toward the door by going limp and dragging my feet, which is not at all a comfortable process. "That's who you are, isn't it? No matter how important a person you are in Rome, they know you met Paolina here secretly last July. I told them, and other people as well. Quite a few." Ah, that caught his attention. "If you do away with me, everyone will know you came back to kill her Monday night. No one will ever believe it was suicide or an accident, not when—"

"Sit down, Signora," said the general. "Pull up a chair for her, Marsocca. I think this woman may have something of interest to tell us."

26
"She Was a Free Spirit"

Carolyn

"**I have been** interviewing visiting chemists, Riccis, employees of their company, employees of the hotel," said the general, "and you, Signora, are the only person to impart any information on the death of Paolina Marchetti. I find that very interesting. How did you, an American, find out that the young woman who died met me here in July?"

"I asked," I replied coolly.

"Whom did you ask?"

"Well, actually, I asked earlier if Paolina had ever been here before with a man. The person I asked thought so but couldn't remember who, until you came this morning."

He nodded. "And who was this person?"

Goodness, I don't want to get Jill in trouble. They might kill her or arrest her. "I really can't say," I replied. "Just someone at the desk."

"You've talked to this person, presumably a hotel employee, several times about this subject, yet you can't remember who it was?" He stared at me. I stared back. "Very well, here is a more pertinent question. Why were you asking about Paolina Marchetti?"

The general looked very grim, as if he thought I might
have killed her. Of course that couldn't be, since he was
the murderer. "Because she was my friend." As I said it, a
rush of grief hit me; Paolina had been such fun. I'd really
enjoyed our afternoon exploring Sorrento. I'd spotted a
number of things I wanted to buy and had expected that
she and I would shop the next day. And the dinner. As horrible as it was, we'd laughed heartily at the plastic duck
and the giant, soggy meatballs. I felt tears rising and
blinked them back.

He was eyeing me suspiciously from under thick, dark
eyebrows, as dark as his hair was silver. "I see." He
frowned at me. "You had known the victim how long? A
previous acquaintance perhaps?" The tone was sarcastic.

"No," I admitted defensively. "We met the day before.
We went sightseeing, and we had dinner together. I liked
her a lot. We—we had a lot in common."

"Indeed." He looked highly skeptical. "An instant rap-
port. Is that what you are saying?"

*Oh, these Europeans! They think you have to know
someone for twenty years before you can be friends.* "And
then I discovered her body in the pool. It was a terrible
shock, and the—"

"What was it you had in common?" he demanded.

"Well, we both like the poetry of Edna St. Vincent Millay. She told me how she read it while she was in convent
school, and I told her how I read it while—while my
mother was dying. And I promised to send her the new
Millay biography, *Savage Beauty.* And we liked to window shop. We were going to buy things the next day. And
we hated the food here." Again I choked up. "It's so sad
to think that her last dinner was that awful roast duck."
Why was I telling him all this? He actually looked rather
upset. Perhaps because he now saw that I'd had reason to
look for her killer. "And don't think you're going to get

away with killing my friend," I announced, staring right back at him. "The police here in Sorrento may be afraid of offending the Riccis and you because you're a big shot from Rome, but you can't get away with killing me too. I intend to see that you—"

"Enough, Signora," said the general wearily. "I was neither the lover nor the murderer of the woman you knew as Paolina Marchetti. I was her father."

"Her—" I didn't believe that! Of all the nerve! Telling me that he was her father. Did he think I was stupid? "If you're Paolina's father, why did you have to meet her here secretly? Under assumed names?"

"Because she also worked for me," he replied.

"Ha! Now I know you're lying," I retorted triumphantly. "She worked for Ruggiero Ricci. She was his secretary."

"Yes," he replied. "She was his secretary, and she was investigating his company."

"Why would she be doing that?" I asked suspiciously, at the same time remembering the Mafia connection. "It's just a chemical and pharmaceutical company. Isn't it?"

"A very profitable one," he said. "We've been investigating them for several years."

"But what for?" I tried to think of what the old, evil Mafia father might have been up to, with or without Ruggiero's knowledge. "Drugs! Were they refining heroin or something like that? Or making methamphetamines? That's a chemical process." Then I had a terrible thought. "Oh, my goodness. The radioactive waste! They weren't making atomic bombs, were they? And selling them to terrorists? I assumed that it was medical waste, but—"

"You have a very lively imagination, Signora, but as far as we know, their profits were coming from watered down prescription drugs and substances labeled as prescription drugs that had no medical value whatever. These were packaged and then sold to third world countries."

"Oh my goodness! That's unconscionable! Sick people were dying because they didn't get the drugs they thought they were paying for? Druggists have done that in our country. You wonder how such people—"

"And there's the possibility that they were planning to ship illegal narcotics disguised as items on their regular product list."

Of course I immediately thought of Sibyl and Hank and their new containers. If the toxic waste fumes couldn't get out, then drug enforcement dogs probably couldn't sniff the narcotics inside one of those containers. I'd have to warn Hank not to do business with Ruggiero. "Do you have any identification to prove that you are an Italian spy of some sort?" I asked. After all, he could have made all this up.

There was a knock on the door, and the short, mustachioed man entered. "The lady is Signora Carolyn Blue, General," he said. "One of the cards is her room card, unless she stole it and the credit card. The other is a card the maids use to get into the rooms for cleaning purposes. That was undoubtedly stolen unless the maid was an accomplice."

He spoke English! And he'd been pretending not to while he was twisting my arm and pushing me around! What a sneak! And now that he wanted to threaten me with the information he'd gathered, he spoke English. "Nunzia had nothing to do with it," I said angrily. "I took the card from her cart because I expected to find Paolina's red leather notebook in your room, General."

"Explain that, please," said the general.

"She carried it with her all the time and wrote poetry in it. You did know that she was a poet?" I studied his face, looking for signs that he, like all the other men in her life, had had no idea of Paolina's depths and talents. "And I would like to see ID, please."

"Loppi, Marsocca, show her some ID," said the general.

"What about you?" I asked. The general opened his wallet and took out a photograph from a pocket that was hard to get into. It was of Paolina and said, "*A Papa*," and was signed, "Lucia."

"Her name was Lucia, Lucia Bianconi. I am Luca Bianconi, her father, and I did know that my daughter wrote poetry. I had a book of her poetry published for her twenty-fifth birthday."

"I'm so sorry," I said, feeling more tears about to embarrass me. "But why would you let her do something so dangerous? Perhaps that's why she's dead—because of her job." Then I had a thought. "But maybe it wasn't murder. Oh, dear, maybe it's my fault!" All three men stared at me, gimlet-eyed. "I mean, I didn't kill her, but I did tell her how Edna St. Vincent Millay died. Of a fall down stairs after the death of her husband. And Paolina, I mean Lucia, had had a disappointment. A—a male friend stood her up. You don't think she threw herself down the waterfall, thinking her favorite poetess had committed suicide over love, so—"

"It was murder," said the general sharply. "Lucia was not the type to commit suicide, certainly not over a man. You ask why I let her join my organization. She was a wild girl, promiscuous, in fact."

"She was a free spirit," I corrected him indignantly.

"That's a kind way to put it, Signora. You evidently didn't know her as well as you thought you did. However, I had hoped to satisfy her need for excitement and intrigue by giving her the job until such time as she matured enough to marry and give me grandchildren." He sighed. "It was a mistake. And now, just to clear this matter up,

Signora, where were you when my daughter was murdered?"

"Asleep, I imagine," I replied. "As I said, we went sightseeing in Sorrento, had dinner together, hugged one another when I got off the elevator on the eighth floor, and then I went to bed. I didn't see her again until I went out to the pool for coffee and spotted her body lying under the water. I dragged her out and tried to revive her, but I think—" I sniffed back tears. "I think she'd been dead for quite a while."

He studied my face, nodded, and said, "Thank you for your friendship to my daughter on her last day. You may go now."

"*Go?* Really, General, if you didn't kill Paolina— Lucia, I should say—I have several other ideas. I have been investigating this, you know."

27
Theories of the Crime

Carolyn

I would have been hesitant to tell her father my theories about Paolina's death since each involved her having slept with a different man, but since he already knew—that thought disappeared from my head when a shocking idea occurred to me. Had he told his daughter to sleep with Ruggiero Ricci? He must have known that she was using her charms, as it were, to get information from the president of the company. Which seemed a little tacky and melodramatic.

But maybe she had fallen in love with Ruggiero, a handsome older man who perhaps reminded her of a father who had always been too busy waging war and running spy organizations to pay any attention to her. After all, he'd left her in a convent school. What a terrible dilemma for her—to be in love with the very man she was betraying to her father.

It sounded like an opera plot. One of the beautiful, new sopranos could sing Paolina; a tenor for Valentino, singing of unrequited love, maybe one of the new tenors from

Mexico or South America; a baritone for Ruggiero, the lover-villain; and a bass for the general.

"You were going to make some suggestions, Signora," prompted the general. He wasn't singing.

What would a female sleuth in an opera be? I wondered. A mezzo? Jason had bought a CD by a fabulous new mezzo, very nice looking. She could play me.

"Signora?"

"Oh, yes. Well, I don't want to embarrass you, General, but Paolina was Ruggiero Ricci's mistress. Maybe he discovered that she was a spy. Or, and again I mention this with hesitation, but his office manager says she slept with someone else the night before she came to Sorrento, someone who visited Ricci in his office and stopped to talk to Paolina on the way out."

"And did the office manager say who this visitor was?" asked the general.

Now this was touchy. "Well, she said it was a foreigner who spoke Italian and was perhaps an American, perhaps a participant in the conference, but that can't be, because the only Americans are my husband, who doesn't speak Italian, except for a few phrases from Italian opera, of which we're very fond, especially Verdi, although Puccini—"

"Yes, yes," said the general impatiently. "Everyone loves Italian opera."

"Not so many Americans, actually, although I think opera is becoming more popular in our country. A number of the smaller cities have companies that do a few performances a year. El Paso, for instance. That's where Jason and I live."

"*Signora.*"

"Yes. Well, back to Jason; he was in Paris until the evening of the next day, as was Sibyl Evers, another American, a professor from Rutgers and, of course, being female and not even knowing Paolina, she wouldn't have killed her. Sibyl's husband Hank Girol is the third American, but he drove in from Rome the morning I found Paolina's body, so I don't think Gracia could have been right about the person being an American."

"I see. Well, thank you, Signora Blue."

"I'm not through," I protested. "I haven't even gotten to the better suspects, the more likely ones. If Ruggiero knew that Paolina took a new lover, he might have killed her out of jealousy, even if he didn't know that she was a spy. He says he was in Catania that night, but who knows? I didn't see him until late in the afternoon after she died, but he could have been here, and since he admits his wife was out of town, she can't vouch for him, nor he for her."

"You asked Signor Ricci these things?" asked Signor Loppi, who probably had some rank, but we hadn't really been introduced, so I didn't know.

"Well, tactfully," I replied. "So as not to alert him that I suspected him. I also asked his wife, but she never answered me." I felt a bit conflicted about implicating Constanza, who could be quite nice and obviously loved her children to distraction. "As I indicated, Signora Ricci-Tassone doesn't have an alibi since she was not in Catania and didn't appear publicly here until late afternoon, but she could have been in Sorrento. Her husband was not a faithful man, as I understand it, so she might have gotten fed up and killed his latest mistress, Paolina.

"And then there was the lover who was supposed to meet Paolina here in Sorrento and called to cancel. I believe I mentioned that. Perhaps he came after all and killed her for whatever reason. He could be anyone." Oh, dear, that wasn't very tactful. "And there's Valentino Santoro, the toxicology expert at the Ricci company. He was madly, evidently hopelessly, in love with Paolina. Maybe knowing about her various lovers just—just pushed him over the edge. Which reminds me, Constanza Ricci-Tassone had hoped that Dr. Santoro would marry their daughter, Elizabetta. Maybe the mother killed Paolina so that Santoro would turn to the daughter for—ah—comfort."

"Are you getting all this down, Marsocca?" the general asked.

"Yes, sir."

Marsocca was very tall and looked quite amusing sitting in a spindly chair, his legs poked up, trying to make notes in a notebook balanced on one pointy knee.

"Ah! I forgot another possibility. Gracia Sindacco, the office manager at the chemical company, told a friend of mine that she thought Signor Ricci's father might have hired a hit man to kill Paolina to avenge the honor of his family when she took a lover other than his son. He was evidently a Mafia person in his younger days. Now I gather he's in ill health and couldn't have committed murder himself. At least, that's what Gracia said, and I see no reason for her to lie. She definitely didn't seem to like him. In fact, she called him an evil old man."

"And to whom have you mentioned this information, Signora?" the general asked me.

"To you. Obviously. Bianca Massoni knows all about it; she's been helping me with the investigation. To Lieutenant Buglione of the Polizia di Stato, although I can't say that he seems inclined to act on anything I've told him. And I offered my insights to Captain Pagano and Lieutenant Vacci of the Carabinieri. They arrived the second day and said they'd interview me after breakfast, but they never did. They didn't even come back to the hotel yesterday that I know of, and when they arrived this morning, they went off to breakfast again. That's what Bianca said, anyway. I was in the gift shop and didn't see them."

"I see." The general frowned. "Well, you have amassed

an impressive number of suspects, Signora," he said. "We shall certainly look into these people. Have you any last thoughts you'd care to pass on?"

Is he making fun of me? I wondered. *Oh, of course not. Why would he?* "Yes, as a matter of fact, I do," I replied.

Loppi rolled his eyes. I think he was trying not to smile. "I saw that, Signor Loppi," I said sternly. "And I see no cause for amusement in the situation. In fact, I take it very seriously. I would not have been assembling information and possibly putting myself if harm's way if I didn't."

"We appreciate your efforts, Signora," said the general, "and your evident concern for my daughter."

"I was not laughing, General," protested Loppi, his olive skin flushing, and his rather large, out-flung ears turning bright red.

"Signora," prompted the general, ignoring his subordinate.

"Well, General." I leaned forward. "It's my opinion that if you find Paolina's red notebook, which has been missing since her death, you will find her murderer. I suppose you'll need warrants to search the rooms of the suspects I mentioned—"

"Did you have a warrant to search my room?" he asked.

"No, of course I didn't have a warrant. I'm not a police officer, but for Paolina's sake, and considering my suspicions of you, I did feel that the search was *warranted*." I was rather pleased with my pun and wondered if he'd caught it. Puns in a language not one's own are probably difficult to appreciate. "Be that as it may, the room in which you find the red notebook will be the room of the murderer, unless, of course, he or she has planted it in some other room to throw suspicion on someone else. One can't discount that possibility."

"Are you, Signora, by any chance a reader of detective fiction?"

"Only occasionally," I replied, then added modestly, "but I have had some experience in investigating murders."

"Have you?" The general gave me a strange look.

Good heavens, surely he didn't think I might be a suspect. But probably not, since he thanked me for my input and escorted me to the door himself. He hadn't even risen to greet me when I arrived, or rather was shoved into his presence. Before opening the door for me, he warned that I should say nothing about the investigation of the Ricci company, and thanked me again.

28
Another Good Deed

Carolyn

As the general and I stood in the doorway shaking hands, I noticed the Carabinieri striding across the lobby, looking well fed. Had they been at the breakfast buffet all this time? They arrived in front of us and saluted sharply. The general returned their salutes, but said nothing. Just stared at them thoughtfully. Captain Pagano introduced himself and his subordinate. The general introduced me. "But you have already met Signora Blue, haven't you?" he asked in English. "Several days ago, I believe."

Lieutenant Flavia Vacci smiled at me. The captain mumbled something that acknowledged my presence and then told the general how honored they were to have the chance of meeting a man who had done so much to investigate the Mafia in Sicily. "We have come to offer whatever humble assistance we can to you, General Bianconi," said Pagano.

"You have interviewed people, gathered information, have you?" asked the general.

"We are at your command," said Pagano, eyes shifting uneasily.

"I believe you had the opportunity to interview this lady," murmured the general, patting my shoulder. "Did you do that?"

"We can do it immediately," said Pagano with alacrity.

"But there is no need now," said the general. "I have done it myself. Signora Blue has been most helpful, a very useful source of information. This case has been ongoing since Sunday, and Signora Blue, a foreign civilian, has given it more attention and developed more theories than any of the authorities in whose hands it has rested. So what assistance is it that you propose to offer, Captain Pagano?"

"Whatever you ask for, General," said the captain, who had begun to look as if his collar were too tight.

"Very well then," said General Bianconi. "You will provide four men of lower rank to keep those who are in some way involved in the crime from leaving the hotel without my permission. Your men will relieve officers of the state police."

"At once, sir."

"Lieutenant Vacci, you may stay and act as my secretary."

"Yes, sir," said Flavia Vacci, not looking particularly excited with her new assignment.

"And you, Captain Pagano. I understand you have been investigating the breakfast buffet here at the Grand Palazzo Sorrento." The general looked at his watch. "Perhaps it is not too late for you to see what the hotel offers for lunch, since that seems to be your area of expertise."

The captain's face turned red, I had to stifle the giggles, and the general, patting my shoulder again, told me that I was free to go to my room.

I was quite exhilarated after my session with General Bianconi and his session with Captain Pagano. And pleased. Captain Pagano had received his comeuppance, and I felt that I had contributed substantially to the investigation, which was all the more satisfying because the general's own daughter, whom I had liked so much, was the victim. Poor man, I remembered him saying that he'd hoped she would marry and provide him with grandchildren. It was hard to imagine the general, who was somewhat intimidating, bouncing a baby on his knee, much less burping one and having it spit up on the shoulder of his beautifully tailored suit. Industrial espionage must pay well. No, industrial espionage was not the right term for the government searching out evildoers in industry.

Ah well, I had been helpful. That was the point. He'd had his aide write it all down, unlike Lieutenant Buglione, who hadn't wanted to investigate anyone. I suppose if I'd suggested that a maid killed Paolina, he might have looked into it, but not when my suspicions landed on a general or a rich industrialist. Probably Ruggiero Ricci practiced industrial espionage in its proper sense of the phrase. After all, Jason had said that the meeting was just an excuse to pick the brains of the conferees.

The elevator, for which I had been waiting, arrived, and Hank stepped out. After we greeted one another, he apologized for his conduct the night before, and said, "I hope I didn't offend you, Carolyn. I'm one of those people who forgets his manners when he's had too much to drink."

It occurred to me that if Sibyl had heard him bragging about his sexual prowess, she would have been even more offended than I. But then, if Hank was talking that way to reassure himself that she wasn't interested in Jason—well, I could hardly blame him for being jealous. I had been. Obviously, I had to forgive him, which I did.

He had been holding the elevator door for me, and I was about to get on when I remembered. "Hank," I said urgently. A couple tried to get past me and through the door, so I stepped back and pulled him aside. "I wanted to warn you."

"Warn me?" He looked puzzled.

"Yes, about Ricci. You shouldn't make any deals with him."

"Why not?" he asked, even more puzzled, frowning, in fact.

"He's being investigated by the general and his aides for industrial crimes, even suspected of planning to deal in drugs."

"He *makes* drugs," Hank pointed out.

"I meant bad drugs, illegal drugs. You know. It would be terrible if he used your containers to transport them and you got arrested."

"I see. Did you tell the general—"

"Of course not. I know you're just interested in the toxic waste, but you can't control what Ricci does with your containers once he's bought them. He could take the toxic waste out and put in heroin or something."

Hank looked quite upset at the prospect. "Thanks for the heads-up, Carolyn. That would be embarrassing. To be caught in Ricci's mess."

The elevator was gone by then, so he pressed the button and put me in the next one when it came. *Another good deed done*, I thought, and advised him to say nothing about what I'd told him to anyone from Catania. He promised not to, and I rode up to Eight, ready for a nice late-afternoon nap. I'd had a stressful day. And I hadn't had lunch. Maybe I'd send for Room Service, although I shuddered to think what they might provide. Left over giant meatballs? A plastic duck sandwich?

29

A French Invitation

Carolyn

"**Carolyn,** where the devil have you been?" demanded my husband, who, much to my surprise, was seated with his laptop on his knees. "I'd have been trying to find you by now if our phone service hadn't been cut off and all of us confined to our rooms."

"No phones?" I asked, surprised. I'd been able to call Bianca this morning, although I wasn't supposed to leave the room.

"Only Room Service, and cops answer the calls. Why aren't you stuck in the room like the rest of us, or did you sneak out? I've been going crazy, cooped up here all day, wondering where you were."

"Did you try sitting on the balcony? The view is spectacular."

"Right, and the wind must be blowing thirty or forty miles an hour, which doesn't tell me where you've been."

"Well, I didn't sneak out." Actually, I had, but I wasn't going to tell Jason that I'd been caught burgling the general's room. "I've just returned from my interview with the general."

"For all this time?" Jason looked amazed. "Mine took about five minutes."

"Well, I had information for him."

Jason groaned. "Carolyn, have you been accusing someone of killing the secretary?"

"Actually, she wasn't a secretary. She was an under-cover agent investigating the Ricci company. They're doing all sorts of bad things, such as sending fake drugs to third world countries."

"I might have known," said Jason with disgust. "This is as bad a meeting as I can remember attending, and don't tell me about the great location. If we can't get out of the hotel, you're not going to be doing any more sightseeing."

I nodded glumly. That hadn't occurred to me in all the excitement of helping the Italian government. "And Paolina was his daughter," I added.

"Whose daughter?" asked Jason, closing down his computer program. "You want to try for Room Service? I didn't get any lunch because the line was busy."

"Me either, but if the hotel provided it, rather than Con-stanza's chef, it was probably awful anyway. Poor Con-stanza. She's going to be so upset when they arrest Ruggiero."

"The sooner, the better," my husband muttered. "Then we can go home."

"No," I said, "we can go sightseeing. You didn't get to because you were stuck in Paris."

"True, but I got a lot of good chemistry done."

I glared at him, remembering the seductively scientific Sibyl.

"So whose daughter is she—Paolina?"

"The general's. She worked as an undercover agent for him."

"God," said Jason. "He's got a shock coming when he finds out that she was sleeping with everyone in sight."

"He knows it."

"You mean she was doing it for him?"

"No, not exactly." I really didn't want to talk about Paolina's wild streak, of which Jason did not approve. Not that I did, but I had liked her. "You mustn't mention the general's investigation of the Ricci company," I admonished Jason. "I wasn't supposed to tell anyone, but since you're my husband—well, shall we see if we can get something to eat?" I asked, to divert his attention from Paolina and my own activities.

We tried and had a hard time ordering from the policeman because he spoke little English. I really had no idea what would arrive, and it was pretty bad, a boring pasta in a watery tomato sauce, a cold, sliced duck salad, the duck probably left over from Paolina's last supper, and some soupy ice cream of indeterminate flavor. Perhaps the general had ordered this meal specially to force one of us to confess, but more likely it was another production from the hotel's Swiss chef.

Jason hardly seemed to notice. Over dinner he told me about an invitation he'd received from Adrien Guillot—to come to Lyon to give seminars, followed by a meeting that Guillot's university was hosting in Avignon.

"You want to visit the Guillots?" I asked, horrified. "I can't stand Albertine Guillot. Her dog urinated on our door this morning, and I slipped and fell right into it. Then we had an unpleasant confrontation at the desk downstairs and—"

"Okay," said Jason. "So I guess you don't want to go to the meeting with me."

"Still," I said, reconsidering, "the papal court was in Avignon for two hundred years. I'd like to see the papal palace. And then there's the Albigenesian heresy to consider."

"The what?"

So I had to tell Jason all about the new slant on Christianity that had arisen in southern France, and the Pope's call for a crusade to put it down, and the French king and his knights riding off from Paris to attack various cities and fortresses in the south. "Southern France might have been a different country today if it weren't for that crusade," I said, finishing my explanation.

"So you *do* want to go?"

"I don't know. How long would it be? I don't think I could stand a couple of weeks with the Guillots."

Jason sighed. "Then you don't have to go."

"Are you saying you don't want me to?" I asked suspiciously. "I suppose Sibyl will be there."

"I have no idea, and it's obvious that I can't win no matter what I say." He stared at me as he finished off his melted ice cream. "Carolyn, you're not going through menopause, are you?"

"Of course I'm not," I snapped, insulted. Then I had to wonder if I was. I'd never distrusted Jason before. But on the other hand, I was only in my forties. It was too early for menopause.

Jason went to bed, and I sat down to write a column, but I didn't get very far because I remembered a part of the Millay biography. Using food as a symbol for sex as it's viewed in Christian cultures, she'd written a play about a society in which it was socially unacceptable to talk about food in public, and people only ate in private. The idea made me so uneasy that I didn't want to write about food just then.

After I'd closed my computer, column unfinished, I thought again about poor Paolina. Had her obsession with sex led to her murder, or was it her investigation of crime? I'd better not mention that thought to my husband. He had enough objections to my own investigations. Of course, I wasn't an undercover agent. I was just a nosy faculty wife and writer about food. I decided to go to bed and listen to the wind hammering against the balcony doors until I fell asleep.

Sleep brought me a terrible dream. The Christian Coalition or someone like that called for a boycott of my column because it said everyone knew what I was *really* writing about, and it wasn't food. Then my book, *Eating Out in the Big Easy*, came out, and I was having a book signing when a crowd of angry ladies stormed in carrying signs about banning books on sex and chased me out into the parking lot, where the National Rifle Association, although how they got into it I can't imagine, was hiding behind cars and taking shots at me. I had just narrowly missed death by dropping behind a Ford Explorer when a very loud explosion woke me up. The wind had blown the balcony doors open.

Trembling, I slipped out of bed and walked barefooted to close them, taking a fearful peek out onto the balcony to see if my enemies were out there, ready to storm our room. They weren't, so I locked the doors, pushed a chair against them, and went back to bed. It was only 12:45 by the clock on the bedside table.

Thursday in Sorrento

Pasta and the Birth of the Four-tined Fork

Two-tined forks were used in Europe during the Middle Ages to transfer meat from platter to diner; otherwise fingers were the means of transferring food to the mouth. The three-tined fork, along with good cooking, was brought to France from Italy by Catherine de Medici, wife of Henry IV, but Ferdinand IV, King of Naples, introduced the four-tined fork, which is still in use today.

Ferdinand was perhaps the city's friendliest, least refined king. He enjoyed mixing with commoners and eating pasta on the street, which was done by taking the pasta in hand, tilting back the head, and dropping the long, dripping strings into the open mouth, a messy business. Still, having fallen in love with pasta, Ferdinand wanted it served every day at court.

His queen, Hapsburg princess Maria Carolina, who had been trying to Frenchify court manners, was appalled. She didn't want the courtiers at her table dropping pasta into their mouths by hand, so to pacify her, the king ordered his steward to devise an implement that would get the pasta from table to mouth without use of the fingers. Thus, the four-tined fork was born. The courtiers loved it and pasta. Their hands may have stayed clean enough to please the finicky queen, but they did tend to splash sauce on the tablecloths. Ah, well.

Carolyn Blue,
"Have Fork, Will Travel,"
Baton Rouge Call-Register

30
A Scream in the Night

Bianca

What a terrible day it had been! First, Carolyn's crazy idea about searching the general's room. I was truly beginning to wonder whether she might not be innocent of Paolina's murder. She hadn't shown any interest in other women since I'd met her, and searching the room of the man who'd come to investigate the death was really insane if she was guilty. Why call attention to herself? Which she had done by getting caught.

Of course my part in the whole thing was less than valiant. What a coward I had been, waddling off down the hall and leaving her to fend for herself against those two determined-looking men who got off the elevator. And what had they done to her? Was she in jail? What had she told them about me? I shuddered to think.

When it came my turn to be interviewed, I didn't tell the general a thing, denied being the pregnant woman in the hall, claimed no knowledge of the dead girl and only a casual acquaintance with Carolyn as a result of two tourist excursions and several scientific dinners. Innocent, pregnant me. He didn't spend much time questioning me, so maybe Carolyn hadn't mentioned my part in the break-in.

As I was leaving the interrogation room, I passed my mother-in-law going for her interview, and she whispered to me that she'd heard he was a very handsome gentleman and "so important." How like Violetta! The general obviously had a surprise coming when he interviewed her. I'd had to stifle a giggle at the thought of that stern man being subjected to the wiles of my mother-in-law. Loppi, the one who ushered me out, gave me a suspicious look because he saw me laughing. Apparently laughter was not proper conduct during a murder investigation.

So upstairs I went, back to the eighth floor and a shocked husband trying to deal with Andrea and Giulia, who were reacting like caged animals to our incarceration. They wanted Papa to play soccer with them. Why couldn't they go into the hall? Why couldn't they ride the elevators? Where was Granny? Why couldn't they use the ice bucket to catch rain on the balcony and pour it over the railing? They wanted something nice to eat. That was the hardest demand of all to answer.

We didn't manage to order lunch at all and had to clean out the refreshments in the refrigerator to satisfy their ravenous little tummies. And dinner! It was delivered by a policeman—plates of overcooked vegetables, some stringy meat that I couldn't identify and about which the children made gruesome guesses: It was the man who delivered the papers to our door in the morning; he had been roasted in the fireplace in the lobby. Or, all the little birds that flew around outside and landed in the bushes beside our balcony had been shot down with arrows and thrown, feathers and all, into a big pot. Where did they get such ideas?

Lorenzo wasn't any better. He said the vegetables

were old auto parts painted to look like squash and egg-plant and that the children should watch out or they'd break their teeth trying to eat the stuff. Of course, they immediately pretended to have tooth injuries and blood dripping out of their mouths and bits of metal digging holes through their intestines. We finally gave up and let them watch television until bedtime, then tucked them in without listening to any complaints, or demands for water, and delayed needs to visit the toilet. Then we went to bed. What else was there to do?

But the ensuing silence revealed a lovely, wild night outside, the wind and rain lashing the hotel, while Lorenzo and I were cuddled together in bed, the children asleep, and even the baby inside snoozing. It had stopped kicking my belly button and jumping up and down on my bladder. I drifted into a blissful doze, which I really needed, and dreamed that my mother-in-law was quizzing me jealously on how much time the general had spent with me. "I'm not interested in the general," I protested.

"Well, I am," said Violetta, "so don't try to flirt with him. We're going to marry and have lots of babies."

I tried to reason with her by telling her that she was past the age of having babies, which she denied, and that having lots of babies was no longer fashionable. She'd hurt Lorenzo's career if she insisted on marrying General Bianconi and having a large family. She gave a loud scream and woke me up. She even woke Lorenzo up. "Did you hear something?" he asked.

"It was your mother," I mumbled, still in the confused stage between dreaming and waking.

"My God!" He leapt out of bed and rushed to the hall door.

"Lorenzo, put on a bathrobe," I called, staggering out of bed myself. I fished the robes out of the bathroom, and we both struggled into them, although they were considerably bedraggled because the children had been wearing them for a game of monks in a religious procession. The hotel would not be pleased.

What we saw was Gracia Sindacco rushing from the end of the hall to the Ricci suite and Constanza leaning against her doorframe, moaning and crying. We closed our door behind us so the children wouldn't be awakened and hurried toward the two women. Constanza was saying over and over, "He's dead. I heard a noise in his room, and I found him dead."

Lorenzo entered their suite as more conference members gathered at the door and then in the parlor. Weren't the Riccis lucky? A sitting room and two bedrooms. They probably had two baths as well. We could have used the two baths but shared one with the children, and we certainly could have used a sitting room this afternoon. Constanza had collapsed on a sofa by then, while Gracia sat beside her, smoothing her hair and consoling her as if she were a little girl. Lorenzo returned from the bedroom, shaking his head, and called the desk to report that Signor Ricci seemed to have died in his bed.

Soon the room was stuffed with people, including Lieutenant Buglione, who took Gracia's place on the couch and questioned Constanza very gently and sympathetically. She said, blotting tears, that her husband must have had a heart attack and described hearing noises and going into her husband's room to investigate, only to find him unconscious or dead.

Gracia muttered to me, "He probably had a woman in there and died in bed with her, after which she ran off, leaving my poor Constanza to find the body. Serves him right. Faithless, cruel man."

While the lieutenant was consoling the new widow, the general and his aides arrived to join the room full of people in nightclothes and hotel robes. We looked like a bathrobe convention. Once he'd ascertained the problem, the general went in to look at the body, decided Ruggiero really was dead, and ordered Lieutenant Buglione to call in a coroner and schedule an autopsy. When Constanza protested the autopsy, he ordered her to bed and offered to send her a doctor with sleeping pills to ease her through the night.

My mother-in-law was the last to arrive, heard the news, and immediately attached herself to the general, saying what a hard day he'd had, and now his sleep had been interrupted in such a sad way. He looked rather surprised and told her that sleep was not something he expected to go uninterrupted on a regular basis. Violetta squeezed his arm sympathetically and murmured that she did admire a man who was willing to sacrifice his own comfort for the good of his country. Did he believe all that? I wondered. Even my husband was watching his mother skeptically.

Later I heard the general murmur to Loppi that a dead Ricci was one less trial the government had to pay for, although he'd have relished the chance to question him and ultimately put him in jail. Very sympathetic, I thought. And what had poor Signor Ricci done that didn't have to do with sins of the flesh? I almost felt sorry for the sharp-tongued Constanza. Had she overheard the general saying Ruggiero belonged in jail? Even stranger, where was Carolyn? And Jason? Had they slept through the whole fuss?

When the general ordered us all back to bed, I headed for her room instead of ours to share the latest news. What would she make of it? Could she have killed Ruggiero because of his affair with Paolina? Out of jealousy? But Paolina was dead, so jealousy was out of date. Perhaps Carolyn hadn't killed Paolina. She'd certainly said often enough that she thought Ruggiero had. When I passed on the news, I couldn't tell much from Carolyn's reaction. She was half asleep and didn't seem to take in my explanation of events. Maybe she'd missed her nap.

31
The Morning After

Carolyn

I awoke the next morning wondering if my brief conversation with Bianca had been part of dream. Was Ruggiero really dead and Constanza really so grief-stricken she had to be sent to bed by the general? Jason's attempts to order breakfast from whichever policeman had room-service duty for our floor had jerked me from sleep. My husband was becoming very frustrated. Since breakfast was our only hope for a decent meal as long as we were quarantined, I grabbed the room-service menu from the bedside table, struggled to the floor in my nightgown, and took the phone from Jason. Then I scanned down the menu picking out the English translations of things both of us liked and reading them off in Italian. The policeman didn't find my Italian easy to understand, but I think he got most of my order. Why hadn't I done that last night? Well, it probably wouldn't have mattered. Dinner was always awful here, unless it was provided by Constanza.

Jason gave me a kiss on the cheek and told me I was "brilliant," always nice to hear from one's husband, and he went off to the shower. I, having remembered Constanza's possible widowhood, now that my empty stomach had the promise of relief, then tried to tell the policeman that I wanted to talk to the general. *"Generale Luca Bianconi—er—grazia telefono Signora Blue."* That was probably Spanish. "Do—you—understand?" I asked. *"Generale Luca Bianconi telefono Signora Blue. Si?"*

"Si," said my policeman, but what did he mean? Then he read back the things I'd ordered. I sighed. After breakfast I'd go out into the hall, where I'd be told to return to my room, to which I'd reply with a demand to see the general. Maybe that would work. I did peek out and retrieve *USA Today* from in front of my door. There were no mementos from Charles de Gaulle, thank goodness. But then, he was undoubtedly quarantined, too. Nothing on the death of Ruggiero Ricci, well-known criminal and Sicilian industrialist, appeared in any *USA Today* headlines, but that wasn't a surprise. When the telephone rang, I was reading an article about a standard French poodle that had been shot to death in Tulsa by an irate neighbor. What had that poodle done? I wondered.

The general had received my message and opened the conversation by asking if I had any theories to pass on about the death of Ricci. Which meant my conversation with Bianca hadn't been a weird dream, so I said, "I suppose he could have died from natural causes, but I did hear him bragging about how fit he was. This was after one of the dinners. On the other hand, if he was murdered, it could have been anyone, given his alleged criminal activities and his well-known sexual proclivities. However," I added, "one does have to feel sorry for his poor wife. I wanted to ask your permission to pay her a sympathy call. Her suite is right down the hall. It wouldn't involve my leaving the floor or—"

"Fine, as long as you don't mention our investigation

of her husband," said the general. "Let me know what you find out."

I agreed to be discreet, and he agreed to tell the guard at the elevator to escort me to Constanza's rooms. Then Jason got out of the shower, and a waiter arrived with our breakfast, which was huge and looked like the items served at the breakfast buffet, thank goodness. I had been afraid the Swiss chef might be enlisted to cook for us in the morning, too, as an added pressure to make one of us confess.

Breakfast was excellent and included the unpronounceable shell pastries. Like a person expecting famine to follow, I ate heartily. Then I told Jason that I had permission to pay a sympathy call to Constanza. He said to extend his condolences as well and to ask the guard at the elevator when we'd be free to leave our rooms. Gracia Sindacco answered my knock and let me into the suite.

Although I had expected to find Constanza lying in bed weeping, I found her, instead, being fitted for a mourning wardrobe by two seamstresses, overseen by a designer, while she talked on the phone to an archbishop in Sicily about the necessity that he himself preside over a high mass at Ruggiero's funeral. Gracia told me what that conversation was about and added that her late employer, considering how he had treated his excellent wife, deserved to be buried in unhallowed ground rather than celebrated by an archbishop.

Constanza finished with the archbishop, nodded to me, and made another call, actually two calls, both of which involved tears and consoling remarks in Italian, punctuated by sharp commands to the nervous seamstresses. She was, according to Gracia, telling the two children the terrible news, consoling them on the death of their father, and ordering them to be in Catania in four days for the funeral. "She is the best of mothers," said Gracia. "Her chil-

dren were blessed by God to have such a loving parent."
Naturally I agreed.

Then while Constanza examined widow's veils—
sheer silk, delicate lace, long and short—she made yet
another call, this one, according to Gracia, to the company
headquarters in Catania. "She makes arrangements to take
over the company, to protect the children's patrimony. The
evil old father must not be allowed to get his hands back
on the power and ruin the company. He is no good in the
mind no more—has a stroke. But still is evil. You know?"

I nodded, thinking that nobody in this room seemed to
be very upset about Ruggiero's death, only about its consequences.

Just as the business conversation, evidently a series of
orders from the widow, ended, Albertine Guillot arrived to
offer her condolences, which segued immediately into a
discussion of the clothes Constanza was ordering. The designer, who, fortuitously, was vacationing in Sorrento, and
the seamstresses, who were locals, pulled out drawings
and swatches of material; Albertine approved of the
dresses but not the long funeral veil. The designer agreed.
Constanza shrugged and explained that in Sicily, and
given her position in society, it was absolutely necessary,
even if it did cover up the top half of an excellent gown.

Albertine nodded and asked how long the mourning
period would be and, when told, said how fortunate it was
that Constanza looked chic in black. While they chatted, I
mused on the absence of Albertine's poodle. Perhaps she
had realized that bringing Charles de Gaulle along on a
condolence call might result in his doing something socially unacceptable in front of the new widow.

Then the whole fashion contingent, including Albertine, departed, and Constanza fell limply into a chair, a
chair, I might add, that was much more comfortable looking than any in our room. She announced that she simply

could not stay in this suite where her husband had died so tragically. *At last*, I thought, *something I can do for her, given that my opinion on her new wardrobe was not solicited*. "Why don't I call the manager, Signor Villani, and see if I can't arrange for you to change rooms?" I suggested.

"My dear Carolyn, how thoughtful of you," said Constanza. "In the absence of my own daughter, you are such a source of kindness and strength. You and Gracia." She gave each of us a sad smile. Gracia rose from her place beside me on the couch—she was already wearing black, had probably been in mourning since the death of her own husband so many years ago. I wondered if half the women in Sicily might not be wearing black for dead relatives.

"Come," said Gracia, "I will help you change into clothes for the move and begin to pack for you."

Off they went to deal with more wardrobe problems while I called the policeman on the room-service phone and demanded to speak to Signor Villani. When I finally got hold of him and explained the problem, he was horrified to hear that such an important man had died in his hotel without his being informed. Perhaps his staff was afraid to awaken him in the middle of the night with such bad news. Signor Villani had to call the general, who said none of us could move off the eighth floor and no one was to enter the room in which Ruggiero had died. As a result, a room that connected to Gracia's was made available to Constanza, and I found myself escorting the moderately grief-stricken widow to her new quarters while a Carabinieri, splendid in white sash and red striped trousers and armed with a large weapon of some sort, stood guard over the crime and/or death scene, and Gracia, with the help of several hotel employees, moved all other Ricci possessions down the hall.

Having inserted the new key card into the slot, I turned

to gesture Constanza in. *Oh my!* I whipped my head right back toward the door because I had caught her shoving something into the sand of a tall ashtray in the hall. Then she sailed past me, evidently unaware of what I had seen. I glanced nervously at the sand, now quite smooth. Had I imagined the whole thing? And if I hadn't, what had she buried there? A gun? Probably not. Ruggiero had not been shot. Nitroglycerine pills? Perhaps he had had heart trouble after all, unknown to anyone but the two of them, and she had replaced his pills with some innocuous substitute, and he had died. Now she was hiding the evidence. I followed her into the room, thinking I needed to talk to the general. Before some maid came along and cleaned out the ashtrays.

"This is not a suite," said Constanza irritably.

I explained the problem with the general, and she said she'd have to complain to his superiors in Rome, but first, having slept not a wink since she discovered her Ruggiero's dead body, she needed to go to bed. I had her in that bed with her shoes off and her robe draped carefully over a chair before she could say another word. As soon as Gracia appeared, loaded down with clothes, I kissed Constanza on the forehead, patted her hand, and escaped.

32

Evidence in an Ashtray

Carolyn

On my way out of Constanza's new room, I decided to look in the ashtray myself, but that didn't happen. A local policeman met me at the door and escorted me to my own door. I did try to tell him that I needed to see the general, but he insisted in broken English that the general was busy. Then I asked for Lieutenant Buglione and was told that he, too, was busy. At least the fellow spoke English, but he also insisted that I go back into my own room. When I stayed outside to argue, he whipped out a key card and opened the door for me. What could I do but enter? However, I was not happy to think that at least four people, counting Jason, now had cards for my room.

Jason was out on the balcony, laptop on a little table, so I began the arduous process of reaching the general through Room Service. He returned my call about twenty minutes later and promised to have someone sift through the ashtray outside Constanza's door—this after I had assured him several times that she did not smoke and had not been eating an apple or chewing gum. Sometimes law enforcement authorities make it very hard to assist them.

I suppose assistance from an amateur seems beneath them or hurts their professional pride. I consoled myself by postulating that a female law officer would be more grateful to and cooperative with helpful citizens. Perhaps I should have called Lieutenant Flavia Vacci, whose voice I could hear in the background as I talked to the general.

I had just curled up on the bed with a book when the telephone rang again. That was fast, I thought, excited to hear what they had discovered in the ashtray. It was Gracia telling me that Constanza had permission from the authorities to gather the conference members and their wives for a luncheon at one o'clock in the meeting room at the end of the hall.

Wonderful! I thought. *We'll have decent food for lunch.* I hastened out to the balcony, catching a gust of wind as I opened the doors, and told Jason that we were to be freed from our rooms for lunch.

"Wonderful," he said. "Maybe they're going to cancel the rest of the meetings."

I wasn't too happy with that thought. I'd never find out who killed whom if Jason insisted on going straight home, but the ticket changes would be expensive, so maybe he wouldn't. On the other hand, staying here at our own expense would be prohibitively expensive, so I didn't say anything to him about his desire to leave as soon as possible. I did suggest that the food would be better since Constanza was ordering it and didn't like the hotel's Swiss chef.

"Excellent," said Jason, and went back to writing an article for a chemistry journal on some esoteric toxin in which he was interested. His only other comment to me was that my hair was messy. As if his wasn't. How could he write in a high wind? Even the wonderful view couldn't persuade me to do that. I went back inside to finish writing the newspaper column I had been unable to continue last night and then to dress for lunch, about which I was quite right. After we all offered our hostess condolences, we were served a promising first course.

Insalata Caprese, of which I can never get enough. However, eating it reminded me that I was unlikely to get to Capri this trip, not while we were immured in our rooms or, alternately, sent home. The only nonconference person at the luncheon was Lieutenant Flavia Vacci, smiling as always, chatting with Valentino Santoro, by whom she was sitting, and obviously enjoying her *insalata* as much as I was enjoying mine. I supposed that she was on duty, assigned to verify that all conferees and spouses were actually there, to listen to everything we said, and to be sure we didn't leave.

While I was eating—I didn't have to take notes on that lovely salad—Constanza tapped her wine glass and announced that the conference would continue—in this very room, once the dishes were cleared. "I know my dear Ruggiero would have wanted you to finish your deliberations. I am only sorry that those of you who are not chemists can no longer enjoy the beauties of our unforgettable Amalfi Coast. However, the police are insistent that we all stay on this floor for the remainder of our time here. Even I, who have funeral arrangements to make, must do so on the telephone." She sighed.

"Valentino Santoro, my husband's right hand, will chair the meeting in Ruggiero's absence." She dabbed her eyes with a handkerchief. "Gracia Sindacco, our office manager, will see that all the conference arrangements are carried out as smoothly as these unhappy occurrences allow. And now please enjoy your food and wine and remember my dear husband in your prayers."

As I went back to my tomatoes and buffalo mozzarella, it occurred to me that Constanza seemed more upset now than she had when I visited her this morning, at which time she seemed much less grief-stricken than Bianca had described her. I was halfway through my salad when Loppi stepped into the room, asked pardon for interrupting our meal, and said the general wanted to see me. Everyone, even Bianca, stared at me as if I was about to be arrested. Jason was particularly taken aback and asked if I wanted him to come with me, which was sweet, but unnecessary. No doubt the general wanted to tell me about the ashtray, even if he did choose an embarrassing time to do it. I rose, about to tell Jason he should finish his lunch, when Loppi placed a hand firmly on my husband's shoulder and said, "Only the signora."

"It's okay," I whispered to Jason, then thought to pick up my salad plate. If I didn't take it with me, it would be gone when I got back.

The general awaited me in the room where we first met. After waving me to a seat, he asked if I had any thoughts on the syringe that had been found in the ashtray stand to which I had directed his men.

A syringe? I gave myself a minute to think while forking up a slice of tomato and mozzarella, and what came to me was the memory of Constanza testing her glucose level. It all became too tragically clear to me then. "Constanza killed him with a shot of insulin," I said. "A shot of insulin can induce a heart attack in a nondiabetic, you know. I remember seeing just that scenario in a police drama on television."

The general looked skeptical. "Perhaps Signora Ricci-Tassone does not watch American television," he suggested.

"Perhaps not, but she is a diabetic. She takes insulin. I saw her use one of those test machines that measures glucose levels. She's a type-two diabetic. She told me so herself, just before she went into the ladies' room to give herself a shot. It was the day we went to Pompeii."

"Umm," said the general. "And why would she kill her husband?"

"Because he was unfaithful, of course."

"His mistress was dead."

"And he was flirting with another woman at the dinner and dance just the other night. Or maybe the noise she heard in his room was a lover, so she went in to confront them, the woman ran, and Constanza killed her husband."

"Because she conveniently had a syringe primed with insulin in her hand at the time?"

"Maybe she had been about to give herself the shot when she heard the noise."

"It seems unlikely that she would be giving herself a shot in the middle of the night, which is when she discovered the body and called for help."

"When she called for help is not necessarily when she killed him. Perhaps the woman in his room could testify as to when Constanza came in."

"We do not know that there was such a woman. That is your speculation, not a fact, Signora."

I had another thought. "Maybe she heard that you were investigating the company and might close it down."

"Did you tell her that?"

"Of course not," I said indignantly, and then tried to remember if I had told anyone who might have told her.

"And killing her husband would deter our investigation of the company? Not really, Signora," he said.

"But she might have thought it would all go away if Ruggiero were dead, and her children, of whom she is so proud and so protective, would then inherit the company."

"Umm." The general tented his fingers and fell into thought.

"You should tell your coroner to look for a needle mark on Signor Ricci's body. That would be the first thing to do."

"And our evidence investigators, if Sorrento has any, must look for fingerprints on the syringe and for insulin inside, if anything is left after the burial in sand." He untented his fingers and stared at me for a minute. "Thank you, Signora. You have been very helpful. My apologies for interrupting your lunch."

That was it? I was to go back to lunch without ever discovering the outcome of my deductions and suggestions? Evidently. The general rose from his chair, although I had not risen from mine, extended his hand, and escorted me to the door.

33
What a Day!

Bianca

For a second day we were cooped up in the room together. Much as I love my children, two days in two
rooms with two bored, unhappy children is more than any
expectant mother should have to endure. Especially one as
pregnant as I. The baby had kicked me for the rest of the
night after Ruggiero turned up dead.

Interesting that he and Constanza don't sleep together,
I mused. *I wonder if the noise that awakened her really
was the sound of another woman in his room. Maybe he
had a heart attack in the middle of adultery and died.* I
could imagine his new love struggling out from under him
and running for her life. Now, that would be a terrible
shock for his lover. And since he hadn't died in a state of
grace, Constanza would have to have a lot of prayers said
for his soul to get him out of purgatory. Maybe, given the
circumstances, she wouldn't bother.

Even Lorenzo was becoming short-tempered with Andrea and Giulia, and of course the stupid police wouldn't
let Violetta come to our room to entertain them. I was so
tired that I locked myself in the bathroom and stretched

out in the tub, soaking in warm water. Probably something the doctor would disapprove of. I've always felt that we mothers know what's good and bad for us and for our babies. So I have to admit that I tend to think of other things when the obstetrician is giving me the "little mother" lectures on how to conduct my life while carrying a child.

Poof! Someone was knocking on the door. Probably Giulia thought she needed to use the toilet. It was time that she stopped that, so I just closed my ears and thought about Constanza, who had seemed genuinely miserable about her husband's death. *What would I do if anything happened to Lorenzo? I'd just die. He's such a sweetheart.*

More knocking. I wasn't sure I could get out of the tub if I wanted to. Lorenzo would have to come in and drag me out. But I'd locked the door. "Go away!" I shouted. "I'm resting."

"*Cara mia*," shouted my husband, "you're not stuck in the tub again, are you?" He rattled the doorknob.

Of course, he was right. I'd done this last month, an embarrassment I'd managed to forget. "Of course not," I shouted.

"Mama, I need to pee pee," called my daughter.

Sighing, I tried to get out, and of course I couldn't. And I'd locked the door. Lorenzo would be so peeved with me, but I had to tell him what had happened, although I waited ten more minutes because it felt so good to lie in the warm water. In fact, I ran more in and ignored the pleas and grumbles from outside. Then I admitted my predicament, and a man from the hotel staff had to be called to take the door off the hinges. Of course the children tumbled right in and cried things like, "Mamma's naked!" and "Look how big her tummy is!" until Lorenzo shooed them and the workman out and extracted me from my comforting soak. That's when I heard that Constanza had invited us to lunch and I had only twenty minutes to dress. The children shrieked about being left behind, and we had to get permission for Violetta to stay with them in our room, and Giulia had wet her panties, poor thing. I felt embarrassed for that, among my other sins, and changed her clothes myself.

What a relief to get out of there, and to have a tasty meal for a change. I could have hugged Constanza, who still seemed pretty broken up, although not as much as she had been in the middle of the night. She ended the speculation about the fate of the conference by saying it would continue, but on this floor in this room. Then we were all taken aback because a messenger from General Bianconi called Carolyn out during the salad. My goodness, was he going to arrest her? Maybe I shouldn't have asked him if Paolina was gay. I didn't know she was his daughter.

We were almost through the main course when Carolyn returned, saying the general had had more questions for her. She didn't seem upset, so maybe my rather outlandish idea that *she* had killed Ruggiero because *he* had killed Paolina had been completely wrong. Carolyn got only a few bites of the fish before dessert was served. Good thing she'd taken her salad with her.

We were enjoying our peaches when the general walked into the room behind a waiter bearing espresso. He apologized for interrupting our meal and waved his two aides in, the short one and the tall one. They walked right over to Constanza and told her they were arresting her for the murder of her husband.

She exclaimed, looking flabbergasted, as the Americans say, "I didn't kill my husband. He died of a heart attack."

"Yes, he did, Signora," said the general, "but that heart attack was induced by a shot of insulin." Constanza turned pale, and I remembered that Carolyn had said she was diabetic. "Insulin from a syringe you tried to dispose of in the sand of a cigarette tray outside your new room."

Constanza turned to Carolyn and cried, "You! I thought you were my friend. I gave you my company and my conversation. And you betrayed me."

The general nodded, taking that as a confession. Carolyn had turned pale, then pink, while the rest of us looked from one woman to the other.

"And for nothing you betray me. I did not kill Ruggiero," Constanza continued indignantly. "I found the syringe beside his bed when I heard him cry out. Of course, I knew he was in there with a woman. The hall door was closing when I entered. I realized immediately that the syringe contained one of those—those drugs that enhance performance. Sexual performance." She herself was more flushed than Carolyn. "How could I let people know that he had died in such an undignified manner? I couldn't, so of course I picked up the syringe and disposed of it as soon as I had the chance. I had to think of my children."

"A very interesting story, Signora, except that the syringe contained insulin, which does nothing for a man's sexual prowess but can kill a man who does not have diabetes. Loppi. Marsocca." He nodded to his aides, and they walked Constanza toward the door. The female Carabinieri, Flavia, was taking all this in, wide-eyed, but the general left without even speaking to her, so she went back to her dessert. Nothing seemed to affect her appetite.

"Carolyn, for Pete's sake—" Jason began.

"Just *don't*, Jason," she retorted, on the verge of tears. "Has it occurred to you that she might have done the same thing to Paolina and for the same reason? Jealousy! She's strong enough to have pushed Paolina over the waterfall. General," she called after the departing federal agents, "you should have Paolina's body examined for a syringe mark and for insulin."

"That occurred to me as well," said the general, and closed the door.

Gracia, who had been seated with us and had tried to follow Constanza out, turned and glared at Carolyn. "That Paolina was a slut. She slept with an American the night before she left Catania. Ruggiero probably found out and followed her to Sorrento to kill her because she was his lover."

"No, he didn't," cried Valentino. "He broke his date with Paolina to visit an old mistress in Catania. I had to call him on his cell phone because of a problem at the plant. He was there, with Maria Falingerno. She answered my call. The man couldn't even be faithful to poor Paolina."

"Whatever Ricci and his young slut were doing that night, my mistress killed no one," snapped Gracia. "She was a good wife to her no-good husband, and she was in Milan visiting designer shops and friends on Saturday and Sunday. She couldn't have killed Paolina, and she wouldn't have killed Ruggiero. *I'd* have been happy to kill him, but it would have broken her heart, so I didn't, but I'm glad he's dead. God will dole out what Ruggiero Ricci deserves: either hell or a long, painful time in purgatory."

Everyone was gaping, including me, and of course Flavia, who was jotting down notes, but not Albertine, who said calmly, "Signora Ricci-Tassone *was* in Milan on Saturday. I saw her coming out of Versace. I must say, I was rather surprised to find her shopping there. The clothing is much too gaudy and daring for a woman of her age and lineage. Of course, she might have been buying for her daughter, but I wouldn't want a daughter of mine wearing—"

"I imagine the Mafia killed both of them," said Eliza Stackpole. "Constanza even admitted that her father-in-law had been in the Mafia, or his father. One or the other. I can't imagine why you'd think Constanza killed her own husband, Carolyn."

Flavia jotted down more notes. Everyone else turned and stared accusingly at Carolyn, who had been continuing to eat her peach. She looked up and said bitterly, "I think you should all tell the general about your theories. I didn't tell him that Constanza killed Ruggiero. I just mentioned that she'd pushed something into an ashtray in the hall, and later, when he asked, I mentioned that she was diabetic."

"I don't see what business it was of yours, Madame Blue," said Albertine haughtily.

"Well, I think we're all finished with dessert and coffee," I said. "I'm going back to my room for a nice nap." Of course, Lorenzo immediately asked if I was having contractions, and I replied, "No, just a great desire to make up for the sleep I lost last night."

After that, the whole group trailed out into the hall, nobody saying anything until Jason reached his door and cursed rather colorfully. Of course we all reassembled and watched him standing on one foot, staring at the bottom of his shoe. I could tell by the odor what had happened and said, "Charles de Gaulle strikes again."

"Mon dieu!" exclaimed Adrien Guillot. "I do apologize, Jason. How in the world did he get out?"

"Maybe you should have a talk with him," said Jason as he used the handkerchief the Frenchie had given him to wipe off the shoe.

Carolyn sent a really mean look toward Albertine, stepped gingerly over what was left on the floor, stalked into her room, and slammed the door.

"I'll do better than that, my friend," said Guillot. "I'll put him in a kennel until we can all leave this dreadful meeting."

"Adrien, you know Charles hates kennels. He'll be devastated," cried Albertine. Her husband grabbed her arm and walked her away while Jason, having given up on his shoe, took it off and reinserted his key card in the door.

"What a day!" I said to Lorenzo as we continued to our room. "Do you think Constanza could have killed Ruggiero?"

"There *are* shots that cause an erection," said my husband, grinning. "And pills. That sounds more likely to me, given Ricci's interest in the ladies. All the ladies. Don't think I didn't see him patting your knee the first night."

I giggled. Nothing got by Lorenzo, but he knew better than to think I'd be interested in another man.

Sorrento is known for its peaches, but surely, since I was not there during peach season, this recipe was not made with fresh peaches, unless the Campania produces several crops, which they do of other things because of the mild climate. Still, fresh or frozen, the following dessert is a delight.

Stuffed Peaches with Mascarpone Cream

- Preheat oven to 400 degrees F. Halve and pit *6 large peaches*. With a teaspoon, scoop some flesh from the cavities, and chop the peach flesh you have removed.

- Combine *3 ounces crumbled amaretti cookies, 3 tablespoons ground almonds, 4 tablespoons sugar, and 1 1/2 tablespoons cocoa powder* with peach flesh. Add enough *sweet wine* to make the mixture into a thick paste.

- Place the peaches in a buttered ovenproof dish and fill them with the stuffing. Dot with *3 tablespoons butter* and pour the remainder of *1 cup sweet wine* into the dish. Bake 35 minutes.

- Make mascarpone cream by beating *2 tablespoons sugar*, and *3 egg yolks* until thick and pale. Stir in *1 tablespoon dessert wine* and fold in *1 cup mascarpone cheese*, which is an Italian cream cheese made from cow's milk. Whip *2/3 cup heavy cream* to soft peaks and fold into mixture.

- Remove peaches from oven and cool. Serve at room temperature with mascarpone cream and dessert wine.

Carolyn Blue,
"Have Fork, Will Travel,"
Atlanta Press

Friday in Naples

The Ubiquitous Pizza

In our time pizza is popular all over the world, its crust thick or thin, soft or crisp, it toppings varying from the early pizza with marinara sauce to pizzas topped with whatever strikes the fancy of the cook and the customer—caviar, pineapple, chili, shrimp, whatever the area provides. Why not? It is the ultimate one-dish meal.

The Italians, however, are not so tolerant of pizza innovation. Neapolitans argue on the street about what constitutes a proper and delicious pizza topping. The Italian government sets standards that dictate how the real thing is to be made. And pizza, after all, is an Italian phenomenon, awarded to Italy by history.

The word *pizza* probably came from *pita*, a flat bread made and eaten in many early societies. The Romans had a baked bread called *picea* that may have been the forbearer in Italy. By the beginning of the 1100s the word had changed to *piza*, a flat round cake baked in a medieval oven—still not the real thing. Enter Naples around 1670, where the crust was adorned with tomatoes, garlic, oregano, and olive oil—*pizza alla marinara*—and the king, Ferdinand IV, who liked to go slumming, joined his poorer subjects in eating the new delight. Pizza hit the big time when Ferdinand wanted it at home in the castle. Maria Carolina, his wife, disapproved, but even a stuffy Hapsburg queen does not forbid her king his desire. She allowed outdoor pizza ovens to be built in the gardens of the Capodimonte palace, and soon not just the king and the commoners were eating pizza. The nobility built their own ovens so they too could eat it.

The first pizzeria opened in Naples in 1830, and the first innovation occurred in 1889 when Queen Margherita, wife of King Umberto I of the house of Savoy, visited Naples and asked for pizza. In her honor, pizza maker Raffaele Esposito, owner of Pizzeria di Pietro, used mozzarella, tomatoes, and basil leaves, the white, red, and green of the flag of unified Italy, and named his new pizza for the queen. She loved it, the Neapolitans loved it, and *pizza Margherita* became a favorite of Naples. The poor made it at home, and Esposito's pizzeria became a popular haunt of the nobility.

Strangely, New York, with its immigrant population, embraced pizza before Rome and Northern Italy. There was a pizzeria in lower Manhattan early in the twentieth century, but Rome waited to approve pizza until the 1970s and '80s. Now it's being eaten in India and China. One wonders what the toppings are. As long as it's baked properly in a woodfired, stone oven, it's still pizza.

Carolyn Blue,
"Have Fork, Will Travel,"
Colorado Springs Bugle

34
The Assignment

Carolyn

I woke up the next morning feeling more than a little depressed. Of course I knew that everyone was angry with me because they held me responsible for Constanza's arrest. But what if she was guilty? Why didn't they consider that? My own husband had complained about how much my meddling—that's what he called my efforts—would hurt his interactions with fellow chemists. I retorted by asking whether Albertine's dog was affecting her husband's relations with his colleagues. Jason muttered, "Damn dog." He'd scraped and scrubbed the sole of his shoe, but the smell was still there. At least he had the good sense to take the shoe off before entering the room. Now the shoe in question was sitting out on the balcony, while Jason, wearing sneakers, was off having breakfast with his colleagues and discussing chemistry. I was left to order my own breakfast.

Should I order and then shower and dress, or shower and dress and then order? One could never tell how fast Room Service would deliver meals to our floor since they had the whole floor to deal with. Our dinner hadn't arrived until ten, although we'd ordered three and a half hours earlier, and when it came, it wasn't even the right dinner. On the other hand, breakfast sometimes arrived in ten minutes. I decided to shower first. If I didn't answer the door, the policeman would probably deliver it to someone else.

When I emerged from the bathroom, toweling my hair and thinking about fennel bread and fresh fruit, the telephone rang, and the general ordered me down to his conference room off the lobby.

"I haven't had breakfast yet," I muttered.

"I'll order it for you. Loppi will be at your door in fifteen minutes to escort you down."

Well, that was nice! He hadn't even asked what I wanted to eat. I'd probably end up with a bun and a cup of coffee. Grumbling to myself, I threw on some clothes and stomped back into the bathroom to dry my hair and put on makeup. Before I could even reacquaint myself with the controls of the hairdryer, someone knocked on my door. I was sure five minutes hadn't passed, but there was Signor Loppi, smiling at me. He had overlapping teeth. Very unsightly. I told him that I had to dry my hair and do a few other things. He told me the general was waiting and wouldn't care how I looked.

So I went downstairs with my hair straggling in damp clumps down my back and my face pale with dark circles under my eyes. The general not only didn't care, he didn't notice. He waved me to a seat, in front of which was placed a little table that contained rolls, coffee, and fresh fruit. No eggs, no fennel toast, but it was better than I expected, and I began to eat without even saying hello to him.

The general didn't greet me either. Instead he began immediately to tell me about a call he had received from Rome. "A tape arrived in my office, addressed to me," he said. "No note. Postmarked Catania, the day Lucia evidently left for Sorrento."

"Lucia?" I mumbled around a mouthful of melon. It was delicious. Maybe from Israel, or could they ripen melons in the Campania at this time of year?

"My daughter Lucia," he said impatiently. "I can see that you are hungry, but this is important, Signora."

I was still thinking of her as Paolina. "Right. What was on the tape?" I asked, and bit into a roll. It had a surprise filling of a fruity cream. *Very* nice. I looked to see if the second one was the same kind, but it appeared to be of a different variety.

"It's a very poor recording. My people think she may have recorded it off the office intercom—Ricci's office. And she must have been in hurry to mail it, because she neglected to include an explanation of what she was sending."

His hard face looked strained, and I felt sorry for him. Had Paolina known she was in trouble even then?

"They're going to try to improve the sound quality and overnight it to me. What they got from it in its present condition was two men talking, no names, but one of them had to be Ricci. And my people think they made out two words. *Radioactive* and an Italian slang word for heroin." He stared at me as I munched my roll and thought about the words. A bit of the fruit cream stuck to my lip, and I wiped it off with the napkin, embarrassed.

"Have you any thoughts, Signora, on who might have been talking to Ricci, and what they might have been talking about?" he demanded.

"Well, Gracia said a foreigner was in Ricci's office that afternoon, the one who stopped to talk to Paolina and may have—well, visited her that night. So that might be the other man on the tape. And *radioactive*—well, Ricci's company may have made those radioactive medicines hospitals use for taking x-rays."

The general nodded. "They do. What else?"

"Ummm—Hank Girol was talking to Ricci one night before dinner about getting a contract to dispose of their toxic waste. That's what his company does. He's the vice president of a toxic waste company. In New Jersey. They're hoping to expand abroad, in Europe and especially Eastern Europe."

"What would that have to do with heroin?"

"I don't know, unless Ricci planned to use their new containers to transport heroin, but he couldn't have been talking to Hank about that, because Hank was in Rome the day Paolina was here sightseeing with me, and he drove down here the next morning, the morning I found Paolina."

The general was silent for a long time. I'd finished my breakfast by the time he spoke again. "Girol has asked permission to take you ladies to Capri today. He seems to feel it's unfair that your husbands and his wife get to continue the meeting, but you ladies can't do any more sightseeing."

"Well, it is, sort of. When you think about it," I replied. "I've really been looking forward to visiting Capri. It's so gorgeous that one of the emperors, Augustus, I think, traded a bigger island for it in Roman times."

"Capri's not going to happen. I'll have to send a policeman, probably Gambardella, along with you, and I don't want him shoved over the side of the boat while you're on the water. Girol's second choice was Naples. I'll say yes to that, and you see what you can find out from him."

"About what?" I asked, thinking of Naples. That would be interesting, sort of, although I'd have preferred Capri—home of *insalata Caprese*, site of Shirley Hazzard's interesting meetings with Graham Greene, one of the most beautiful places in the world. Still, I wasn't going to turn down Naples. It was bound to be better than staying in the room all day by myself. And although I'd heard it was quite dangerous, those warnings are usually exaggerated; no doubt Hank and Sergeant Gambardella could take care of us.

"I'll go, but maybe you could be clearer about what you want me to ask him."

"I don't want you to *ask* him anything, Signora. I want you to lead him into conversation. See if you can get him to knock down his own alibi. Find out what he thinks about Ricci's death. Show an interest in his business connections with Ricci. You seem to have collected a lot of information since my daughter died, but most of it regards motive; motive doesn't help us in court without hard evidence. Try to find out some facts, Signora."

I was a bit peeved, really. I hadn't told him anything that would stand up in court? Why would he say that? "How do you know he's going to invite me to go to Naples?" I asked. "Everyone's mad at me since you arrested Constanza."

"Trust me to see that he does," said the general. "Now go back to your room and think about how you're going to approach him. And you might do something with your hair. It looks—" He searched for a word.

"Wet?" I suggested. "Loppi showed up too fast and wouldn't let me dry it. He said you were in a hurry and wouldn't care what I looked like."

"I don't," said the general, "but Girol might."

Although I was supposed to be thinking of questions I could ask Hank, should he invite me to go to Naples, I couldn't help thinking about Naples itself and everything I'd read about it. Of course, I did want to see the archaeological museum since it housed the artifacts from Pompeii, but the city? Its reputation was mixed at best. A city where people hung their washing above the streets? Didn't it get all dirty again? A city where homemade pasta was hung to dry outside on lines so that it could be preserved for times of famine and war? How sanitary was that? But probably they didn't do that anymore.

Then there are all the wars, plagues, earthquakes, and volcanic eruptions over the years, some in recent times. One period of violence that the Neapolitans avoided was the devastating raids of Saracen pirates. While the rest of the Campania suffered from these predators, the Neapolitans cultivated them as friendly trading partners and evidently weren't bothered at all that they were "infidels." The Pope, however, was bothered and excommunicated the whole city.

Aside from the attacks of all the conquering armies that besieged Naples, including the Nazis and the allies during World War II, there were the little wars—the rebellion of the population against the "vegetable tax" imposed by the Spanish Viceroys, the modern "family" warfare among various branches of the Camorra, which is the Mafia of the Campania; it has no central organization. A bishop actually organized a local "army" to fight the Camorra gangs in Naples in the 1980s, although the effort failed. And once a cabal of artists led by the Spanish painter Ribera terrorized noncabal artists to eliminate the competition for art contracts, but that was in another century.

It is said that there is no law in Naples, where crime and graft are rampant. Even professors at the university accept expensive stays on Capri paid for by the parents of their students when oral-exam time comes up. Those factors made Naples less alluring than it might have been given its castles, palazzos, museums, and its opera house, the San Carlo, which is the largest opera venue in Italy. It

was founded by a king who didn't like opera, and its patrons are given more to conversation than attention to the
performance. In other words, it's beautiful but noisy.

Also, to the eyes of a Protestant American, maybe even
a Catholic American, Neapolitans are bizarrely superstitious. The city's patron saint is San Gennaro, a bishop
who arrived to support Christianity early in the first mil-
lennium and was sentenced to death by the local Roman
leader, Timotheus. On pronouncing the death sentence,
Timotheus was struck blind. The kindly Bishop Gennaro
prayed for the return of his tormentor's sight, God
obliged, and five thousand people were converted by the
miracle, although the Roman leader was not one of them.
However, Gennaro was not an easy man to execute. He
survived a fiery furnace and hungry wild beasts in the amphitheater. Finally he was beheaded, which did kill him,
but the stone on which his blood fell was saved, and his
blood was collected in vials which are still shaken on cer-
tain feast days in order for the miracle of liquefaction to
occur and forecast a good year for the city. The dark blood
spots on the stone brighten to red. When the blood does
not liquefy in the vial or turn red on the stone, Neapolitans
expect to be visited by volcanic eruptions and defeats of
their soccer teams, and the saint is cursed by the populace.

Furthermore, Neapolitans believe in the evil eye. They
have amulets to ward it off, and some have more than a
passing interest in numerology and black magic. Not that
I believe in any of those things, but did I really want to
visit the most superstitious city in Europe?

Then there is the Neapolitan character. The men adore
their mamas but pride themselves on their ability to seduce women who are not their mamas. Neapolitan women
are guarded by their men in old-fashioned ways. Wives
who work as maids for bachelors are accompanied by
their husbands, who sit outside scowling. Sisters are chap-

eroned by their reluctant brothers. Yet there are women of power in the Camorra, in politics, and in the arts. A lawless, schizophrenic society. *Do I really want to go to Naples?* I asked myself, while trying to repair my hair with the hotel's hair dryer, away from which the general's minion had dragged me.

Then Hank called, and I accepted. After all, it was my civic duty.

35

Escape to Naples

Bianca

"Thank you, Holy Mother," I said fervently as I put down the telephone. My children looked up hopefully, astonished to see me looking pleased. "Guess what?" I cried merrily. "You can spend the day with Granny; the general said so." They both cheered, believing that they had been granted a fine gift, which they had. Any change from being locked up in this room looked good—to them and to me. We gathered up toys, books, and a change of clothes in case of accidents, and I hustled them out into the hall. Of course, the policeman guarding the elevator spotted us since we were heading his way, and told us to stop right there. I paid no attention.

"Signora, you are not allowed—"

"The general says we can spend the day with Granny," Andrea told him. "Ask the general."

The policeman looked confused. He wouldn't let us on the elevator, but he did call the general's number. Probably terrified he'd get in trouble with Rome if he inadvertently countermanded General Bianconi's wishes. After some questions and answers, he handed the phone to me.

"I was told I could go to Naples with the others. No one said the children could go." My children looked downcast. "Museums and churches," I whispered to them, and they cheered up. They preferred Granny to museums and churches. "Therefore, I have to leave them with their grandmother." I was talking to Flavia Vacci, not the general. "Ask your new boss." She did and then conveyed a message to the Sorrento policeman, who let us on the elevator and told me I had five minutes to drop them off and return before he came after me. *Dear God*, I prayed silently. *Let her be there. Let her want to take the children.*

She was. She did. She thought the general was such a sweet man. I had to agree since he was letting me go to Naples.

We all congregated in the lobby, and there were two more than I expected. The first was Sergeant Gambardella, our escort, who looked as happy to get out of the hotel as any of us. Probably he resented the addition of Carabinieri officers to the guard force because they had prettier uniforms. And, second, Charles de Gaulle, mooning after Carolyn, who was saying, "I thought he was going into a kennel."

"Adrien couldn't get him a place until tomorrow," said Albertine angrily. "He won't bother you; he'll sit beside me and be a perfect gentleman, although I don't know why you're included in this outing. After what you did to our hostess, who is quite innocent of—"

"Now ladies," Hank intervened. "We're out on parole. Let's make the most of it. We even have our own escort." He grinned at Sergeant Gambardella, who tipped his hat and smiled happily. "Carolyn, I'm sorry it couldn't be Capri, but maybe I can talk the general into that tomorrow."

"Naples sounds good," she said, but not with the enthusiasm she had shown for Capri. "How are we all going to fit into the car?"

"Well, we're putting a chair in the luggage compartment—it opens out like an old-fashioned rumble seat. The sergeant can sit there and keep an eye on all us suspects. Bianca has to sit in front because she can't get in back. I'm driving so I'm in front, and I thought you could sit in the middle."

"Fine," Carolyn agreed.

"I'll sit in the middle," I offered.

"Not at all," she said. "I don't mind the middle."

"It's not as if I can get a seatbelt over my stomach, Carolyn. You might as well use it." Hank agreed to that, but then Carolyn said she wasn't sitting in front of the dog because he'd drool on her, and she wasn't sitting beside the dog in back either. Obviously Albertine, the dog, Hank, and I couldn't all squeeze into the front. So we had to talk Sergeant Gambardella into sitting between Albertine and Eliza, with Charles de Gaulle behind them in the luggage compartment.

The chair placed behind for the sergeant was collapsed and returned to the hotel. I wondered whether they had realized that Hank commandeered it. Hank lifted the dog into the back, and the rest of us squeezed onto the two bench seats. I really felt bad for the sergeant because the happy dog, when he wasn't sticking his head over the side, ears streaming in the wind, which upset Albertine, laid his head on the sergeant's shoulder, drooling on his uniform and gazing wistfully at Carolyn, who was sitting in front of Albertine. Still, I enjoyed myself to no end on the drive to Naples, although Carolyn didn't have very much to say. I talked to Hank until just when we were getting to wherever he was taking us. Then there was a clap of thunder—I'd hardly noticed that the sunshine with which we'd started had disappeared—and rain began to fall.

"There are restaurants over there," Hank shouted at us. "See the plastic tents? Run for it."

We piled out after he pulled the car up onto a curb. He stayed to get the top up before his convertible became a catch basin for an inch or two of rain. Carolyn grabbed my arm and assisted me safely across the cobblestones. The other two and the dog ran off and left us with Sergeant Gambardella, who seemed unnerved when the people he was guarding split up without his permission. Eliza did hold the plastic flap open for us when we got to what had been a sidewalk café before its owners spotted the imminent deluge and raised a square canvas and plastic room beyond the sidewalk that fronted their restaurant. In fact, the whole street was now half covered with these rooms. We just took the first one we came to and fell into uncomfortable iron chairs that wobbled on the rounded stones. When Hank and the sergeant arrived several minutes later, pretty well soaked, they pulled two tables together, seated us all, and we breathed in the lovely aromas of pizza and pasta and other good Neapolitan dishes cooking inside.

A nice lady in a red, green, and white apron dashed out of the restaurant and across the sidewalk to offer us menus and napkins to dry ourselves off as best we could. "You're parked on the curb," Carolyn pointed out to Hank, who had taken a seat at the head of the table with Albertine and Eliza between us and him. The sergeant sat at our end.

I hated to think where the dog was. If under the table, there was going to be trouble. No, there he was at the corner between Albertine and Hank. He was staring at Carolyn, but he couldn't get to her as long as Albertine held his leash. We all ordered hot coffee and hot dishes. No salads on a day like this, except for Carolyn, who said she just had to have one more *insalata Caprese*, in case the general wouldn't let us go to Capri. She also ordered *pizza Margherita* because it was the favorite of Neapolitans, according to Hank and the waitress.

Her salad arrived, and she had just taken the first bite when suddenly Charles de Gaulle popped up beside her and thrust his long nose into her plate. Tomatoes and mozzarella disappeared before her eyes. The dog licked his chops and slurped down the rest of her salad. Then he licked up the olive oil. Coming out of shock, Carolyn whacked him on the nose with her fork, and Albertine, scolding in French, leapt up and rescued him from his weapon-wielding true love. The dog whimpered sadly while being dragged away, and Hank, ever the diplomat, rose with his plate of *fritti*, insisted on changing places with the sergeant in order to share with Carolyn, and explained to her that Neapolitans were always ready to feast on little, fried antipasti as they waited for the main course.

He then fed her delicious bits of fried dough dotted with seaweed, tasty tidbits of battered, fried vegetables—asparagus, zucchini, eggplant, artichokes, and not the least, *crocche de patate*—potato croquettes, which are about the size of the first joint of my finger, coated with breadcrumbs and fried. I'd have sacrificed my soup to the dog if it meant sharing Hank's *fritti*. So interested in the lecture and the tidbit tasting did Carolyn become that she stopped glaring at Albertine and her salad-thieving dog and gave herself over to tasting and note taking.

When her *pizza Margherita* arrived, that simplest of Neapolitan pizzas—dough, mozzarella, tomatoes, a few basil leaves, and olive oil—Carolyn wasn't all that impressed. She said that actually she thought the sun-dried tomato and pesto pizza at Ardovino's in El Paso was much tastier. Of course, she was stuffed with *fritti* before she ever tasted the favorite pizza of Naples. Both Hank and I agreed that her comments constituted sacrilege, but I'm not sure she heard us. The rain was falling so heavily during our meal that conversation was almost impossible.

When the storm abated, Hank paid the bill before we could order dessert and insisted that we return to the car. "I'll get you as close as I can to the Archaeological Museum before it starts again," he said. He did, and it did, so we had to climb the steps in the rain, but Carolyn didn't seem to mind. She was very excited about the museum and wanted to see everything, but particularly the things from Pompeii that the guide and Constanza had mentioned.

"I don't know how you can say that after you got the poor woman arrested," said Eliza. "She might have been here with us, if you hadn't—"

Carolyn pointed to a painting of Medea and said, "Do you see that? Constanza mentioned it to me. She said she'd never understood why Medea killed her children when it was her husband she should have murdered. And furthermore, Constanza approved of the fate Medea arranged for Jason's bride-to-be."

"I don't know what you're talking about," said Eliza resentfully.

"Medea sent the princess a wedding dress that burned her alive. It makes you wonder whether our hostess didn't do away with Paolina before she got to Ruggiero."

Eliza looked shocked and had no more comments. Hank said, "Now, now, ladies. Let's try to enjoy the day out." Albertine had had to stay in the lobby. They wouldn't let the dog into the exhibition rooms, and she wouldn't leave him out in the rain by himself. I wondered whether she liked her husband as much as she did Charles de Gaulle. Of the two, I'd pick Adrien. He seemed nice enough—for a Frenchman—while Charles de Gaulle was absolutely intolerable.

After we left the museum, we walked along a narrow street of butcher shops with dirty water running down the curbs and bloody hunks of meat hanging from hooks. To my encroaching heartburn was added nausea. At the corner, we turned and came upon shop after shop selling crèches in all sizes, full of wonderful shepherds and wise men crowding around brown, mossy mangers. I just had to stop and wanted to buy one for the children, but Hank asked where I thought we'd put it on the way back to Sorrento—in the luggage carrier with the dog? Everyone agreed that there was no taking a crèche, even a small one, back to the hotel.

"But I have to bring something for the children," I protested.

"Maybe we'll see something small that you can fit in your purse," Carolyn suggested.

"No more shopping," Hank announced, and insisted that we return to the car because it was time to be heading home before the traffic got too bad. So that was the visit to Naples, a lot of rain, a quick meal in a tent, a long visit to the museum, and my shoes were ruined from walking through the dirty water on the butcher and crèche streets. Not as delightful a day out as I'd anticipated, especially since my ankles had swelled again. I blamed it on the marble museum floors and Carolyn's limitless enthusiasm for every statue, pot, mosaic, and painting she saw.

36
Crime in the Streets

Carolyn

Of course we ladies wanted to shop, but the sergeant agreed with Hank that it was time to be getting home, so we walked back toward the car, Eliza and I holding Bianca so that she wouldn't slip on the cobblestone streets. Wet cobblestones make for dreadful walking. It's a wonder that large portions of medieval populations didn't die from compound fractures that festered, while the other half slipped once too often and became cripples for life. It was a great relief to get to a large concrete piazza, comfortable and safe underfoot, even though the sun had come out, and the area was very crowded. I don't know how many times passing pedestrians bumped me, but I certainly remember the last time. We were within ten yards of some tree-shaded benches at the far edge when I took a hard, but not painful jostling. Then, to my astonishment, Hank punched the seedy-looking man who had bumped into me. The poor fellow fell in a puddle, his nose gushing blood.

"Hank, I'm not hurt," I assured him. "I'm sure he didn't mean to—"

The man made an effort to scramble up, but Hank stepped on his wrist and said, "Give her back the camera." He said it in Italian, and Bianca translated, quite excited by the confrontation. The rest of us were all wide-eyed with shock, even Sergeant Gambardella.

The fellow in the puddle then spoke at length in a frantic, wheedling tone. "He says he doesn't have a camera," Bianca translated. "Did you notice that he started by calling Hank *Dottore* and worked his way up to *Commendatore*? Hank obviously isn't impressed by Neapolitan flattery."

I, however, was impressed by Hank's fluent Italian. I remembered him saying that he knew all the good restaurants in the area. Obviously he had visited before, but his command of the language—my thoughts were interrupted when Sergeant Gambardella tried to remonstrate with Hank, but to no avail. Hank shifted his considerable weight, and the alleged thief screamed as the bones in his wrist cracked audibly.

"Why do you think he took my camera?" I cried, letting go of Bianca and reaching into the outside pocket of my purse to prove that the camera was still in my possession. *This is dreadful*, I thought, for I had spotted a Neapolitan policeman hurrying toward us. Hank would be thrown in jail unless I could find the camera, which didn't seem to be in the pocket where I thought I remembered putting it. No, that wasn't right. If I *had* my camera, Hank would be jailed for assaulting an innocent man. What was I to do? I didn't want to be the cause of another person in our group being arrested, but on the other hand, I couldn't lie to the Neapolitan police.

While I was fretting over this moral dilemma and unsnapping my purse to search inside, Hank leaned down and grasped one of the very large pockets in the man's pants, ripped it completely off, and handed me my cam-

era, which the Neapolitan policeman immediately confis-
cated as evidence. Then he hauled the whimpering thief
up by his coat collar and marched us all off to a police
station.

What a welter of misunderstandings that was. The police did not speak English. Hank and Bianca had to translate, but the officers were loath to believe their
translations. Everybody shouted; nobody got to sit down
except Bianca. They were probably afraid that she'd give
birth on the spot if they didn't find her a chair. Charles de
Gaulle tried to lick a captain's hand and was immured in
a cell as a "dangerous canine." Albertine all but attacked
the captain—in French, of course. Eliza said the thief was
probably a Mafia soldier, which didn't go over well, since
organized crime, and everything else in Naples, is run by
the Camorra, not the Mafia.

Then several unpleasant remarks were made about
President Bush, although I had thought that the Italians
were our allies. Bianca explained to me that a sergeant's
cousin had been killed in Iraq, so I offered my condolences to the sergeant and said that I, too, disliked the war
and feared that my own son might have to go if the draft
were reinstated in our country. All the shouting stopped
while Bianca translated my remarks, which I followed by
saying that I could prove the camera was mine and would
swear that I had not given it to the alleged thief.

The captain demanded to know if I had a sales receipt
for the camera on my person, which of course I didn't, but
I did manage to convince them, through Bianca, that I
should have the camera returned to me for the time being.
Then everyone crowded around to see the pictures on my
little digital screen. They passed the scenes from hand to
hand, identifying the restaurant where we ate—the sergeant knew the lady who ran it; the museum with Albertine and Eliza standing on the steps, Charles de Gaulle

pulling at his leash; Bianca at a crèche shop pointing to
call attention to a favorite—Hank had taken that picture;
and all of us in the lobby of the Grand Hotel Sorrento—
the captain had stayed there on his honeymoon.

There was even a picture of Gwen that came up when
someone pressed the wrong button and started the pictures
from the back—all the young officers were enchanted
with Gwen and asked if she had come to Sorrento with
me. One insisted that I zoom in so he could see her face
better. Then he sighed rapturously as if he had been af-
flicted with love at first sight. Such romantics, these Italians. I only agreed to work the zoom feature because my
daughter was safely back home in the states.

The upshot of all this international photo viewing was
the arrest of the man who had stolen my camera, the taking of all our names as witnesses—we didn't bother to
tell them that all of us would be going home soon, except
Sergeant Gambardella, who had liked my daughter too—
and our release. We were even given a ride back to the car,
where Hank found, under his windshield wiper, a soggy
ticket for parking on the curb. "Fucking *vigile!*" Hank
snarled. I was offended, Bianca said a *vigile* was a traffic
policeman, and our police chauffeur laughed uproari-
ously, clapped Hank on the shoulder, and tore up the
ticket. Too bad. I had been about to tell Hank that I'd
warned him.

Since the rain had returned, the luggage compartment
could not be opened, and Charles de Gaulle had to sprawl
across the laps of Eliza, Sergeant Gambardella, and Albertine. I was left to reflect glumly that I had not and
would probably never, during this trip, get a chance to
question Hank about his connections, if any, with Ruggiero Ricci. The general was going to be very disappointed. In fact, he might think I had accepted the
assignment only for the opportunity of a trip to Naples,

which wouldn't be fair. It hadn't been that wonderful a trip.

Beside me, Bianca was giving Hank a detailed description of the heartburn that accompanied late pregnancy. I provided her with an antacid tablet. Since she was dubious about taking an American medicine about which she knew nothing, I read the instructions on the roll. "There," I said, having made my way through the directions for usage and a list of off-putting ingredients. " 'Safe for pregnant women.' You can chew it up without a qualm."

After the heartburn episode, we had a fairly peaceful interlude, if travel on that highway, the A3, could be considered anything but traumatic. Eliza mentioned that she and Francis were planning to spend several days in Rome before flying home and asked Bianca's advice on what new things had opened in recent years that they might not have seen. Bianca suggested Nero's Golden Palace, which had been excavated.

"Oh, I couldn't go to see that!" Eliza exclaimed. "What a dreadful man. Imagine playing one's violin when the city was burning down."

"Actually, he wasn't a violinist," I told her. "He was a really bad singer, who wanted to win the Olympic singing contest."

"I've never heard of a singing contest at the Olympics," Eliza protested.

I shrugged. Neither had I, but I remembered the story very clearly. "He came to a music festival in Naples to further his ambition and sang his way right through an earthquake. As bad as he was, he got a good round of applause from an audience who couldn't leave while the emperor was performing and were greatly relieved to be alive at the end. They left, and the stadium immediately collapsed."

Bianca laughed. "What was it? His singing or the earthquake that knocked the stadium down?"

Before I could say I had no idea, that there had been a bad earthquake the year before that might have started the undermining of the theater, Eliza, who hadn't laughed, asked whether he ever went to the Olympics.

"Oh, yes," I replied. "And he won because he wouldn't stop singing and no other competitor got to."

"Well, that's not fair," said Eliza, "although it's not as bad as the fiddling story." After that we were all quiet for a while.

The next problem was, to no one's surprise, Charles de Gaulle. His head was in Albertine's lap, she nodded off, and he stuck his nose over the seat. I shrieked and gave the nose a light bop, which, for all Albertine's complaints, was just the right thing to do. The dog kept his nose to himself for the rest of the trip, although his stomach took to rumbling, and I think we all worried that an accident of a nontraffic nature might be in the offing.

My pill evidently helped Bianca. She dozed off. So did everyone else, except Hank and I. Now was my opportunity. "I like Rome better than Naples," I said.

"Have you seen that much of Naples?"

"No, but I love Rome. I should have stayed over when I found out Jason wouldn't be able to get to Sorrento from Paris. Were you able to do any sightseeing before you drove to Sorrento?"

"Nope," he replied. "I got into Fiumacino, booked a room at an airport hotel and a car, caught as much sleep as I could, and headed for Sorrento early in the morning."

"Too bad," I said. "I was just thinking of how nice it would be to sit in the Piazza Navone, eating gelato and looking at the fountains. I'll bet it isn't raining there. Are the airport hotels nice? I've only stayed in the city."

"About what you'd expect," he replied. "On the expensive side for what you get."

Well, I hadn't found anything out so far. Could he have talked to Ricci, slept with Paolina, flown to Naples, driven to Sorrento to kill her, headed back to Rome to rent a room and car near the airport, then driven back to Sorrento? The answer was, probably not. "What hotel did you stay at?" If I kept asking questions, he was going to get suspicious, except that innocent people had no need to be suspicious.

"A Best Western. I get a discount there," he replied.

So much for that, I thought, and mentioned that I'd stayed at a Best Western in Tours and found it very comfortable, with edible food.

"Edible, huh? Now there's a testimonial they'll want to put in their ads."

I had to laugh. "You don't know what the rest of the food was like on that trip. *Edible* was a high point." After that, while trying to think of another question, I dozed off myself.

37
Another Ticket

Bianca

We must have been about halfway back to Sorrento when I woke up with cramps in my left foot and my right calf. Pregnant women get those along with nausea and heartburn. You name it, I had it with that pregnancy. The rain was coming down like the end of the world without an ark. I pressed the cramping foot hard against the hump in the floor, wishing I hadn't offered to sit in the middle where I couldn't stretch my legs out and the gearshift limited my mobility further. The foot eased up a bit, but my calf—oh, it felt as if the pain would eat it up. I guess I groaned because Hank asked what the problem was.

"Nothing, nothing," I mumbled. I could see that he had his own problems. With rain flooding the windshield, the wipers weren't keeping up. I couldn't see a thing and hoped his view of the road was better than mine. Biting my lip to keep from crying, I let up pressure on the foot and tried to stretch my wretched calf out. Both of them spasmed, and Hank muttered curses under his breath, as if he could feel my pain. Or had I interfered with his driving? I was on the right side of the floor shift, and he was reaching for it.

In trying to scoot further over, I woke Carolyn up. She mumbled something I didn't catch because not only was I suffering from two cramps again, but also the convertible roof had started to leak down my neck. Oh, perfect. I'd probably catch a cold.

"I've got to pull over to the side," said Hank, grabbing the stick shift and catching a piece of my skirt. "I can't see a damn thing."

"Thank God," I said. "I've got to walk around."

Carolyn, now fully awake, asked, "Where? You can't get out in this rain. I'd have to get out too, and we'll both be soaked."

Hank was edging cautiously over, but who knew where to? I certainly couldn't tell. "I've got to walk," I insisted.

"Are you going into labor?" asked Eliza. "They made me walk when I—"

"*Mon Dieu!*" cried Albertine. "You can't have the baby here, Bianca."

"I'm not." I could feel the car sliding. Hank turned into the skid. "My legs are all cramped up," I complained. "It really hurts."

"Jesus," said Hank. "Everybody shut up before we drive into a ditch."

But we didn't. The car came to a stop, and a sheet of water washed over us from another car passing, so we must have made it off the road. "I've got to get out!" I insisted.

Carolyn groaned and opened the door, saying, "I knew you shouldn't have sat in the middle." Then she tumbled out into the deluge. "Come on," she shouted at me.

Of course my leg hurt so badly I couldn't move, so she reached in and pulled me out while Hank pushed. Shades of the first time we met in the hall, when I couldn't get up off the floor. Carolyn, not very gently, stood me up, moved me to the middle of the opened door, and slid back inside. I started to cry. She was going to leave me out in the wind and rain by myself when I could hardly stand up.

"Start moving your weight from foot to foot," she ordered.

"We're getting wet back here," Albertine complained.

"Too bad," said Carolyn, who had taken my hands in hers and was saying, "Move, move."

I moved. The damn door only shielded the middle of me. My feet were squelching in mud, my chest and head were completely soaked, and I hurt. Oh Holy Mother, I did hurt!

"Any better?" Carolyn shouted.

Now I was hearing sirens and didn't bother to answer her. I just kept shifting my weight and sniveling because it hurt so much that I felt faint. Another wall of water roared over us, and I thought I'd be washed away, but Carolyn was hanging onto me so hard my hands hurt almost as much as my foot and calf. Ahead of the car I thought I saw flashing lights. Help had arrived. Maybe. No one was coming to *my* aid. "Over here," I yelled into the rain. "I'm an expectant mother. Help me." Thinking back, that sounded pretty stupid, but I was hoping for an ambulance. A nice, dry ambulance with a cot I could lie down on and medics to massage my poor legs and assure me that my baby was just fine.

But wouldn't you know? It was the police. And no one came to rescue me. An officer in a big rain hat and coat splashed over to Hank's side of the car and knocked on the window. He was shouting that we couldn't park here; it was illegal. That infuriated me so much that I stamped harder and harder, ready to go right around the car and tell him a thing or two. And the cramps let up. Oh, blessed Mary Magdalene, the pain was almost gone. Just that lingering soreness in the muscles. I moved cautiously to see if it would come back.

"You're okay?" Carolyn yelled. She'd paid no attention to the policeman who was trying to knock Hank's window in, while Hank just leaned his head on the steering wheel as if he'd had more than enough of all of us. "Get back into the car," Carolyn ordered.

I got back in, noticing that she, having moved over, had her knees under her chin because of the hump. Not that I was going to offer to change places this time.

"Keep your legs stretched out and move them from time to time," she advised as I pulled the door closed behind me. And did we look terrible, like two drowned cats ready to snarl at the first person that gave us trouble. And that was the policeman yelling at Hank and pounding on the window. *What the heck*, I thought. *I'm already soaked.* So I got out again and yelled over the car, "Hey you. Officer. Get over here before I go into labor."

The idiot heard me because the rain had let up a bit and no cars were presently passing. He splashed around the car, ready to yell at me until he got a look at my stomach.

"What's wrong with you?" I asked. "We're about to drown or get washed away, and you're not even offering to help."

"This is not a parking zone. I must see the ownership papers and the driver's license to drive," he insisted.

"It's a rental, he's an American, and I'm getting soaked. Why don't you just go away if you're not going to help?"

"I will have to arrest all of you," he said, peering into the back seat, where two women, a large French poodle, and Sergeant Gambardella were peering back. "If you don't cooperate, I will have to—"

Hank had passed his license to Carolyn, who passed it
to me. I shoved it at the officer, who took it up under the
shelter of his plastic rain hat and said, "This is in a foreign language."

While I was re-explaining that the driver was an
American so the license was in English, Hank was going
through his coat pockets, looking for the rental papers.
Finally he said, "They must be in the glove compartment," and reached across Carolyn.

"I'll get them," I shouted, ducking back in the car. "No
use everyone getting wet." I opened the box and shuffled
through the papers, looking at each carefully so that I
could stay out of the rain for a minute while Hank kept
offering to do it himself. Then I stuffed some papers back
in that didn't seem to be what the officer was looking for,
inched the door open, and handed out the rental contract.
It got a bit soggy between my hand and his hat brim, but
he read it over carefully, probably highly relieved to see
something in Italian.

Then he leaned down, and I edged the door open
again. "I don't like the foreign license, but the rental
seems all right. Now I will write a ticket for the illegal
parking."

For me that was the last straw. I shoved the soggy papers at Carolyn, from whom Hank grabbed them and
stuck them in his pocket. Now, that was going to do his
sports jacket a lot of good! Fortunately, his clothes
weren't my problem. Pushing the door open again and
shoving the officer back, I heaved myself out. "You're
going to give a ticket to a man who pulled off the road because he couldn't see and didn't want to kill me and my
baby and everyone else in the car?

"This isn't America, you know. Killing unborn babies
is illegal here, and it would be your fault. So we'll all go
back to your police station, and I'll tell your superior how

you've treated a pregnant woman, mother of two, who is this close to giving birth." I held my thumb and finger about a quarter inch apart and pushed them right under his nose. "What real Italian man would keep an expectant mother shivering in the rain, probably endangering both her health and the health of the child? You must be a Yugoslavian immigrant."

I could hear Carolyn behind me hissing, "Just take the ticket, for God's sake." In the back seat Sergeant Gambardella was roaring, "Let *me* talk to him."

"I'm not getting out in that," squeaked Eliza.

"You there," shouted the sergeant. "I am a sergeant of the Polizia de Stato in Sorrento, escorting these important visitors back from Naples. I intend to file a complaint against you for endangering my charges and myself, not to mention the unborn infant of this good lady."

The eager writer of parking tickets backed away, throwing up his hands, stamped around our car and back to his, and sped away, sending a shower of mud onto our windshield. I got back into Hank's car and said, "That was impressive, Sergeant Gambardella. I'm going to tell your lieutenant that you must be the best officer in his department." The sergeant flushed with pleasure, and Hank muttered that now all he needed to do was clean the windshield, change the wipers, and we'd be on our way.

Carolyn and Eliza were discussing the neon shrines they'd seen in Naples. Neither of them thought neon was a tasteful example of religious décor.

Lorenzo, my dear husband, was all kindness when I dripped into our room at the Grand Palazzo Sorrento. He helped me out of my wet clothes and into a warm shower, then tucked me into bed and fed me hot soup. It was heaven to be warm, dry, and free of leg cramps, with my children fast asleep and my husband sliding into bed, curling up behind me, and wrapping an arm around my shoulders.

"You know, Lorenzo," I said after I had related the high points of the adventurous trip to Naples. "It's the weirdest thing. I'm sure that while I was dozing I heard Hank tell Carolyn about flying into Fiumacino, getting a car and an airport hotel room, and then leaving early to drive to Sorrento for the meeting. But the rental papers I had to get out for the stupid policeman said Hank had rented the car in Sorrento the day before."

"You're sure of the date?" Lorenzo asked sleepily.

"Well, I was wet, and I was dripping on the paper, so I could have misread that, but I know it said Sorrento."

"He probably had trouble with the car coming down from Rome and turned it in for another one," said Lorenzo. "Remember the car we rented in Spain? Fifty kilometers into the countryside and the transmission broke down."

"And the children were crying, and that farmer came along, towed us to his house, and gave us a really bad wine to drink with some of his own olives." I laughed at the memory.

"Girol was lucky he made it to Sorrento. He could have been stuck anywhere along the way."

"Umm," I agreed. "And since he's American, there might have been no friendly farmer to give him a tow." Then we both dozed off, all comfy and warm.

When it rains in the Campania, one is best advised to stay safely inside a waterproof building or vehicle. I'd almost forgotten how wet an unwary tourist can become when confronted with a real thunder storm. I returned from a trip to Naples on such a day, sneezing and feeling on the verge of a terrible cold. Certainly I was not up to eating anything prepared by a Swiss chef, which would be our lot at our Sorrento hotel. I called the kitchen and begged them to provide us with something made by an Italian. A pot of vegetable soup arrived at our door. Never did anything taste better on a wild night after a comfortless day. My husband and I had three bowls each and went to bed. I am pleased to say that the fine Italian soup saved me from viral infections.

Ribollita
Italian Vegetable Soup

- Heat *3 tablespoons olive oil* in a large saucepan. Sauté gently in the oil for 10 minutes *2 chopped onions, 3 sliced carrots, 4 crushed garlic cloves, 2 thinly sliced celery stalks, and 1 trimmed and chopped fennel bulb.*

- Add *2 large, thinly sliced zucchini* and sauté for 2 minutes more.

- Add a *14-ounce can of chopped tomatoes, 2 tablespoons pesto (which can be purchased at your grocery store), 3 1/2 cups vegetable stock, and a 14-ounce can of drained pinto or navy beans.* Bring to a boil, reduce heat, cover and simmer gently for 25 to 30 minutes, until vegetables are tender. Season with *salt and pepper.*

- Sauté *1 pound young spinach leaves in 1 tablespoon extra virgin olive oil* until wilted.

- To serve, place *slices of crusty white bread* in soup bowls, top with spinach, ladle soup over spinach, and serve with extra virgin olive oil, which can be drizzled onto the soup, and *Parmesan cheese shavings* sprinkled on top.

Carolyn Blue,
"Have Fork, Will Travel,"
Milwaukee News-Register

Saturday

Yearning for Capri

The one place I particularly wanted to see during my trip to southern Italy was Capri. I had heard so much about its beauty, not to mention its food. A friend of Italian ancestry in El Paso told me that the one thing I had to eat, even if I didn't get to Capri, was *Torta Caprese*, which she said was "truly a dessert to die for." Here is a recipe, which I made when I got home. My husband and guests loved it.

Torta Caprese

- Chop as finely as possible *8 ounces of cooking chocolate and 2 cups of almonds with skins on.*

- In a bowl, beat until creamy *3/4 cup and 1 tablespoon of butter and 1 cup of sugar.*

- In a separate bowl beat *6 eggs* completely and add to the butter cream.

- Add chocolate and almonds and then stir in *2 1/2*

level teaspoons of baking powder and 2 tablespoons of a liqueur such as strega.

- Butter a springform cake pan, 22 inches in diameter, pour in mixture, and bake in a preheated oven at 350 degrees F for approximately 50 minutes.

- Turn the *torta* onto a wire rack to cool and then dredge in *confectioners' sugar.*

- Decorate with mint leaves and shaved chocolate (optional).

Carolyn Blue,
"Have Fork, Will Travel,"
Zanesville Bugle

38
Finally Capri

Carolyn

"**W**ake up, sleepy head," said a disgustingly cheerful voice in my ear.

Although I'd fumbled for the phone and mumbled something into it, I hadn't opened my eyes. Now I opened one, held the phone away from my ear, and eyed it with intense dislike. It seemed only a moment ago that Jason had awakened me with cheerful whistling in the bathroom, which was all very well for him; he hadn't gone through a trying day on the road and in Naples. He hadn't had to fend off thieves and policemen who did not believe it was their mission to serve the public. He hadn't been pummeled with heavy rain time and again. He hadn't been awakened from a deep sleep at eleven at night by a phone call from an irate general who wanted to know what I'd found out during my trip to Naples and who wasn't the least bit sympathetic about the rain and the dog and the police and the thief and the whole dreadful situation that had prevented me from asking Hank more than two questions the whole trip.

"As far as I can tell," I had said, "he was where he said

he was when Paolina died, in a Best Western Hotel near Fiumacino and then on the road to Sorrento in that miserable convertible. Surely there's someone in Rome who can check that out for you. And what have *you* found out about Constanza?" I asked sharply. I'm not all that cheerful when awakened from deep sleep.

"The people she claims to have stayed with in Milan have left town, so no one can confirm her alibi. Shopping won't do it. She could have shopped and taken a plane to Sorrento afterward. On the other hand, we have a good evidence-based case against her for killing her husband."

"Wonderful," I'd said and hung up. Not very helpful of me, but I'd never been more tired in my life than I was after that trip home from Naples.

And now some idiot was saying, "Wake up, sleepyhead" in my ear! I sneezed and said into the phone, "Who *is* this?"

"Hank," said the hoarse voice. He sounded as if he had a chest cold. "If you can get dressed and down to the entrance in twenty minutes, we can go to Capri. I've hired a boat and made reservations for lunch at a great Caprese restaurant. I even used the hotel's hair dryer on the car, so it's habitable."

"But what about the general?" I asked.

Hank laughed. "I didn't invite him. No, seriously, it's okay. We don't even have to take Gambardella along. The general must have crossed us off his list of suspects. So do you want to go or not? Bianca's game."

"What about Albertine and Eliza?" I asked, but without much enthusiasm.

"Didn't invite them. I've about had it with Albertine's dog and Eliza's plant-and-Mafia fetish, not to mention too many people in the car."

"Amen," I said. "Twenty minutes?"

"Right. Take the elevator that goes straight down to the

ground floor. I'll have the car out front on the turn-around."

"But what about breakfast?" I asked plaintively, thinking that surely there would be time for a piece of fennel toast and—

"Breakfast in Positano, lunch in Capri. Get moving. We don't want to miss the boat." And he hung up.

Capri! I thought. *Finally!* It's amazing how fast exhaustion can fall away when you have something wonderful to look forward to. I took note of the sunshine outside the balcony doors, showered and dressed in ten minutes, left Jason a note, and dashed out into the hall. Bianca was waiting at the elevator—no police guard to tell us we couldn't leave the floor. Hank was waiting outside, top down, not a cloud in the sky. I wouldn't even need the umbrella I'd prudently brought along.

With me in the back, taking pictures at every opportunity, and Bianca in front, stretching her legs to ward off cramps, asking how long we could spend shopping in Positano, and announcing that she was going to gorge on fish when we got to Capri, we were a merry threesome. Even the lingering odor of Charles de Gaulle blew away as we sped across the peninsula, and then onto the cliff highway.

Positano was a delight—white villas stepping down the steep cliffs right to the deep blue water below, winding streets, cafés, ceramics shops, fashion boutiques, cooking schools. I could see why it's called the Pearl of the Amalfi Coast. Under a striped umbrella, sitting in cushioned chairs in a café overlooking the town and the sea, we sipped espresso and devoured rolls veined with hazelnut paste. Then we shopped while Hank sat on a bench and coughed.

Bianca bought herself a beautiful lavender blue dress to wear after the baby was born. I had to wonder how many months it would be before she lost enough weight to get into it, but she was confident. Then she bought a brightly colored, round bowl that she intended to fill with candy for the children. While she was buying candy, I found a delightful sun hat with red and green streamers, a lovely shawl as delicate as a spider web, and a huge ceramic platter for which I had no use in mind and no idea how I'd get it home, but I couldn't resist. I could have stayed all day, but Hank insisted that we'd miss our boat if we didn't hurry. He stowed our purchases in the rear luggage compartment and hustled us into the car.

"Couldn't we have caught a boat from here?" I called from the back seat as I passed a cough drop forward. Obviously he hadn't used soup to stave off the effects of yesterday's rain.

"There's an overlook I wanted you to see, so I made arrangements to board further along the peninsula," he replied, sucking on the cough drop, which seemed to help. When we turned from the main coast road onto one that wove downward, the traffic almost disappeared.

"I wondered why we were going through Positano. It seems out of the way," said Bianca.

"Some sights aren't to be missed," said Hank. "Another half hour on the road is nothing compared to a view you'll remember until the day you die."

I had to agree with that sentiment, clutching my camera in anticipation. Still, how could any place be more beautiful than Capri, whose mythology involved Lucifer stealing a piece of heaven and planting it in the blue waters off the tip of the Sorrento Peninsula? "Will there be time to see the Blue Grotto?" I asked eagerly, having read of its ethereal light.

"Depends on the weather and finding a boatman to take us there," Hank answered, his cough starting up again.

"So what are you planning to eat on Capri, Carolyn, now that you've had *insalata Caprese* at least twice?"

"Yesterday hardly counts," I muttered resentfully. "Charles de Gaulle got most of mine, and I haven't forgotten that Adrien said poodles were hunting dogs and meat eaters. Have another cough drop. You may need to see a doctor."

"The dog wanted to eat out of the same plate you'd eaten from," said Bianca.

"That dog is not in love with me!" I insisted. "I think Albertine turned him against me and then sicced him on me every chance she got. When she's in her hotel room, she probably trains him to do awful things to me."

Hank laughed. "He's a young, male dog. Don't you remember how little boys expressed their affection? By being as obnoxious as possible." He pulled off a few miles along the way and we got out on a narrow stone path between two towering rocks.

"Maybe I'll have *ravioli Caprese*," I mused. "It's a two-cheese ravioli in tomato sauce, and for dessert— what else?—*torta Caprese*. It's a cake made of almonds, chocolate, and strega. Have you ever had strega, Hank? It's a local liqueur."

"Sure," he answered. "It's great."

"Or maybe I should have Rum Baba. Capri is famous for it." From the car we were picking our way through even larger rocks and around vegetation.

"It has an interesting history. A Polish king, Stanislaus, liked to dunk pieces of a favorite German cake with some unpronounceable name in rum, so the king's baker developed a method for soaking the cake in alcohol ahead of time to save his monarch the trouble. The king named it after Ali Baba in the *Arabian Nights*—although I have no idea why. Maybe it was his favorite bedtime story. Anyway, Stanislaus lost his throne and went to France—you know, I think his daughter was the queen there—and his dessert became popular in the French court, from which it was transported, with all things French, to the kingdom of Naples. Actually, since it's really French, maybe I'll stick with the *torta Caprese*." At that moment we came to the edge of the cliff.

"Capri," Hank said, pointing to the shadowed rise of the island from the sea. "Best picture you'll get of it," he promised.

I was enchanted and reached for my camera while Bianca looked over the cliff hundreds of feet down to the water crashing below. First I took several pictures of the island, then of foaming surf, bracing myself against a rock lest I fall.

"Now ladies," said Hank. "I have another surprise for you."

I turned, my head full of beautiful scenery and rich desserts, and he was pointing a gun at us. *A gun!*

"We can hardly be seen here from the road. Perfect choice on my part, isn't it?" he said, fishing a handkerchief from his pocket and blowing his nose with the gun-free hand.

I was stunned speechless. What in the—

"So you each have a choice. You can jump now, or you can lie down, and I'll throw you over one by one. And I'll take another one of those cough drops, Carolyn."

He looked quite serious about both the cough drops and killing us. Of all the nerve! He could cough until he choked before I'd give him another one of my Eucalyptus lozenges, I thought, incensed. In fact, maybe if his cough continued to worsen, we could overpower him. Or not. He was *so* large.

39

The Price of a Mistake

Bianca

Frightened out of my wits, I stared at Hank Girol, who was leaning against a rock, coughing and pointing the gun in our direction, while we, fools that we were, stood at the edge of the cliff. I realized too late that I had made some very serious mistakes. First, I should have taken that rental contract seriously. Second, even if I didn't take it seriously, I shouldn't have jumped at the chance to go to Capri. And third, I should have at least told Carolyn about the contract so she, who was not addled by advanced pregnancy, could have taken it seriously and refused to go anywhere with him. "You're kidding, right?" I asked hopefully.

"No, I'm not," he replied, no charming smiles or good-natured banter now. "Jump or lie down where you can't be seen if anyone should come down the road."

Carolyn hesitated, then lay down. For goodness sake! Wasn't she even going to argue for her life? At least she didn't lie down on the edge of the cliff where he could roll her off. She carefully eased herself down onto her stomach so that her head was directly in front of his feet.

Hank laughed. "Throwing yourself at my feet, Carolyn? Or is that just the best you can do, besides hogging the cough drops, to make things difficult for me? I hope you realize, my nosy little detective, that I'm granting your wish. I'm pretty sure that you'll be going to Capri. You should wash up there in a day or two."

"Why are you doing this?" I demanded. I was the one who'd be pushed over, obviously. No way could I lie down, certainly not on my stomach. Terror forced the blood into my face, and I felt as if I'd suddenly developed a high fever.

"Don't play dumb, Bianca," he chided. "You know why it came to this. You just had to read those rental papers, and then as soon as we got back, you had to tell Carolyn. You practically dragged her into the elevator so you could pass on the news."

"I did not," I protested. Oh, God! I was getting dizzy. I couldn't faint! I took a quick peek at Carolyn, who was untying his shoes. Why? Hoping he'd trip while carrying one or the other of us to the edge of the cliff. "We were both soaking wet and wanted to get to our rooms," I protested. "I didn't tell her anything." I side-stepped away from the edge so that I could put my back against a tall, safe rock. Hank just laughed at me.

"Then it's too bad she came along," he said, "but since she's here, she goes over too. No way I'm going to let you put me in Sorrento the night Paolina died." He wiped his nose as he scowled at me.

"Then you killed her?" Even at this point, I found it hard to believe that he had killed Paolina. "Why would you?" I was taking deep breaths in between each sentence, trying to overcome the dizziness induced by abject terror.

"The bitch had the intercom on, making notes on a conversation I had with Ruggiero in Catania. She snapped the machine off as I was coming out the door and shoved the notebook in her desk. Probably thought I didn't notice."

His voice, hoarse and angry, gave me the shivers, as if I wasn't already terrified. Still, I had to keep him talking because Carolyn, when I glanced at her, was now messing with both his shoelaces. I didn't know what she was up to, or what good it was going to do, but maybe we had a chance if I could keep him from looking down.

"Couldn't you have stolen the notebook? Or bribed her to keep quiet?"

"Not too bright are you, little Miss Italy." Another spasm of coughing hit him. "I did try to get the notebook," he snarled. "Ruggiero and I searched the office after she went home, then I followed her home and fucked her, and searched her apartment as soon as she went to sleep. No notebook. After that I told Ruggiero, who isn't much brighter than you are, not to meet her in Sorrento. He thought no way would she snoop on him; she was in love." Hank laughed derisively. "Like hell she was in love. Not with him. Not with anyone.

"I followed her to Sorrento, searched her room, still no book, so I caught her at the pool and dumped her over. The book was in the pocket of her robe. Just like I thought, it had notes on what we'd said, those and some stupid poetry. So with Paolina dead and the book in my hands, the problem was solved, or would have been if Carolyn hadn't kept sticking her nose in when Constanza almost had everyone convinced it was suicide. She probably thought she was protecting Ruggiero."

He snickered, which brought on his cough, but as soon as he mentioned Carolyn, I started toward him so he had to keep looking at me. "D-did you kill Ruggiero too?" I stammered.

"Sure. Once the general showed up, I couldn't trust Ruggiero not to try for a plea bargain by implicating me."

His mouth pulled into a cruel line, and he said, "Enough talking. Are you jumping, Bianca? If not, lie down. Right now."

"I can't lie down! In my condition, it looks like four miles to the ground. And I certainly can't lie on my stomach. Look at it." *And keep looking at it*, I thought. *Don't look at Carolyn.* "Are you really going to kill a woman carrying a baby? It's almost ready to be born. It's got fingers and toes and feelings and——"

"Shut up!" he snarled, and tried to take a step forward. Carolyn rolled out of the way as he fell, flinging out his arms in a futile attempt to maintain his balance. Still coughing, he rocketed headfirst into the rock behind my back. If he'd been shorter, he'd have missed the rock and hit the ground, but he was a very large man.

If I hadn't sidestepped, he'd have hit me. I just stood there, dumbfounded. "What did you do?"

Carolyn had jumped immediately to her feet and was running toward him. "Tied his shoelaces together," she said, kneeling beside him. "I can't believe it worked."

I got the giggles. Hysterical giggles. Tied his shoelaces together? That was something children did to each other. But I could see the blood leaking out from under his head. Still, what if he was conscious? With great difficulty I leaned over to pick up a rock, which I'd drop on his head if I had to, but then I wasn't able to straighten up. I could have cried.

"He's unconscious," she said. I turned my head sideways to see her rolling his eyelid up. Then she felt for a pulse and said, "But still alive." She glanced at me—bent over, clutching my rock in one hand, and trying to push myself up with the other. "What are you doing, Bianca?"

"Well, I was trying to get a weapon, but now——"

"The weapon was a good idea. I don't see his gun anywhere." Looking worried, she glanced at Hank, then walked over to me and hauled me upright.

"So what do we do now?" I asked. "We could leave him here and drive off."

"Do you have a cell phone?" She was brushing dirt off the front of her flower embroidered knit shirt and her matching slacks.

"No, I was in such a hurry to get ready for the trip to Capri that I forgot all about it."

"And I," said Carolyn, "don't have one at all. Jason doesn't believe in them."

I was astounded. "Everyone in Italy has a cell phone. In a few years I'll be getting one for the baby." I patted my stomach.

"Maybe *he* has one," said Carolyn, looking down at Hank. "On the other hand, maybe we don't want the police here. They might put us in jail and let him loose. I guess I'd better untie his shoelaces. That way it will look like he fell naturally."

"But if he wakes up and they're untied, he can push us over the edge," I protested.

"What we need to do is lock him in the luggage compartment and take him back to the general," Carolyn decided.

We both heard a car whoosh past and looked nervously toward the road. The car didn't stop. "He's huge, Carolyn," I pointed out. "There's no way we can get him to the car, much less into the luggage compartment, which may not be large enough to hold him. It would attract attention if there was a leg hanging out."

"You're right," she agreed. "We have to flag down a car and get someone to help us."

"Help us what? Put him into the luggage compartment? How are we going to explain that?"

"Into the back seat. We'll say he fell, and he's your husband. You can act all hysterical."

"I feel hysterical," I muttered.

Carolyn nodded. "And they'll put him in the back seat for us, and we'll drive home."

"Praying he doesn't come to while the Good Samaritans are getting him into the car," I added.

"Or while we're driving back," Carolyn agreed. "One of us will have to sit in back with a rock and knock him out again if he regains consciousness."

"Well, if you can get me in the back seat, I'll sit *on top* of him. No way he can get up with me using him for a chair. And I wouldn't mind hitting him. Actually, maybe we should just roll him off the cliff."

"How will we explain it to the general when we come home in Hank's car but without Hank?" Carolyn asked.

"I wonder how he was going to explain coming home without us," I retorted.

"And we have to deliver him to the general, or the general will continue to think Constanza is the killer."

I sighed. "You're right. We have to take him back. We can't leave Constanza in jail."

"But there's another problem," said Carolyn. "I can't drive a stick shift."

I groaned. How was I going to get my stomach behind the wheel of the car and still reach the pedals? "I vote we roll him off the cliff and worry about the explanations later."

"But that's murder," Carolyn objected.

40
On Handling a Large,
Unconscious Man

Carolyn

I offered to walk to the road and flag down a car, but Bianca didn't want to be left alone with him, so she went, and I sat down on a rock, ready to hit him with a more portable rock if he woke up and hoping not to be caught in the act by any strangers she might inveigle into helping us. As I waited, I mused on the things he'd said. Something about a car rental that Bianca obviously knew about but had neglected to tell me. And he'd admitted to both killings. Could he be convicted on our testimony? Undoubtedly he'd deny having confessed.

After about fifteen minutes I began to worry about Bianca. What if she had passed out, or fallen and hurt herself, or gone into labor? Maybe she was suffering from heat stroke and was too weak to wave down a car. I felt overheated myself. After studying Hank carefully and detecting no signs of returning consciousness, I decided that I could afford a trip to the car for my new sun hat, which proved to be a good decision. I felt much more comfort-

able with it on my head. I'd give Bianca another fifteen
minutes and then—what? Leave him here and walk to the
road? I couldn't do that unless I found his gun. He could
wake up and come after us with it. So I had to find it, but
it didn't seem to be anywhere in the area, not under or on
top of any of the rocks.

I thought back to his fall. The gun hadn't gone off
while he was trying to maintain his balance. Maybe it was
underneath him. The thought of trying to retrieve it sent a
shudder through me. However, if Bianca came back with
help, and they lifted him up and saw the gun, they'd know
something was wrong with our story. People in Europe
aren't like people in Texas; they aren't allowed to go
around with guns in their glove compartments and pockets. Which made me wonder how Hank had gotten hold of
his. He certainly hadn't brought it with him.

I stared down at him with dismay. He was *so* big! I
made another search of the area for the gun. It definitely
wasn't here, and the chances that it had flown over the
rock on which he'd hit his head and fallen into the sea
were minimal indeed. Biting my lip, I leaned forward and
tried to nudge him over. No luck. It was going to take
more than a nudge. I knelt and tried again with a hearty
shove. Still no luck. What I needed was a lever. Alas, the
only thing I could think of was my beautiful platter in the
trunk, and I needed the car keys to get into the trunk.

Gritting my teeth, I stuck my hand into his trouser
pocket, expecting that he would leap up and grab me.
Thank God, he didn't, and the keys were in that pocket,
although very difficult to extract. I had the ring, but a key
must have caught on something. Desperate, I gave the
ring a sharp tug, heard the sound of cloth ripping, and the
key ring came free. But now his pocket had a noticeable,
jagged tear. Would the hoped-for rescuers think that

strange? At least, Hank still seemed to be unconscious. So far, so good.

I walked backward to the car, thinking he could wake up any minute, unless he was going to die. Oh dear, would tying his shoelaces together with malicious intent constitute murder? Or self-defense? Did they have a self-defense plea in Italy? I opened the trunk, pulled it toward me, and peered in—and what did I see? Besides the clutter of our shopping trip, a tire iron. Perfect. I wouldn't have to ruin my platter. I almost fell into the trunk trying to retrieve the tire iron. What kind of a car was this anyway? Convertibles were supposed to have bucket seats. This one had bench seats. Convertibles were often two-seaters. This car seated six if you didn't mind being squished together. And the luggage area worked more like an old-fashioned rumble·seat. While I was hanging over the edge, my legs dangling, I expected Hank to come up behind me, shove me inside, and lock me up. To avoid that, I kept a tight grip on the keys.

Then I rushed nervously back to my prisoner and tried various methods for levering him at least halfway over. Just working the tire iron under him and pulling up on the free end didn't work at all. My second idea was to put a round rock in the middle of the iron, work the iron under him, and push the rock closer and closer to his body. Then finally I pushed on the free end of the iron. His body lifted a bit in the center. I sat down sideways on the iron beyond the rock, and Hank lifted a few inches more. I think I may have broken one of his ribs in the effort.

Keeping my weight in place, I bent forward and spotted the butt of the gun. Although I thought I could reach it and still keep the lever in place, I didn't want to get my fingerprints on the gun and perhaps smear his. As the rod holding Hank's weight pressed painfully against my thighs, I pondered the problem. There was nothing for it.

I took off my sun hat and pulled my knit shirt over my head. Then I covered my hand with the shirt and dragged it through the dust toward Hank's body and the gun just showing beneath it. And it was such a pretty shirt, too, with bluey-purple irises and green leaves embroidered on it.

I was leaning to the side, sliding my hand and wrist under Hank, when my weight evidently lifted enough from the iron to allow Hank's weight to snap his end of the rod down. I fell off, the rod rolled off the rock, and I was trapped with my hand, still clutching the gun butt, and part of my forearm under the unconscious body. I was lucky my arm hadn't broken in the accident. Gritting my teeth, holding the gun fast, I finally wormed my arm out from under him. Then I sat and trembled for a while as I massaged my gun hand and arm. When I had recovered enough to remember that Bianca might be coming with help, and me in my bra and nothing else above the waist, I put the gun down and pulled the tire iron out from under Hank's body. That was even harder than getting my arm out. I had to rest on my hands and knees, panting.

That's when I heard voices coming down the trail. Panic! I shoved the tire iron under a rock, grabbed the gun, jumped up, and slipped it into my waistband. Then I pulled the filthy shirt over my head and smoothed the back over the bulge made by the gun, all the while trying to look unflustered while Bianca and three men edged by the car and walked into the clearing.

"Bianca," I cried, plucking up my sun hat and plopping it onto my head, "I've been so worried about you. Are you all right?" Then before she could answer, I added, "And I'm even more worried about your husband. He hasn't come to."

She tried to look frightened and tearful, rather than re-lieved, eyed my shirt with a puzzled glance, and introduced me to the three Italians who had agreed to help. Evidently, once they got a look at the man they were expected to get into the car, they decided that it would be wiser to use one of their cell phones to call an ambulance. Bianca promptly burst into tears and floods of Italian, not to mention wild gestures, many of which included her stomach.

I guess they decided not to argue with a hysterical, pregnant woman, who, for all I knew, had terrified them by threatening to go into labor. The poor fellows had a terrible time getting him to the car, and even more trouble lifting him over the side and stuffing him into the back seat. Then there was another long discussion. I think, from what little Bianca translated, that they offered to follow us to the hospital, while she insisted that they had already been so helpful that she wouldn't dream of asking them to go out of their way. She finally got rid of them by shaking their hands, kissing their cheeks, and motioning for me to do the same, both of us weeping and thanking them for their kindness in two languages.

They trudged back to the road, and Bianca leaned weakly against the car. I looked into the back seat to see how Hank was doing, his upper body flat on the seat, his head oozing blood onto the upholstery of the seat back, and his legs bent awkwardly to fit into what little space was left. He was still unconscious.

"I found a tire iron," I said, trying to sound cheerful. "And the gun." I carefully covered my hand with my shirttail and fished it from the waistband of my slacks, thinking, belatedly, that it could have gone off and killed me while those men were trying to be more helpful than we wanted or needed.

"Great," she said. "Then you can sit in front with me. If he wakes up you can reach back and hit him with the tire iron or shoot him with the gun. I don't think you'll be able to get in with him once we've moved the front seat back far enough that I can get both me and my stomach behind the wheel."

That certainly proved to be the case. Once we were in, another problem developed. The seat was so far back that Bianca couldn't reach the pedals. "You don't think you could *learn* to stick shift, do you?" she asked hopefully.

I shook my head. I'd tried on a car of Jason's before we were married, and it had been a disaster—literally. I did something terrible to the ignition after putting it into the wrong gear and backing into a tree. Or was it the gears that I destroyed?

What we finally worked out was bizarre, to say the least. Bianca sat sideways so her left foot could reach the clutch pedal. I sat in the middle with one leg on the far side of the gearshift so I could work the gas and brake pedals. Since I was sure we'd be killed before we made it back to Sorrento, I now wished fervently that we hadn't chased the three men off. Then, on top of all our other problems, we couldn't get the top up. If Hank awakened and I had to hit him or shoot him, presuming I got turned around in time to do it, I'd have to attack in full view of anyone on the road.

We scraped both sides of the car backing out between towering rocks, were almost smashed by an oncoming car while trying to get across the road into the lane to Sorrento, ground the gears shifting from reverse to first, shouted at each other, both panic stricken, and then began the long, slow, terrifying drive home. Bianca had to shift, steer, and ease the clutch in and out. I was the gas-and brake-pedal person. I did not press hard on the gas and had trouble reaching the brake. A lot of people honked at us and passed us in dangerous fashion before we ever got off the reasonably empty road and onto the coast road.

41
Prisoner in Route — Driver in Distress

Bianca

We weren't doing too badly once we got on the coast road. I shifted gears as seldom as possible, which was hard on the car, but who cared? It was only Hank's rental car, that scoundrel. I should have been wary of all that charm in an American. Eventually everyone behind us risked their lives to pass, and we ended up behind a tour bus. It wasn't one of those that stopped at every path down the cliff to a small hotel. If it had been, I'd have had a nervous breakdown. I was hoping it would go straight back to Sorrento, clearing the way on the sharp curves with us behind it.

The worst problem for a while was the exhaust that blew in our faces. Carolyn was coughing, and I was trying not to because I didn't want to stir up the baby. He evidently liked my position, body turned partially to the right, left leg stretched out to reach the clutch, foot tucked away from Carolyn's share of the pedals. The baby had gone off to sleep as soon as we got moving, whereas, while I was waiting at the edge of the road for a car to flag down, he'd been giving me boisterous kicks. My back felt as if it were broken and my poor stomach was bruised on the inside by the time the Good Samaritans came along and stopped.

They were pretty surprised when I stood up, and they saw the monster tummy. I suppose they thought they were coming to the aid of a pretty young thing, not a super fat mother-to-be. But what could they do? Drive off and leave a pregnant woman on the road? No way. They were Italians, and I'm adept at playing the mother card. After three pregnancies, I should be. Maybe I should get my tubes tied, since Lorenzo and I didn't seem to be able to practice birth control successfully, although I blame Giulia for the last slip-up. How many Hail Marys would I have to say to make up for a tubal ligation? Maybe they'd kick me right out of the church.

Then our situation changed abruptly. That was no baby kick! That was a contraction! "Carolyn, get ready to speed up. I'm going to pass the first chance I get."

"I'll do no such thing," she said, turning her head from the strained position that allowed her to keep tabs on Hank. "We should stay right behind the bus. Even though we may require respiratory therapy when we get back, at least we have a chance of making it to Sorrento in one piece."

"I just had a contraction."

"One contraction doesn't mean anything," she assured me. "One contraction is false labor, a common, but non-predictive event."

"Not this contraction. Take my word for it." I spotted a gap in the traffic and swung the wheel, yelling, "Give it the gas." Carolyn screamed, but she didn't put her foot down. "Damn it, if you leave us out here, we're dead." She saw a car down the road hurtling toward us and pressed down on the gas. I got past the bus, just barely, and swung in sharply. The bus driver laid on the horn. The driver coming toward us slammed on the brakes and laid on his horn. Carolyn started to cry. I said, "Stop sniveling and pay attention. And don't let up on the gas unless I tell you."

Finally we approached the turnoff that would take us across the peninsula. "Faster," I yelled, and swung in front of an oncoming car, across the oncoming lane of the crossroad, and back into my own lane. "Now, don't take your foot off the gas," I ordered, a little less stridently. Contraction number two hit. *Oh, Holy Mother. That is much too close to the first one. Please, please let the baby lose interest and go back to sleep*, I prayed.

"You have to do everything I tell you to do, and no arguing," I ordered, having finished my appeal to the Holy Mother. "Carolyn, are you listening? We could end up on the side of the road with me giving birth. Do you know how to deliver a baby?"

"No," she admitted in a voice so soft and quavering I could hardly hear her.

"Then pay attention, and press down on the gas. This is the best chance we'll have to make some time, even if this is an awful road."

She obeyed, and we arrived at the coast road on the other side of the peninsula with only three more contractions. But they really, really did hurt! I was sweating when I swung wide to the right and almost clipped a Mercedes truck. He slewed off the road and back on, and, of course, he honked loudly and repeatedly. Italian drivers think of their horns as another gear or pedal.

Okay, I'm on the last stretch to Sorrento, I told myself. *I'm going to make it to the hotel.* Later I wondered why I wanted to get to the hotel. I should have been looking for a hospital. "Keep your foot down on the gas, and take a look at Hank." We kept moving. In fact, we sped up when she turned her body. I didn't complain. I passed the car in front of me. Carolyn saw what I was doing and gasped.

The driver honked. The woman in the Japanese car on the other side honked, and I pulled back in. All up the coast this side of the peninsula I could see the black clouds building. Why couldn't this have been the one afternoon it didn't happen? Then it started to rain. As if we didn't have enough problems. As if we knew how to get the top up, even if we could stop to do it.

"I have an umbrella," said Carolyn. "Should I put it up?"

"Thanks," I said, "but I don't think that would work." Another contraction hit. Number—what, five? Six? What was I going to do?

"Hank's still unconscious," said Carolyn, probably trying to cheer me up. "I hope the rain doesn't bring him around."

"Well, don't bother with the tire iron if he wakes up. Just shoot him. But be careful where you aim. We don't want a bullet in the gas tank or a tire, just in him. I think—" I gasped as another contraction wrenched my stomach and twisted my spine. "I think the best thing would be to lean over the seat and shoot straight down at his chest or head."

"But my foot might come off the gas if I—"

"Oh, don't worry. We'll face that problem if we come to it. Speed up!"

She pressed down, I swung out, everyone honked, and we made it back into our own lane. *Oh, for a wide, wide autostrada*, I thought, imagining myself weaving in and out of many, many lanes.

And there was the sign for Sorrento. We were going to make it. "Let up some on the gas," I ordered as I headed off the coast road and over the hill that would take us to the hotel. "Brake!" She braked, I shifted and swung in, and we pulled up nose to the entrance doors, having knocked over two large cement pots and torn down a bush in the central garden through which we passed because I couldn't make a sharp enough turn to catch the actual circular driveway. Then I closed my eyes and leaned my head against the back of the seat.

"Bianca," said Carolyn. "We're here."

I just kept sitting there, waiting for the next contraction, wondering if I'd have to roll out of the car to let the baby out of me. Could a baby being born get through panties and slacks? Doormen rushed over to us. They made frantic calls upstairs to the lobby. Neither one of us moved. We didn't even look back at Hank, but he didn't move either, so that was all right.

Hotel employees from the lobby rushed off the elevator, followed by the general, Marsocca, Loppi, Lieutenant Flavia Vacci, and Lieutenant Buglione. *Word gets around fast*, I thought, feeling dazed. Hitting those pots had been jarring, even though we didn't hit them head on. More like glancing blows. Still—

The general stuck his face right into mine and shouted, "You did not have permission to leave the hotel."

"I'm in labor," I mumbled.

"Don't shout at Bianca," said Carolyn, rising up on a knee and shaking her finger at him. "We've brought the murderer back. He tried to kill us because Bianca found out he was in Sorrento when Paolina died."

"You did not have permission—"

"He killed them both—Paolina and Ruggiero. See. He's in the back seat."

The general looked into the back seat, then looked again. "What did you do to him?"

"I'm having a baby here," I said. "I need to lie down. I can't have a baby sitting up in a convertible, in case you people don't know that."

42
A Tale to Tell

Carolyn

Amid all the hubbub, I suggested to the general that we needed two ambulances. Agent Marsocca made the call on his cell phone and announced that there would be at least a ten-minute wait because all the local ambulances had been called out.

"I don't have ten minutes," gasped Bianca, who was panting through a contraction. "For God's sake, get me upstairs. I don't want to deliver down here by the road."

The general took charge, ordering his aides to see that Hank was taken to the hospital when the ambulance arrived and guards put on him while he was there. "What happened to him?" the general asked me.

Meanwhile Lieutenants Buglione and Vacci organized men to carry Bianca to the elevator. I wanted to go with her, but the general wanted an answer, and Bianca couldn't wait.

"Well," I began, embarrassed, "He told us you gave us permission to go to Capri. Then he took us to an overlook for a view of the island, pulled a gun on us, and said we either had to jump off the cliff or lie down on the ground so we couldn't be seen from the road while he threw us off one by one. I lay down directly in front of him, hoping I could do something to save us. Bianca argued because lying down on the ground was almost impossible for her, especially on her stomach, and there was the baby to consider—lying down on rocky ground wouldn't be good for the baby, and so forth. Anyway, she kept him talking, and I—well, I tied his shoelaces together."

The general gave me a very peculiar look, which I rather resented. In my position, I doubt that he could have come up with anything better. "It's not as if I had a weapon or know anything about self-defense," I said. "I did the best I could under the circumstances."

"So it would seem," said the general. "Please go on. I'm most interested to hear what happened next."

Was he being sarcastic? I hardly thought I deserved that attitude. After all, I'd delivered the murderer to him. "Well, as I said, Bianca kept him talking. She asked questions and complained about his planning to kill the baby and all. He said he killed Paolina because he caught her with Ruggiero's intercom on. She was taking notes, although he didn't say about what."

"He was selling Ruggiero a container in which heroin couldn't be detected," said the general. "We got that off my daughter's tape. Your Hank Girol is Enrico Girolamo. He has Mafia connections in New Jersey, and Ricci was going into a different kind of drug business."

"I had it right then!" I exclaimed, quite pleased with myself. He could have congratulated me, but he didn't. Probably jealous that I'd figured it out without the cleaned-up tape. "And then he killed Ruggiero when you showed up because he didn't want him—Ruggiero—getting arrested and trying for a plea bargain by getting him involved—him being Hank." The general was frowning. All those masculine pronouns were no doubt confusing him. Although I'd been careful to identify the antecedents. "Anyway, instead of agreeing to lie down or jump, Bianca started toward him, which was very brave of her, and I rolled out of the way. When he tried to grab her, he fell forward because his feet were tied together. He hit his head on a rock and passed out."

"I can't tell you how unlikely that story sounds, Signora," said the general.

"Well, if you don't believe me, I can take you back to the scene, because his blood is on the rock. He fell quite hard, and he's probably seriously injured if the time he's been unconscious is any indication."

"How long is that?" asked the general.

"I have no idea, but it seemed like hours," I replied. "While Bianca was on the road getting help, I had to find his gun so he couldn't wake up and shoot us." Should I admit that I might have broken Hank's ribs? I didn't want to, but the truth is always best, so I added, "You may find that he has broken ribs. I found a tire iron in the trunk, so I used it to turn him over—at least partially—since the gun wasn't anywhere to be found. I was right, as it turned out. It was under his body, but I did hear a funny sound while I was levering him up with the tire iron. Of course, I didn't mean to cause him any further injury, but what was I to do? No one wants to risk being shot by a criminal.

"Then Bianca flagged down three men who lifted him into the back seat of the convertible, but driving it was a problem for us. I can't drive a stick shift, and Bianca, in order to fit her tummy behind the wheel, could only get one foot on a pedal. So she shifted, and I pressed the gas pedal and brake. It was very awkward and uncomfortable, not to mention dangerous. And then, of course, she went into labor, so we had to speed up and pass cars, which was terrifying, and finally it started to rain. Being rained on in an open convertible, whose top refuses to close, is dreadful. We both found it a very stressful trip back to Sorrento, and I hope you'll explain to hotel management that we didn't mean to destroy their garden." I waved at the tipped, cracked pots and the crushed bushes. "They are so picky about ordinary things. Goodness knows what they'll say about our driving through their landscaping and breaking their pots."

The general, who had been leaning against the remains of the rental car, watching the removal of Hank from the back seat and listening to me, started to laugh.

"That, Signora, is a story that will live in memory in my department. You'll have to dictate it for the record, and I may well have the typed testimony framed and hung in my office. Perhaps with suitable drawings."

"Very funny!" I snapped and walked away without permission. I'm happy to say that he didn't try to stop me. Perhaps he realized that my duty was now to Bianca—or that laughing at me was not a very tactful thing to do.

43

In the Manager's Office

Carolyn

When I arrived in the lobby, there was a terrible hulla-baloo. Signor Villani was insisting that Bianca be taken back down to await an ambulance. Bianca insisted that she be taken into his office so that she could give birth with some privacy.

"Signora, you cannot have a baby in my office," cried Signor Villani. "It is not proper. There is no midwife or doctor. I'm sure it is against hotel rules."

"Don't be a fool," said Albertine, who was at the desk for whatever reason. "The woman needs to lie down. Do you expect her to give birth on the floor of your lobby? If so, I shall certainly file a complaint with your head office. In Geneva, isn't it? Here, Madame Blue, give me a hand. We must help her into the office while there is still time."

So we walked poor Bianca, who seemed to be having one contraction after another, if her moans were any indication, through the door marked "Pietro Villani, Man-ager." After all his objections, we discovered that he had not only a sofa, but a chaise longue, of which Bianca said, at the end of a wail, "That one. Get my slacks and panties off."

"I don't know how to deliver a baby," I protested, weak-kneed with fright. "Do you, Madame Guillot?"

"No. But you must call me Albertine, both of you. This is certainly not the most formal of situations. We are three women, pulling together at a time of—"

"Oh, shut up, and call Gracia," snapped Bianca. "She'll know what to do. I don't want to have to direct my own delivery."

"Of course," I agreed. "Six sons. She'll—"

"Now," ordered Bianca. We had both been trying to relieve her of her lower-body clothing while she thrashed around.

I ran to the telephone, got Jill on the line, thank goodness, and told her that Bianca was giving birth—

"Right now?" gasped Jill.

"Yes, and we need Gracia Sindacco. This very minute."

Freed of her clothes, Bianca half leaned against the back of the chaise longue, drew up her knees, gave a shriek, and asked if she was crowning. I'm embarrassed to say that I didn't want to look. My experiences with childbirth had involved numbing shots, giggle gas, and a doctor out of sight behind the draperies. It had been a somewhat distant experience once I was no longer in pain and telling people that I'd changed my mind and didn't want to have a baby after all. I'm told that is a common reaction, that and shouting curses at one's husband, which, of course, I'd never do under any circumstances. What a way to welcome a child into the world.

Fortunately, Albertine, who'd never even had a baby, was braver than I and took a peek. "*Oui*, I think that might be a patch of the head showing. Should you be bearing down now?"

"How should I know?" Bianca groaned. "Someone always told me what to do."

Then, thank goodness, Gracia arrived, took a look, and said, "Why should I help you people, who are responsible for my mistress being arrested?"

"No, no, Gracia," I cried anxiously. "We've cleared her. The general will have to release her immediately because the murderer confessed, and Bianca and I brought him back. He has a serious head injury, I think, but the general knows now that we're right. So please, please, help Bianca."

Gracia snorted and began to issue orders, in Italian in a crooning voice to Bianca, in English in a not very friendly tone to us. We heated water in the manager's coffee pot; we got towels from the manager's private bathroom and wet washcloths to bathe her face. If Gracia had told me to begin flamenco dancing to entertain the patient, I'd have tried and insisted that Albertine join me.

"A girl," said Gracia brusquely. "Too bad. A boy is always preferable." She handed the baby, who was all messy, to me and ordered me to clean it up and return it to Bianca. I was terrified. The child was amazingly teeny considering how huge Bianca had been. What if I injured it? But Gracia gave me a mean look, and I hurried into the bathroom, thinking she could have given Bianca's newborn daughter to Albertine. My feelings wouldn't have been hurt.

There was a good-sized, but shallow sink in the bathroom, but the baby was so slippery, not to mention the fact that she was wailing noisily. She probably realized I didn't know what I was doing. I couldn't just put her in the sink and turn on the water. What if it came out hot or freezing? I sat down on the toilet lid and shifted her carefully to my shoulder with my hand holding her head and my arm flattened against her little body. Then I rose shakily and used the other hand to run and test the water and stop up the sink, all the time humming in the baby's ear, which didn't seem to make her any happier, and thinking that my blouse and maybe even my slacks were never going to be the same.

"Okay," I said softly, lowered her into the shallow sink, and splashed water over her. She didn't like that either. Gwen had loved baths, but then she'd been older. A knowledgeable nurse probably administered Gwen's first bath. Well, this wasn't working very well. The water was getting all messy. I opened the drain, turned the tap at exactly the place it had been before, and grabbed a washcloth. Better. She was still wailing, but I had her pretty well cleaned up. Now for a towel. The bath towels were gone. We'd used them all, so I draped a hand towel on my shoulder, placed the baby there, and draped another hand towel on her back.

Then I took her out to her mother, feeling quite proud of myself.

"Good God, Carolyn, I was afraid you'd drowned her," said Bianca, who was lying flat and reaching for her baby. "Oh, you sweet, beautiful thing you," she crooned, bringing the towel bundle down on her chest. The baby immediately stopped crying. Now *that* hurt my feelings.

"We'll call you Gracia, won't we?" Bianca beamed at Gracia. A stream of baby talk followed from Bianca while Albertine and I stood around, smiling but useless, and Gracia did midwife-type things. Rubbing Bianca's stomach and whatnot. Frowning. Why was she frowning? The baby had seemed fine to me. Then Bianca let out a shriek, and the baby started to cry again. You can't blame her for that. There she was, all clean and warm and cuddled against her mother, and there's this dreadful shriek.

"I thought so," said Gracia. "There's another one coming. How many did your doctor say?"

"One," said Bianca. She looked pretty disgusted. "Four children? We'll never live this down. Everyone in the department will be whispering behind our backs. Oh God! Carolyn, take the baby." Her back arched, and she thrust little Gracia toward me. However, Albertine stepped forward and grabbed the baby.

"Carolyn will need to take care of the new one," Albertine said, and plopped the shrieking bundle of towels against her shoulder.

"We're out of towels," I moaned. "Completely out."

"Then get some," said Gracia as she went about delivering a second child.

I ran to the door and called out into the lobby. "We need more towels. Immediately. Lots more." People started running around. I considered running away but decided that wouldn't be a very nice thing to do.

"And a blanket and sheets," Gracia commanded. I relayed that.

Five minutes later Bianca gave birth to a son. In all the excitement, we never even thought to call Lorenzo out of the meeting. Lucky Lorenzo.

44
A Postnatal Gathering

Carolyn

Once we'd done all the work, the ambulance arrived. Violetta, with Andrea and Giulia in tow, learned from lobby gossip, in this case Eliza, that Bianca had given birth. Violetta then called Lorenzo out of his meeting, and the whole family trooped after the stretcher carrying Bianca and the two babies. Giulia could be heard thanking her mother, as the family squeezed into the elevator, for having two babies, one for each sibling. She thought her brother might have wanted to share little Gracia if a boy hadn't arrived for him. "No trouble at all, sweetheart," said Bianca gaily. Then she called to me before the elevator doors could close.

"I owe you an apology, Carolyn," she said.

"Whatever for?" I asked.

"I thought you were the one who killed Paolina."

"Me?" I echoed, astounded. "Why in the world would you think that?" But I never got an answer because the closing doors separated us.

Eliza then told me that I really needed to change my clothes—as if I didn't know it—but that I must come straight back to the lobby and tell her what had happened. Absolutely, Albertine agreed, and warned me that if I took a nap, as I had announced I intended to do, I'd have nightmares. She said what I needed was conversation and several stiff drinks to bolster me after our mutual ordeal. *Mutual ordeal?* I thought. *She didn't have to wash off two slippery babies in the manager's sink.* Signor Villani had rushed back into his office once we'd vacated it. How I'd have loved to see his reaction to the state of his chaise longue and bathroom, not to mention the piles of towels tossed onto the carpet.

Since a stiff drink sounded good to me, I did return after showering and changing clothes, and we three ladies went into the bar and sat in comfy chairs with cocktails in our hands while I told my story. Of course, they were horrified at what Bianca and I had been through and impressed with my innovative solution to imminent death. I was impressed myself. So far only the general had found my strategy laughable. Eliza did remark that if Hank hadn't been a fellow American, I might have realized earlier that he, not Constanza, was the murderer.

"Oh?" I said. "And when did you suspect him?"

"I'm always suspicious of people who won't stop the car when I come upon an absolutely smashing plant," Eliza replied.

She never had a clue, I thought, but I let it go.

Albertine asked if Constanza had been released from hotel arrest, an arrangement that had to be explained to me. It seemed that the general had sent Constanza to another hotel under guard, where she was held and questioned in the comfort befitting her noble ancestry. In fact, word had come back that she liked the food in her new hotel much better than anything the Swiss chef could produce and had announced to Agent Loppi that if Ricci Chemicals held any more conferences in Sorrento, the

Grand Palazzo Sorrento would lose its place to her new favorite. Agent Loppi was of the opinion that Signora Ricci-Tassone had no firm grasp on reality if she thought Ricci Chemicals would even survive after the general got through with it. However, no one on the general's staff had thought Constanza guilty of anything but murder.

My, how police business does get around, I reflected. *Even federal secret agents can't keep their mouths shut.* The general dropped in and had a drink with us. "Girol has a fractured skull," he announced. "They're operating on him now. Of course, he may not live to face trial for the two murders, but I congratulate you, Signora Blue, for wheedling a confession out of him while you tied his shoelaces together." And the general started laughing again. I was about to say something I might have regretted, when he stopped laughing and said, "I hope the bastard stays alive long enough to feel some pain, a lot of pain, for what he did to my daughter."

For a minute there I'd forgotten that the general was in mourning. He was so stoic. I patted his arm and said, "She was a delightful young woman. And extraordinarily beautiful."

"Thank you," said the general. "She was, wasn't she?"

"In fact, I have pictures of her on my camera. If you would you like to choose some, I'll have them printed and sent to you."

"That would be very kind."

We were all looking at pictures of Paolina when the chemists finally got out of the meeting and joined us in the bar. That's when I realized that someone was going to have to tell Sibyl that her husband was not only in the hospital with a fractured skull, but also that he had committed two murders. I let the general do it. He'd only gotten as far as the fractured skull when she burst into tears and threw herself into Jason's arms.

It was at that moment that my jealousy of Sibyl ended. My husband looked completely flummoxed. He stared at her in dismay, this woman who, because she was much taller than he, was putting a crick in her neck in order to cry on his shoulder. Then he turned to me with the most helpless look. If ever a man needed rescuing, Jason was that man. I wouldn't have chosen myself for the job, considering that I was more or less responsible for Hank's condition, but Sibyl didn't know that. She hadn't heard a quarter of the story. I pried her gently away from my husband, murmuring sympathetically, patting her on the back, providing tissues, and suggested that she'd want a cab so that she could go straight to the hospital to be with Hank.

She was very grateful and went along with me to the desk and then downstairs to the entrance where the cab pulled up much more promptly than the ambulances had. I helped her in, handed her a whole pack of travel Kleenex, and sent her on her way. I suppose I should have prepared her for the double-murder part of the story, but there were police there to guard him. She'd hear. And after all, I had been one of his intended targets. How much more could be expected of me?

On returning upstairs to the bar, I discovered that in my absence my husband had been apprised of my adventures and was very upset. "You weren't even supposed to leave the hotel, Carolyn," he said reproachfully. "I didn't even know you were gone. Why would you ignore the general's specific orders and—"

"I didn't know about the general's orders," I interrupted. "Hank said he had permission. And I really did want to go to Capri. How was I to know Hank planned to toss me off a cliff and let the tide wash me up on the island? I was expecting to take a boat."

"For shame, Professor," Albertine scolded. "Do not upset your wife when she has had such a trying day. I am distraught myself, and I only helped with the delivery of the babies. Poor Carolyn did that *after* surviving a terrifying attack on her life and a very dangerous auto trip back to Sorrento with a murderer and a woman in labor."

Jason looked embarrassed. Adrien asked, "What babies are these that you and our good Carolyn helped to deliver?" an incredulous smile on his lips.

"My grandchildren," trilled Violetta, fluttering up to the group and linking her arm through the general's. She leaned forward to drop kisses on my cheek and Albertine's. "How can we thank you? Such beautiful babies. And to have them on a chaise longue with you kindly ladies in attendance." Then she rifled through her handbag and lifted out hospital photos of the newborns, who looked as newborns usually do, red-faced and wrinkled. "Aren't they adorable?" she asked the general.

He looked sadly at the pictures. "They are indeed, Signora. You are a lucky woman. Now that my Lucia is gone, I can never hope to welcome grandchildren into the world. Signora Blue, perhaps you would be so kind as to show Signora Massoni the picture of my lovely daughter, the one you took in the Piazza Tasso."

My camera and the baby pictures were passed around the ever-widening circle—Agents Marsocca and Loppi had joined us, not to mention Lieutenant Flavia Vacci, who was cooing over the twins. Violetta squeezed the general's arm again and said, "You poor, dear man. To lose such a beautiful daughter. It is so tragic. But you shall share my adorable grandchildren. You must come to visit us, once we are all back in Rome."

Valentino told the general that he had loved Paolina to distraction and would have been a happy man could he have called the general father-in-law. Then he offered to take everyone out to dinner at the expense of Ricci Chemicals. The general confused him by advising him that he should be looking for work rather than spending company money that might soon belong to the government.

After that, we all walked down the hill to a restaurant recommended by Violetta. She had eaten there with an admirer during this visit. The food was wonderful, as was the ambiance—all lattices and trailing vines in the dining room, which was reached by a wide staircase from the first floor. I felt much more cheerful, especially since Jason said no more about my misadventures.

Epilogue

Carolyn

Jason was already in bed when I finished my preparations to retire. "Why don't you open the curtains so we can see the night sky and the volcano," he suggested as I draped my robe over a chair. I padded barefoot to the balcony doors to draw the drapes and then the sheers back. The night was so beautiful. The afternoon clouds had lifted, and the moon shone so brightly that I could see its light glimmering on the water below, while the shadow of Vesuvius loomed against the night sky. The Amalfi Coast, the Bay of Naples, they had to be the most beautiful places in the world. Not that I'd have cared to be tossed into those lovely waters.

I turned away and climbed into bed beside my husband. "Guess what?" I said.

"What?" he murmured sleepily.

"I forgive you for spending all that time with Sibyl."

Jason sat bolt upright and said indignantly, "Carolyn, she's a colleague, not a—a girlfriend. Did I get jealous because you spent so much time with Hank? At least Sibyl wasn't a murderer."

I was laughing, but said, "You never know. She might have been in on the container-for-heroin scheme."

"What scheme are you talking about?" Jason asked, looking down at me.

Poor man, he didn't know the half of what I'd discovered. "I think I'll go with you to France after all. Albertine's not so bad, and presumably we won't see anything of Charles de Gaulle."

"Right," said Jason, lying down again, "and you won't want to miss the Albigenesian Heresy or whatever it is."

"I'm afraid it's over, Jason," I said giggling. "Just a distant, but painful memory."

"No more storming castles and *autos-da-fé* in the street? That's good to know. And I have to say, love, that it's nice to see you in such a good mood. You've been pretty grumpy lately."

"Why wouldn't I be? You're always telling me what I can and can't do."

"Well, I worry about you." He pulled me into the curve of his arm.

"And you think I don't worry about you?" I retorted. "But did I nag you all these years about working with toxins, which are at least as dangerous as the occasional murderer?"

"Point taken," said Jason and, pulling me closer, curved his body against mine.

It felt like old times. Better times. I guess romantic Sorrento was finally working its magic.